Praise for Jack Skillingstead
and for *Harbinger*

"Jack Skillingstead takes the reader on an acid-induced trip through a place where the many-worlds theory and quantum entanglement collide with new age mysticism at the far edge of the world."
—Brenda Cooper, author of *Reading the Wind*

"Jack Skillingstead is fearless. No one in SF writes about death, sex, loneliness, and love with such searing honesty. In *Harbinger* he does something astonishing: In a story that spans hundreds of years, multiple planets, and shifting realities, he somehow renders an intensely personal portrait of one man struggling to understand himself. The effect is like reading classic Vonnegut or Dick, but with an emotional punch that is uniquely Skillingstead."
—Daryl Gregory, author of *Pandemonium*

"Jack Skillingstead's fiction always delights and surprises."
—Kristine Kathryn Rusch, author of *The Disappeared*

"Jack Skillingstead plays with big ideas, Olaf Stapledon big, but he plays with them on a personal scale. *Harbinger* is like reading the life of a huge oak by taking one, thin slice out of the middle, but the whole tree is there. This is a book that blew me away."
—James Van Pelt, author of *Summer of the Apocalypse*

"Jack Skillingstead shines a floodlight into the writhing hollows of the human condition."
—Ted Kosmatka

HARBINGER
A Fairwood Press Book
September 2009
Copyright © 2009 by Jack Skillingstead

Fairwood Press
21528 104th Street Court East
Bonney Lake, WA 98391
www.fairwoodpress.com

Cover illustration by Adam Hunter Peck
Book and cover design by Patrick Swenson

ISBN: 0-9820730-3-8
ISBN13: 978-0-9820730-3-2
First Fairwood Press Edition: September 2009
Printed in the United States of America

For Nancy
Everything is Simultaneous

PART ONE:
REGENERATION

"The process of evolution can only be
described as the gradual insertion of more
and more freedom into matter..."

—T.E. Hulme

CHAPTER ONE

A soap bubble the size of a Volkswagen Beetle drifted over my bedroom. I opened my eyes in the dark. Strange how I knew it was there. But I was a strange boy back in 1974, the year I graduated from high school.

Jeepers, my Border Collie, was standing erect at the foot of my bed. And he wasn't the only erect thing. My body tingled, my skin was coated with sweat. An intense, longing arousal possessed me. I stripped off my pajama top (canary yellow with red piping; don't ask). My heart thudded alarmingly.

I was scared. It was as though I would die if I didn't somehow complete the suddenly urgent equation of my biology. The room tilted when I stood. I fell against the cheap bookcase packed with science fiction paperbacks. The *Sirens of Titan* hit the floor face up. I closed my eyes and tried to calm down. Dad was snoring in the next room. My mom used to nudge him awake and make him stop. But Mom had been gone for years. Just like my big brother Jeremy. At the time of the accident he had been seven years older than me and on leave from the Army. I missed him badly, because sometimes I needed a nudge, too.

There was a scrabbling sound, and I opened my eyes. Jeepers was chasing his tail in a tight circle, reminding me of the Tasmanian Devil cartoon character.

"Jeepers, sit!"

Jeepers didn't sit. He kept running around in that circle, like something wound up and let go. The moon streamed through the cherry tree outside my window and cast a bony shadow over him. It was kind of horrible. In the winter, without its blossoms—all gnarled and black in the night—that tree used to scare me. I mean when I was a little kid.

wasn't winter; it was June.

ring from leg to leg, I yanked on a pair of jeans. My brother's US Army duffel coat hung from a hook on the door, and I grabbed it and shrugged it on over my bare shoulders. As I said: I was a weird kid, and constantly wearing my dead brother's army coat was just one of the weird things I did to prove it.

I felt better outside in the fresh air. The dizziness retreated and my heart settled down to a lugging rhythm. Some power had changed me that night, made me unlike any human being in history. But all I knew at the moment was that I felt different in an indefinable way. Also, for the first time in my life I had a destination, though I didn't know what it was.

The cherry tree was in full leaf. I stared at it as if it were an optical illusion, then I started walking the night streets. At first I looked frequently into the sky, which was a pale wash of moonlight over a dim star field. The day would arrive, some hundred and eighty years hence, when I would find myself sailing outbound toward one of those stars, in the belly of a vehicle so incomprehensibly immense that it would have boggled my easily boggled seventeen-year-old mind. But I had no inkling of any such journey on that June night in 1974.

Clouds blotted the stars in the near distance, but the sky was devoid of giant soap bubbles. After a while I ceased looking for them. My feet stopped walking at about the same time, and I found myself standing in front of a green frame house with a big madrona tree in the yard.

Blue television light pulsed behind one curtained window on the first floor. Big white moths fluttered around the porch light, making shadows ten sizes too big. I knew whose house it was because I walked by it practically every day. I even knew which of the dormer windows belonged to Nichole Roberts. Passing by, I'd once caught an unforgettable glimpse of white bra and creamy breasts. Now some kind of groaning urgency compelled me toward her, but what the hell? We knew each other, had lived within a couple of blocks of each other most our lives, but she wasn't my girlfriend. Far from it. She was dating a guy named Roy Hathaway, who was on the wrestling team. I'd never even *kissed* a girl. So I was a late bloomer, which turned out not to matter in the extremely long run of things.

I'd seen a guy on TV throw pebbles at a girl's bedroom window to get her attention. So I looked around on the shoulder of the road for some pebbles of my own (our neighborhood had no sidewalks; Nichole's two story house was almost grand by local standards, even if it did need a paint job). I hunkered and came up with a handful. The window opened before I could pitch even one.

"Ellis?"

I crossed the lawn and stood under her window, face upturned.

"How'd you know it was me?"

"I recognized the coat. What are you *doing* out there? And where's your shirt?"

"I don't know."

"To both questions?" She chuckled.

"Just the first one," I said and dropped the pebbles, slipped my hands in the pockets of my brother's duffel coat, and pulled it closed in front.

"Hey, it's like that play," Nichole said.

"*Death of a Salesman?*"

We had an English Lit class together, and Mrs. Forslof was hell on plays. We read them out loud in class, and most of the kids thought they were idiotic. But not Nichole. She had real intelligence and sensitivity, and she wasn't afraid to acknowledge those qualities in herself.

"*Romeo And Juliet*, silly," she said.

I nearly made the egregious error of trying to quote Shakespeare, but stifled myself.

"Oh," I said.

"Ellis?"

"Yes?"

"I feel strange. I mean I woke up feeling strange."

"Me, too."

"Why don't you come in?"

"Up there?"

She nodded.

"Okay." It was like some kind of dream. Or waking up, finally, from another kind of dream. Nichole wasn't my girlfriend but I was in love with her in that way of virginal teenage boys who know they don't have a chance. "Is the door locked?"

"Climb up."

"What?"

"Come on, climb up, Romeo."

I looked at the madrona tree. A limb bent like a flexing arm within hopping distance of the roof, if I stood in the elbow crux. Or so it appeared. Probably I wasn't such a great judge of distance at the moment, though. Or of anything else, for that matter.

I monkeyed up into the tree, a feat that required my full attention for a minute or two. When I was on a level with the roof I noticed the gap was greater than I'd estimated from the ground.

"Come on," Nichole said.

She had lighted a candle. Her face was lovely, almost angelic in the glow. Auburn highlights gleamed in her long hair. Her mouth was broad, full-lipped, inviting. I jumped—borne up by some kind of ethereal vision—and missed the roof by a foot.

Flat on my back on the lawn, I waited for the wind to find its way back into my lungs. Presently Nichole's face leaned over me.

"God, are you all right?"

When I could inhale I said, "I'm excellent."

We entered the house by the front door, which required less acrobatic skill. There was a weirdly herbal smell.

"Where's your mom and dad?" I whispered.

"My mom doesn't really live here. She's staying with a friend or something. My dad. I guess he's asleep."

We were creeping up the stairs.

"What if he wakes up?"

"He won't."

"He might."

We reached the top of the stairs. She stopped and looked at me. She was only about five foot one to my five eleven. She was wearing an oversized blue T-shirt and no bra.

"Ellis, he's kind of drunk? Passed out on the sofa. That's why my mom isn't ever here."

"Oh."

"So it's safe."

"I wasn't scared. I just wondered."

"Okay."

In her bedroom she closed the door and locked it. The walls were mauve, and the ceiling wasn't flat like mine but had quirky angles and was sprinkled with hand-painted silver stars. She had a Gerard turntable and a shelf of record albums as long as my arm. A *Madman Across The Water* poster was thumbtacked over the turntable. It was basically the graphic from the album cover. I liked it that she didn't have a picture of Elton John doing some flamboyant shit. I thought the poster was classy.

"Wow, you're really sweating," she said. "You want to take your coat off?"

"I don't know."

She reached out and pushed the coat off my shoulders, and I let it slip to the floor.

"You're all flushed."

"Yeah," I replied.

We sat on the bed, which had the rumpled look of having recently been slept in. Nichole smoothed her hand over the white bedspread between us. I could *smell* her. My hand floated up to her face. I touched her cheek and then I took her hair in my fingers.

"Do you want to kiss me?" she said.

"Yes."

She tilted her head, lips slightly parted. I leaned forward and kissed her mouth, just as if I'd been doing it my whole life. Oh, she was sweet. *Lie back,* I think she said, though it might have been my blood speaking. She stood up and removed the big T-shirt. I continued to breathe, but just barely. Her breasts were perfect, the nipples like pink eraser heads. She wore sheer beige panties, damp over a pubic shadow.

She straddled me and began moving her hips.

"What's in here?" she said, playful.

"My sock monkey?"

She giggled. "Let's take him out," she said.

"___"

The zipper, the tugging down, the cool air, her hand firmly squeezing, thumb caressing. She stood long enough to slip out of her panties, and then she straddled me again, only this time I was inside her, where I belonged.

Time unwound, infinitely—for about fifty seconds. Afterwards we held each other while I fought a contradictory impulse to be away from her. Gradually that impulse retreated, and I thought I'd never want to be away from her again.

"It was your first time, wasn't it?" she said.

"Sort of."

"How can it be 'sort of'?"

"Well, it was my first time with another person in the room."

"Ellis, can I ask you something?"

"I don't think so."

"He was *really* mad, wasn't he."

"Yeah. Nichole?"

"Hmm?" She was fiddling nervously with the radio dial again.

"Why him?"

She shrugged. "I don't know, Ellis. Because he's strong and uncomplicated and knows what he wants. Because he wants me, but kind of acts like he doesn't care and treats me like shit. And I *know* it's screwed up, so don't tell me."

"It's not that screwed up," I said, thinking of her father passed out drunk on the sofa in front of a hissing TV screen and her mother gone off somewhere. Not really that screwed up at all.

A pine tree air freshener dangled from the rearview mirror. I flicked it with my fingernail, and Roy Hathaway pulled up on Nichole's side. We were just coming to the big four-way intersection by Sea-Tac Airport. The light was yellow.

"*Shit.*" Nichole had been slowing to stop, but now she took her foot off the brake, hesitated, then jumped the gas again. The hesitation is what did it. The light had gone red, and we rolled into the intersection without conviction.

A black sedan struck us first, broadside just behind my door, and the Nova spun around. Nichole screamed. Time seemed to attenuate. The air freshener was still swinging wildly when the bus came on. I glimpsed a pair of headlights higher than my head, started to turn, caught a hurtling wall of silver, and then it smashed into us. My door frame buckled like pasteboard. The Nova launched into the air, tumbling. Hotels and lights and traffic and even a landing 737 flipped upside down, right side up, upside down. The windshield fractured like a sheet of ice. My lap belt dug painfully into my waist, unbearable. Then, in an instant, the force broke my restraint and flung me through the windshield.

An interval of darkness. Out of it, very distinctly, my brother said: *Don't be afraid, Ellis*. Which was dumb, considering.

Then somebody let there be light. But no noise. A black puddle with a rainbow sheen on its surface. In the puddle lay a human hand severed raggedly at the wrist, white dowl of bone protruding, the pinky finger erased to a bloody nub. It didn't strike me as particularly horrible; I felt pretty detached myself.

Without moving my head I looked around. I mean 360 degrees. The Nova was flipped onto its roof, windshield gone, and Nichole was hanging from her lap belt, hair falling straight down, mouth open. Her eyes were closed, but I knew she was alive and mostly unhurt. If she were dead, we'd both be looking around with Super 360 Omnivision, right? But she wasn't dead, and somehow looking at her I could feel her strong heart beat and even sense the quiet electrical impulses of her brain. She was unconscious and undreaming.

My brother Jeremy and my mother had died together in a car wreck. October thirty-first, 1968, coming back from the store with a load of Halloween candy. Some teens driving around in monster costumes and drinking beer crossed the center line and hit their car. A policeman came to the door to tell us. I stood behind my dad, still wearing my dumb homemade Star Trek uniform. My mom had glued shiny gold sequins onto the officer's patch, and she'd helped me make Spock ears out of cardboard and "flesh" colored tape. I was a little old for trick-or-treat, I guess, but this was my last time. My brother had been away in the army for almost a year, and I'd missed and idolized him. As soon as he got back from the store, he was going to walk with me around the neighborhood. My big brother. I remember looking at that policeman and thinking his uniform was a costume, thinking that until my father burst into tears. Trick-or-treat. Now I wondered if my mother and brother had witnessed a muffled tableau similar to the one I was seeing tonight.

It was fascinating, outside of time. The glitter of glass and blood. The way the Greyhound had ended up, right angles to the direction it had been traveling when it struck us. The people on the bus, their boiling states of anxiety and confusion and fear, the driver's paralyzing shock as he stared at the body in the street (mine?). Hathaway's pickup had jumped the curb and struck a power pole. I got nothing from him. Dead air.

I wanted to explore every detail. I wanted to *see*. I was like a baby in a bassinet. A nice well-fed baby—a being of pure experience, absorbing every facet of the world.

That was me: Baby Ellis. Goo goo—*gah*!

It did seem strange that I couldn't depart from this one place, intriguing though the place may have been. Weren't the dead supposed to be able to ghost around unfettered by physical limitations? *Was* I dead?

Here came the cars and trucks with pretty flashing lights. And a crowd was gathering. I recalled that Ray Bradbury story, where it's always the same crowd, appearing out of nowhere at accident scenes, eager to claim a new member. Was that my fate, to die and join The Crowd?

And wasn't it strange that there should be trees among the people. Eight foot tall, leafless trees swaying out here in the middle of the intersection. I saw my brother speaking with one of them. Jeremy was smoking a cigarette, just like he used to do in life, holding it between his thumb and first two fingers, the glowing end turned inward when he pulled it away from his lips.

I wanted to see my mother, too. All of a sudden I wanted desperately to see my mother. I was the baby in the bassinet and I began to cry.

At once emotion overtook me, drowning my sublime detachment. And then pain. Unimaginable pain. Something inside me— upper left abdomen—was on fire. There was a dreadful pulsing at my wrist.

Noise burst upon me. Sirens. Jet engines. People yelling, hard shoes gritting on pavement.

The smell of gasoline and scorched rubber. I lay on my back, staring at the washed-out star field, my omnivision lost. A soap bubble the size of a Volkswagen Beetle drifted above me, and a shadow moved inside of it.

Someone touched my arm and I screamed.

CHAPTER TWO

I had a cartoon hand. Bandaged, wrapped and gauzed to outsized proportions. And endlessly throbbing, itching. For the first few days they kept the room subtropical. Okay, a slight exaggeration. But it had been hot in there. The doctor told me that heat was necessary to keep the blood vessels dilated and prevent clotting after my "hand replantation."

Now more than a week had elapsed. The room was cooler, but I still found it stiffling. I had a new scar on another part of my body, as well, where they'd cut a vertical seam starting just below my breast bone through which they had reached in to remove my ruined spleen. That one hurt, too, and itched. Inside. Which was strange, according to the doctor.

I was heavily drugged and drifting in and out of soft-focus reality. During one drift cycle the room was empty and then it was not. Over by the moon-glazed window something loomed like a tree with twisted branch arms and legs. I lifted my head off the pillow, blinked slowly, and the tree was a gnarly man. One more slow shutter blink and watery morning light was flooding the room and rain was tick-ticking on the window.

A doctor I'd never seen before came in. She was tall and thin with a narrow blade of a nose and black framed glasses.

"I'm Dr. Jane," she said, and proceeded to read my chart and examine my war wounds. My brain slogged around in a swoony bath of nausea juice. I focused on her lapel pin, blue enamel with the stylized letters: *UI* in silver.

Dr. Jane partially unwrapped my hand, snipping first with a small pair of scissors. She breathed mostly through her nose, a quiet rasping. The rasping halted for a beat when she revealed my wrist and forearm scars, which had already faded, making the stitches stand

"I don't get it."

"The doctors say you aren't healing right."

"But I feel great!"

"Yeah. But they think you shouldn't feel so great. Or I mean that your healing is abnormal. I'm not saying it right, you'll get the full picture from that lady doctor. But they say it's important, what's happening to you."

I stared at him. "What's important about it?"

He started walking around the room. "You know, this place is pretty nice. Not everybody gets treated like this, especially when there's no insurance. You have to think about that, too."

"I just want to get *out* of here."

He nodded again. That nod. Even when he was there he was absent.

"The thing is," he said, "I signed papers that say you have to stay for a while."

"What? Even if I'm not sick I have to stay? I'm not staying here."

"Well . . . The way the doctor's put it, it's best for you to stay a while longer."

"That's bullshit, Dad!"

He stood with his back to me, staring out the window at the night garden, his head bobbing slightly. Silver hairs curled down the back of his neck; he needed a cut.

"I guess I could talk to them, but I already signed the papers. I mean it's a done deal."

"I don't care about any papers."

"You're still a minor, for another six months anyway."

"Dad?"

He turned around. "What's the big deal?" he said. "You're out of school, this place isn't that bad, is it? Can't you just relax? It's like a vacation or something. Don't they treat you good? I know they do."

"I'm not staying here six more months!"

"Nobody said six more months."

"*You* just did."

"I didn't mean it like you were going to be here that whole time."

"What *did* you mean?"

He put his cap back on. "I got my shift in the morning." He

worked the grill at an IHOP on Pacific Highway. It was one dead-end job after another since Boeing laid him off. "That doctor will explain it better," he said. "And I'll talk to them about the papers, I'll do that. If it bothers you so much."

Suddenly I didn't want him to leave. I didn't want to be left in this dreadful, lonely place by myself. I touched his shoulder and he turned back to me.

"Dad—"

My tears started. Dad was never any good with tears. Fumbling in his back pocket he said, "I've got something for you. I'm not supposed to give you stuff like this, but the hell with it."

He handed me a square, white envelope, the kind that holds a greeting card. The only other thing he'd brought me in the last three months was my high school diploma, which he'd mounted in a cheap frame and propped on my bedside table. My name and home address were printed on the front of the square envelope in blue ink. It was from Nichole Roberts. The post date was more than a month old.

"Why aren't you supposed to give me my mail, Dad?" It was hard to keep the anger out of my voice.

"We'll talk tomorrow, with the doctor. I got to go." He fussed with his cap, patted my shoulder, and left. I waited for the usual click of the lock being engaged, but it didn't come.

I tore the envelope open. From its shape I'd expected a Get Well card (and it would have been my first), but this was a Miss You card depicting a harlequin sitting cross-legged holding out a pair of ballet slippers by the laces, a forlorn expression under the white makeup. Inside it said:

I guess this will be my last letter, Ellis. I'm not even sure why I bother, since you haven't answered any of the others. I wish you'd at least tell me what's going on. Your dad won't talk to me. I've been to your house, and I know he's in there some-times, but he doesn't answer the door. Am I such a pariah? (only Nichole could use a word like 'pariah' and not sound self-conscious). *Anyway I hope you're all right. I guess that's all. I just hope you're all right.*

Her signature appeared under a scribbled heart.

So it was time to check out. I'd been thinking about it for weeks. What had stopped me, always, was the idea that there was nothing waiting for me. In retrospect that is exactly the way Langley Ulin had *wanted* me to feel. I'd thought obsessively about Nichole, but her silence finally wore me down to a lethargic nubbin. After reading her card I was suddenly restored to a number 7 Ticonderoga with a needle sharp point, and I was ready to pencil myself back into life.

I had no street clothes. The staff provided me with flimsy tie-in-the-back "gowns" to sleep in plus one pair of baggy hospital greens and cotton slippers for my morning strolls, which is what I was wearing at the moment.

I let myself out of the room. The corridor was empty, the other doors shut. A stainless steel caddy was parked by one of those shut doors, stacked with neatly folded towels. Down there at the far end of the corridor was an elevator. I started walking toward it. Before I got there it dinged and the doors slid open and disgorged an orderly type with a ring of keys in his fist.

I quickly diverted to the stairs, trying to look purposeful as hell, like I was one of the staff. Maybe I could have pulled it off if I'd been older and dressed in real clothes.

The orderly reached out and hooked my arm. He was big and round, with a flat-top crew cut. He smelled like some nasty cologne "Hold up," he said, and I wrenched loose and ran for the stairs.

He was big but I was fast. In the stairwell visions of every prison escape movie I'd ever seen flashed through my mind. Wailing sirens, search beams crisscrossing the "yard," armed guards in the towers, and slobbering bloodhounds snarling and straining at their leashes.

The stairwell was just as antiseptically clean as the rest of the hospital. I took the steps two and three at a leap, my good right hand sliding down the rail. The door above me banged open. The orderly's big shoes stomped and echoed after me.

"Hold up!" he kept saying, "Hold up, kid!"

The hospital was only three stories. I came out in the lobby. A woman at the admissions desk looked my way but didn't say anything. She had been talking to a guy in a charcoal suit and black tie. I hesitated then broke for the door under the green EXIT sign, hit the crash-bar, and was *out*.

There weren't any guard towers or search lights. Machine gun fire did not strafe at my heels. A sweep of grass bordered by a low wrought iron fence lay before me. The fence lacked even a token coil of razor wire.

I vaulted the fence and crossed the road into pine woods. They'd brought me here in a private ambulance, a long morphine-saturated ride. I recalled sitting up as we passed through a small town shortly before arriving at the hospital. So that nameless town was my goal.

I tramped along, paralleling the road, and I felt every pebble, root and twig through the soles of the cotton slippers. Behind me voices suddenly rose. My breath and I halted. Three flashlight beams crossed and jiggled in the wooded distance. No bloodhounds, though.

I moved farther away from the road, found some dense brush, and balled myself up in it, white face hidden behind my arms. The hospital clothes were dark green. I waited and hoped for the best.

A man passed within a dozen yards of where I hid. I risked a peek. A flashlight beam swung and bobbed, seeking, but it never touched me. I remained in my hiding spot a long time. There were no more voices or flashlights.

I called Nichole collect from a payphone outside a 7-11 store in Shelton. It had taken me forever to get there and it was almost morning. I had no idea what day of the week it was. All I was counting on was that Nichole's father would be passed out on the sofa, that he wouldn't answer the phone.

Nichole picked up on the fourth ring and accepted the charges. She sounded wide awake.

"When the phone rang," she said, " I just knew it was going to be you. Isn't that weird?"

"Yeah."

"So where are you, and *how* are you, and why didn't you ever call me before now?"

"I'm in Shelton," I said. "I need you. And Nichole? I need some clothes, too. Any kind of clothes."

"I'm there," she said. No hesitation. "I got a nine a.m. class," she said, a couple of hours later when she picked me up in her dad's Mercury. I'd been waiting for her in a park. A police cruiser had passed through the park once, but that was it. Otherwise it had been me and the jungle gym, and now I was grateful to be sitting in a comfortable car with the radio playing and a beautiful girl in the driver's seat. My girl.

"You're in college, huh?" I said.

"Not really." She lit a Winston with the dash lighter. "It's just community college. Killing time college. Fuck it. You look like an escaped mental patient. How's your hand? I can't believe what happened."

I showed her the hand, and she looked a little disappointed.

"I thought there would be, like, Frankenstein stitches and all."

"There were but the scars faded."

She looked more closely. "But there's *no* scar."

"I know. It's weird. I think that's why they had me in that hospital. That and the finger."

"What finger?"

I told her about the pinky. "Holy shit," she remarked. Then: "Are you going to be in trouble?"

I shrugged. "My dad signed some papers, but they can't force me to stay. Nichole? Thanks for coming."

"Jesus, no problem. What else was I doing? Hey, your stuff's in the back."

I twisted around to look. My brother's duffel coat was neatly folded on the back seat. There was also a blue sweatshirt and a pair of beat up Nikes. I teared up at the sight of the coat. "How'd you get this?" I said, grabbing it.

"Your dad doesn't always lock all the windows when he goes out. I should have snatched some jeans, too, but I got scared."

"You're the greatest. Don't worry about the pants."

A car passed us slowly, and the driver, a man in a sport coat, looked over.

"We better go," I said.

Nichole put her cigarette in the ashtray and moved the shifter into Drive. I felt okay again, because I was with my girl and that's all I wanted.

That first day we drove for hours. Nichole seemed to pick roads and highways and exits at random. She smoked a whole pack of cigarettes. She told me how her mom finally moved all the way out of the house and how awful it was now, and how her dad never had more than two words to say to her. So I told her about how my dad signed me up to be some kind of guinea pig without even asking me first. It was hard for me to follow a critical line on my father for long, though, because I could see him in full 3-D vision.

"What do you mean 3-D vision?" Nichole asked.

"I mean I can see things from his point of view. I know how tough it's been for him, losing his stupid Boeing job *and* my mom and brother."

"Well, you lost them, too. Except for the job."

"I know."

"So why does he get a special pass to be an asshole?"

I winced inwardly. "He's not really an asshole. Not a total asshole."

"*My* dad's a total asshole. And my mom's a flake."

Steering with her left hand, she felt the empty pack of Winstons with her right, crackling the cellophane, making certain the pack was empty.

"My mom's a complete fucking *flake*," she said, throwing the crumpled pack into the passenger footwell.

We slept on the sand in Long Beach, Washington. Nichole had brought a couple of sleeping bags. We zipped them together and snuggled into them behind a driftwood windbreak. Bonfires blazed up and down the beach. Silhouetted figures holding beer bottles capered before orange and yellow flames. Smoke chugged into the night sky. We were part of it and remote from it at the same time.

We had been talking a lot, but now in the double bag we stopped talking. The stars were diamond hard. So was I. Well, not *diamond* hard. But pretty damn hard. It was my first unequivocal erection since my operations. Of course there had been the physical trauma of the accident followed by the deliberate trauma of scalpel and stitch. But lying in the bag with Nichole I realized that I'd also been depressed, maybe even *clinically* depressed. And now I wasn't. Just like that. It had been like the ambulance ride to the first hospital. The medics had stanched the blood gush from my wrist with a tourniquet. I'd kept staring at the soaked gauze wrapped over my stump, and I knew a piece of me was gone. Even in my deep fog of pain, I knew I wasn't whole and never would be again (at that point I hadn't known they'd put my hand in a cold box right in the same ambulance or that there was a chance surgeons could successfully reattach it). A profound sadness and sense of loss had descended upon me—and abruptly lifted the next day when I saw that I had my hand back.

Nichole had been severed from me for *three months*.

"Hmm, down boy," she said in the bag, reaching into my underwear and taking me in her hand. I whimpered a little, but in a manly way, of course.

"Do you know why I invited you into my room that night?" she said.

"Not really."

"Because it was like I remembered I *knew* you."

She fell asleep first, all tangled up with me in the hot bag, her head snuggled against my chest. I gazed at the stars, the taste of Nichole still on my tongue, the smell of our sex enveloping us like another bag. I fell asleep with the minute knitting of muscle and tendon tingling in my pinky.

In the morning I woke before Nichole. The sky was a pastel suggestion of lime. I watched Nichole's sleeping face and I took her hair into my fingers. I used my left hand because the right one was trapped under her shoulder. It was a few moments before I realized that all my fingers were working, that I'd regained, in my last sleeping hours, the full function of my hand. And for the first time in weeks the tingle-itch was absent. I held the hand up to the pale dawn and flexed the fingers experimentally. Then I stared at the pretty sky and waited for Nichole to wake up. She did, but it was a while before I realized it. What clued me in finally was her mouth kissing my mouth. Her breath was sweet even at that hour— sweet enough, anyway.

"Where were you?" she said.

"Right here."

"I don't think so. Your eyes were open, but you didn't hear a word I said, did you?"

"Sometimes I kind of zone out," I said. "Mom called them my autistic vacations."

"Yeah?"

"Yeah." But I didn't want to think about my mother, so I asked Nichole what she wanted to do.

"Let's go see my flaky mom," she said.

It turned out Nichole's driving had not been all that random. Her mother was in Long Beach, staying in one of the cottages a friend of hers rented to the tourists.

"I'm warning you," Nichole said. "She's a total flake."

I said thanks for the warning.

The cottage was charming in a deliberate way. Cedar shake walls, flower boxes under the windows overflowing with color. A porch with two Adirondack chairs angled toward the sound if not the sight of the ocean.

At the slamming of our car doors Mrs. Roberts appeared. Standing on the porch she looked like some kind of gypsy queen in a diaphanous purple skirt (through which the good shape of her legs was visible), bright paisley scarf, hoop earrings, African bracelets that clicked woodenly on her wrists, and so forth.

"There's my baby! she cried, then added, turning to me, "And who's this? *Your* baby?"

"Mom," Nichole said.

"I'm Ellis Herrick," I said.

"Oh my God, the boy in the accident?"

"Yeah."

She looked at my left hand then at my right.

"It's this one," I said, holding up the left.

"It looks so normal."

"It's pretty normal," I said.

"Ellis just got out of the hospital," Nichole said.

"And they wouldn't give you your pants back?" Mrs. Roberts said to me, staring at my baggy hospital greens.

"I left in kind of a hurry."

"Well, both of you come in. I've got tea, wine, and cannabis. English muffins, too."

"Jesus, Mom," Nichole said.

I had tea but really wanted a Pepsi. Nichole also had tea, and her mother lit up a joint. She embarrassed Nichole, and I could see why, but I liked Mrs. Roberts. Her features were similar to her daughter's, and at forty-five or whatever, she was practically as beautiful. Plus the dope didn't make her act sloppy or stupid. It seemed to *enhance* her.

"You have the most astonishing aura, Ellis," she said to me, and I had to ask what an aura was. She described it as an "energy nimbus" that glows off everyone but is invisible to those who aren't willing to look at them. Nichole rolled her eyes, but I was interested.

"What do you mean not willing to look? People just see or don't see stuff, right?"

"The eye is a physical organ," Mrs. Roberts replied. "It will see whatever there is to see in the strictly physical realm."

"Uh huh," I said.

"But there are realms other than the physical, Ellis."

"Like other dimensions?" That was me and my science fiction fetish.

She drew thoughtfully on the remaining scrap of a joint, holding it in a fancy silver roach clip.

"Other dimensions, yes," she said. "A Master recently told me that everything is simultaneous. Don't you find that profound?"

"Everything is simultaneous?" I said.

"Very profound, mother," Nichole said.

"What's a Master?" I asked.

"Actually, this one referred to himself as a Harbinger, not a Master."

"A harbinger of what?" I asked.

"Consciousness evolution. I saw him out on the beach one night. About a month ago. I saw him with my physical eyes, but I think he was existing simultaneous to the physical. He came down out of the sky in a big bubble, like Glinda the Good Witch? Remember Glinda in The Wizard Of Oz?"

"Sure," I said. "I remember."

Nichole and I exchanged looks. See? Nichole's look said: a total flake. But I was recalling my soap bubble dream of a few months ago.

"What did the Harbinger thing look like?" I asked Mrs. Roberts.

She laughed. "That was so odd. When I saw him I was actually scared for a minute. He looked like an old larch tree we had in the backyard of my house when I was a kid. A big old gnarly larch tree. Let's order a pizza, kids. I'm starving."

Nichole and I slept in the cottage that night, but not in the same bed, or even the same bag. I doubt Mrs. Roberts would have objected, but Nichole whispered to me that it would be too "creepy" with her mother right in the next room.

There was only one bed in the cottage anyway. So Nichole slept on the sofa and I unrolled the sleeping bags on the floor, one on the bottom for extra padding. In the dark the air was salted and the ocean surf a constant susurrus calling me out.

I lay on my back, fingers laced behind my head. Moonlight ivoried Nichole's face, her cheek squashed and lips puckered in sleep on the sofa cushion. I was going out, and I thought about touching Nichole, waking her to come with me. But I decided to let her sleep.

I walked the night beach. The surf was luminous. At this hour there were only a couple of fires. I removed my sneakers. The dry sand was cold under my feet, the wind off the water blew sharp. Was it here that Nichole's mother had seen a bubble like the one Glinda The Good Witch had ridden down to Munchkin Land?

I gazed upward, not really anticipating a visitation. The wind whipped my thin hospital pants. I hunched inside the comforting bulk and dusky smell of my brother's army coat.

Sensing someone behind me, I turned. A figure walked toward me from the direction of the cottages. At first I thought it was Nichole. I mean I was all but positive it was Nichole. She looked so much like her mother.

"I thought I saw you come out here, Ellis," Mrs. Roberts said. And I wondered how that could be. Her bed was in the back of the cottage where no windows faced toward the beach.

"In my dream I saw you," she said, as if reading my mind. "And then I sat up and realized it wasn't a dream anymore."

"Okay," I said.

Mrs. Roberts was wearing a rain parka. She produced a pack of Salems and offered me one. I shook my head. Back then it seemed like practically everyone smoked, but not me. Even later, when I knew for a fact that nicotine held no lethal threat over me, I refrained from the habit. I learned to smoke other things, but not cigarettes.

I watched Mrs. Roberts light up, the way she cupped her hand over the lighter to protect the flame and inclined her head, cigarette between tight lips, toward it. The light flickered briefly on her face—and there was Nichole's future of lines, of slightly pouched skin under the eyes, of a jaw gone soft. Time's alchemical insult, slowly transforming precious youth into something withered and mortal. It was more than a simple resemblance between mother and daughter. It moved the blood coldly through my heart.

She let the lighter go out, raised her chin to the stars and drew on the cigarette.

"I know what you are, Ellis," she said, wind tearing smoke from her lips.

"What do you mean?

"The Harbinger told me."

I stared at her. "So what am I?"

"You're one of the impossible things. A pointer. You're like a crop circle or a UFO. You're a precognitive dream, synchronicity, something meaningful and inexplicable. Something that is but shouldn't be."

"I don't understand."

She chuckled, blowing smoke that the wind tore away. "To tell you the truth, neither do I. And please call me Adriel. That 'Mrs. Roberts' stuff makes me feel old."

fected me; I simply didn't recognize it). But in the dark, in our creaky, narrow bed, it was a world composed only of our skin and our smells and the myriad inarticulate intimacies of our touching. It was the place where there *was* no place and no Time. But eventually I began to withdraw, experiencing the touching and tenderness on the outside only. I hated this withdrawing and couldn't understand or deny it. Certainly I never associated it with the deaths of my mother and brother. Especially in the dark, I began to experience Nichole as something separate and other, girl flesh and bone and an enclosing intimacy that was like a straightjacket.

And then there was Darcy on the loading dock.

"Are you really eighteen?"

"Sure," I said, then realized it wasn't a lie anymore. October twenty-fifth had come and gone almost unnoticed, and I really had attained the age of majority. If the war hadn't recently concluded I would have now been eligible to get my guts shot out in Vietnam.

"I mean I really am," I said. "Now."

Darcy grinned. She had one of those mouths that seemed over-crammed with very white and very even teeth. A Carly Simon mouth, to mention a performer popular at that time. A mouth designed to gobble you right up.

"When was your birthday?" Darcy asked.

"A couple of days ago."

"We're both Scorpios!" she said. "I'm a Halloween girl."

"Great!"

"Did you get any good presents?"

"Not really." Of course I'd gotten *no* presents, since no one in my little Bremerton world even knew the day had occurred. Not even Nichole.

"Do you have a girl, Ellis?"

"Yeah, sort of." Even this mild equivocation struck me guiltily as a betrayal of the quasi-mystical bond between Nichole and me. But a battalion of suddenly aroused hormonal soldiers had their own ideas of betrayal and conquest.

"Oh," Darcy said. "I guess you wouldn't want to come over after work for a birthday drink, then?"

"I don't know. I mean I guess it couldn't do any harm." At this point I wasn't really in charge of my tongue—or much of anything else.

Darcy smiled toothily. I remember it didn't smell very good on that loading dock. The dumpster's lid was open and fat bags of garbage overfilled it. One of the bags had split. A ripe, wet smell, underlined by the indolent buzz of the flies.

The apartment was a one bedroom with wall-to-wall carpeting, burnt orange. The drink was rum and Coke. I'd been drunk exactly once in my life, in a tent at Saltwater State Park with a bunch of other fifteen-year-olds. All I retained from the experience was the popping sound of rain on canvas, the smell of human sweat, and the taste of bile in my throat, where it didn't belong. Oh yeah, and when I'd closed my eyes the spinning sensation had intensified. So in the present situation I planned to take it easy with the rum; the weak self-deception that it was a drink I'd come seeking at Darcy's apartment had dropped to the wayside even before I left work and got into her Charger for the ride over.

"China Road" was on the radio in her apartment. Framed travel posters (Hawaii, Bali, Cayman Islands) hung on the walls. In the bathroom a blue macramé thing with wooden beads supported a spider plant in a kiln-fired bowl.

After splashing my face with cool water, I stared at myself in the bathroom mirror. My eyes failed the trustworthy test. Howdy, wretch. I couldn't even claim inebriation as an excuse. The rum and Cokes went down like Coke that had never even heard a rumor of Mr. Bacardi. Taking it easy wasn't an issue. At the time I ascribed this weird resistance to alcohol as "nerves." But of course my body was processing that rum with preternatural alacrity and efficiency, just like it had the pain killers.

Back in the living room I said, "I have to call somebody."

"Surely. Phone's in the kitchenette."

Darcy had opened a few buttons on her white peasant blouse. She sat on the puffy yellow sofa with her legs crossed and a big tumbler of Bacardi and Coke in her left hand. There was so much rum in the mix that the Coke wasn't much more than a diluted suggestion of moderation. The curvature of Darcy's breasts appeared in the loose V of her blouse, swelling from pink bra cups.

I called Nichole, standing next to the refrigerator with an urgent hard-on in my pants. I had to call her, though, or she would worry at my absence. Portrait of a conflicted moron. Maybe I should have placed the call before leaving the roadhouse.

"It's me," I said.

"Hi, Me. How am I?"

She had to be cute. Guilt clouted me in the solar plexus.

"I'm going to be a little late," I said.

"How come?"

"A bunch of us are going out after work."

"A bunch of you, huh? Where are you going? I wanna come, too."

"We're—" Darcy appeared in the kitchen doorway. Her blouse was completely unbuttoned and she had unsnapped her jeans and dragged the zipper down revealing her creamy belly and the pink waist of her panties. A few shiny pubic hairs curled over the top. She leaned against the jamb, cupping her right elbow in her left hand and sipping from the almost clear glass of rum and Coke. I very distinctly heard the ice click against those bright white teeth.

"You're what?" Nichole said in my ear.

Darcy's belly button squinted at me.

"Ah, going to this bar? One of the guys thinks I can get in. I mean he knows the guy at the door and he says he won't check my I.D. But I mean he might check yours. I don't know."

Darcy raised her eyebrows, took a big swallow of her drink, placed the tumbler on the counter and walked over to me. She did something with her walk, too. Something obvious and fairly devastating.

"Is something wrong?" Nichole asked.

Darcy stood in front of me and stroked her hand between my legs. There was plenty wrong, all right. All you required was a loose definition of "right."

I wound up walking back to the motel. Darcy had pounded the rum until there was nothing but a clear puddle in the bottom of the bottle. I doubt I could have wakened her. Nor would I have been stupid enough to climb into a vehicle with her behind the wheel. I'd had one big accident and didn't feel like tempting Fate any further.

The industrial stretch of road on which the motel stood appeared particularly dismal in the aqueous light of dawn. A discarded Slurpee cup from a nearby 7-11 store rolled around the parking lot, playing coy with the cigarette butts, candy bar wrappers and other assorted trash.

Speaking of butts, I felt like one myself, and was at my lowest ebb. It wasn't even five o'clock in the morning and the burgundy

Mercury was not parked outside the familiar green-painted door with the tarnished #7 nailed to it; Nichole was gone.

I let myself into the room. One of the dresser drawers stuck out like an idiot's drooping lip. Nichole had taken her clothes and personal stuff but left the little touches she'd applied to make the cheap room more welcoming and homey. The garlands of gold and silver tinsel she'd thumbtacked in loops around the walls and window. The Happy New Year cone hats she'd topped the TV's rabbit ears with. A plastic bowl full of glitter and rainbow confetti. The Richard Nixon Halloween mask on the door to the bathroom. All this acquired from a novelty store near The Donut Hole.

And there was a Donut Hole box on the dresser, too. On Fridays Nichole always brought a box of doughnuts to the motel for us to eat while we lay in bed watching Johnny Carson or Nightmare Theater—our low rent version of decadence. Christ, we were a couple of kids, that's all.

I flipped the lid up on the box. Three plain cake, two maple frosted, and this week's Surprise Fat Bomb: a strawberry Danish. There was always one Surprise Fat Bomb, and I was supposed to guess what it was. Staring into the box now I realized she must have *hated* doughnuts, after working in that place all those weeks. Yet she kept up the Friday night ritual. I pictured her waiting for me, short legs stretched out on the bed, watching TV. And then I pictured her calling The Wild Boar and asking where Ellis and his pals had gone. And then I noticed I was crying. Liars always think the people they're lying to aren't clever enough to figure it out. But in the case of someone who loves you (and aren't they the ones we most often lie to?) that isn't the case at all. It's because they *want* to believe you. You're like a story of goodness they are telling themselves, and they strive to suspend disbelief.

I stared at the bed, where we'd turned even cuddling into a transcendental experience. I was not alive. Once, between bites of doughnut, Nichole had told me about her alcoholic father. "The AA people are always saying fake it till you make it," she said. "That's me, Ellis. I'm not a drunk, but I always fake it, like with Roy. You're the only one I never had to fake it with. I guess that's why you used to scare me, before that night. I always thought faking it was *better*."

Her lips dusted with white powder.

*

Ulin's voice was almost hypnotically unperturbed and soothing. He sounded so reasonable, a voice of mature and empathetic authority. The kind of voice the dead man in the house had once upon a time possessed. I had to go with that voice.

The interior of the limo was another world. A privacy screen separated us from the driver. Ulin directed him by speaking into a microphone grill built into the door frame. "Go ahead, David," he said into the grill, and the big car pulled onto the road. In the passenger compartment I barely sensed the forward motion. Diminutive fans cycled the air. The light was soft and intimate—theater light. We sat on plush rolled leather. For a while we drove in silence, then Ulin said, "You're father was a stubborn and principled man."

I looked at my hands.

"I didn't know him well or long," Ulin went on, "but I could tell he possessed a deep vein of personal integrity. Unfortunately it did not end up serving him well. We had a business relationship, Ellis, and when it happened that he was unable to uphold his end of the arrangement your father refused to accept my offer to fulfill my end until he could make good. Do you know what the object of our arrangement was?"

"I was the object, I guess. I don't understand it, though."

"To put it simply, I've been waiting my entire life for someone like you to appear," Ulin said. "And I always knew you would appear, eventually. I knew it in my gut."

"What's so special about me?"

"We believe your unique physiology holds the key to indefinite longevity."

I wasn't really following him. My mind had returned to hunker over the memory my father. I shouldn't have left him alone with a stranger.

"I want to go back home now," I said.

"Of course." Speaking into the grill: "David? Young Mr. Herrick would like to go home."

The car made a turn.

"You're alone in the world now, Ellis. Have you considered what you will do with yourself? I'm in a position to offer you an opportunity you'd be reckless to refuse."

I kept looking out the window for Jeepers, remembering how dad brought him home a couple of months after the accident that killed my mother and brother. Remembering, as Mr. Ulin put it, how alone in the world I was now.

"I want to go *back*." I said.

"But we are back, Ellis."

The car pulled onto the shoulder and stopped. The driver opened my door, and I saw my house. There was a police car parked in the driveway behind the Plymouth. Before I got out, Ulin handed me a card. "Call," he said. "Things were handled badly before. Don't make a hasty judgment based on past experience. You can sign your own contracts now."

I stuffed the card in my pocket without looking at it and climbed out of the limo. The bald man passed me on the way up the walk. He nodded but said nothing. Inside the house a female police officer with a clipboard was waiting for me.

By noon the following day I was completely overwhelmed. Calls had to be placed, legal issues dealt with, papers signed, decisions made. Adult decisions. I looked in the mirror and didn't see an adult. A couple of times I picked up the phone and started to call Nichole, but couldn't bring myself to dial the number. I'd betrayed her. And worse, I'd betrayed something bigger than her, some mystic bond.

I looked at the card Langley Ulin had given me. It was thick gray cardstock with a series of burgundy numbers embossed on it. A phone number, nothing else. Impulsively, I picked up the phone again and dialed. Probably I would have hung up after a couple of rings. I was that iffy. But it didn't get to a couple of rings.

"Hello, Ellis."

"Hi."

"How are you handling things?"

"Not that great," I said.

"Yes, I understand."

That voice. So comforting.

"I'm—" My throat tightened with emotion.

"Ellis, why don't you let me handle the arrangements."

I breathed out.

Two days later I was sitting on a folding wooden chair next to Mr. Ulin in the little cemetery in north Seattle where my mother and brother were already buried and where my father was about to be interred. Dad's casket rested in front of us on a covered frame work. I was uncomfortable in my new black suit. Besides us, there were about twenty people in attendance. A few of them looked vaguely familiar. Everyone must have thought Ulin was my uncle or something. I had no real uncles, and the one aunt I was aware of lived in Massachusetts and wasn't anywhere in sight. Aunt Sarah was a little intense about funerals. She had stayed at my house for a couple of weeks after my mom and brother were killed, and was mostly hysterical the whole time, which had frightened me. I'd mentioned that to Mr. Ulin, and maybe that was why she wasn't there. I said, in a low voice, "Who are all these people?"

"Friends of your father. Former co-workers, for the most part."

Afterwards the men all shook my hand and the women gave me brief consoling hugs. Some of them said they remembered me from when I was a baby. It started to rain. Everyone left. Mr. Ulin and I sat in the limo.

"Home?" he said.

I was staring out the open window, across the grass, at my father's casket. Now I'd seen my entire family put in boxes. I never again wanted to get within a hundred miles of a funeral. Never.

"Or would you like to come with me now?" Ulin said.

I looked at him. "Come where?"

"First to a facility in Oregon. No, nothing like that hospital you were in."

"What kind of facility?"

"A medical research facility. There will be some tests and a few invasive procedures. I can't promise you won't be uncomfortable at times. But after that, if things appear as promising as I believe they will, you can come and live very comfortably in a little coastal village for a while. Perhaps a long while. You'll have everything you could want or need."

"Would I *have* to live there?"

"For a time. It's a controlled environment, Ellis. A safe environment. You would be my employee. Everyone in the village is an employee, or a relative of one. And of course you will be very well paid."

"For doing what?"

"That would be largely determined by the results of the tests I mentioned. Essentially we'd be harvesting various organic samples."

My mind skipped over that one. I looked out the window. The casket gleamed darkly in the rain. A couple of guys in work clothes stood discreetly off to the side, waiting for us to leave. I wished I could talk to Nichole, but she felt gone to me, as gone as a dead person.

"Okay," I said. "Let's go."

"Good choice, Ellis."

The smoked glass window slid up and the car began moving.

Snapshots:

—My first ride in an airplane, and me glued to the window of the Lear, watching the world I'd known my whole life shrink away into dollhouse irrelevancy.

—My first view of the "medical research facility," thinking it looked like the Adams Family Mansion, from the outside, anyway. Inside it was as modern and gleaming as any hospital. The weirdness of that contrast.

At the end of the week, after being probed, siphoned, sliced, diced and microscopically examined, I found myself sitting in a conference room with a bunch of serious men and women in business attire. There were pictures of me on the walls. Big color photographs ten times life size of my post accident, preoperative body. Dr. Jane gave some kind of lecture while she walked around with a pointer and, well, pointed. It was weird sitting in my jeans at that big mahogany table with all those adults looking at me splattered over the walls. I drank my whole glass of water and reached for the urn to pour another. My hand was shaking.

"In short," Dr. Jane concluded, "complete regeneration of damaged and removed tissue, including the entire spleen."

"In short, Doctor," Langely Ulin said, "Ellis Herrick is a God damn miracle."

She looked at the leash then scanned around the empty beach. "Taking Jeepers for a walk?"

"Yeah, it's kind of our last walk."

"Oh, don't say that."

Jillian was a sweet girl. Her yellow hair was cut short and her cheeks got red in the cold. She had a sturdy frame, ample breasts, a frequent smile. She wasn't my type, which is probably why I picked her. There had been other girls, all of them Blue Heron locals and none of them my type. It was pretty messed up, but there you go.

"Did you ever see that TV show *The Prisoner*? I asked Jill.

She shook her head. "I don't watch much TV. Mostly just *Miami Vice*."

"*The Prisoner* was about this guy who was a secret agent or something, and he winds up captured by the bad guys, and he has to live in this village where everybody works for the bad guys, only it's unclear. You know? It's all kind of mixed up and goofy, so you don't know what's real and what isn't. Plus nobody has a name."

"No names?" She smiled uncertainly

"Yeah. Everybody has a number instead. The secret agent guy was Number Six."

"It sounds weird. Are you sure you're not making it up?"

"It was a BBC show," I said.

"Well no wonder!"

I nodded, looking past her down the shingle where the land curved away. "What would happen," I asked, "if I kept walking along this beach for a long time?"

"I guess you'd get tired."

"What I mean is, would I be allowed to?"

"What's to stop you?"

"I don't know. Giant white balloons and guys in golf carts, maybe."

"What?"

"Never mind."

"Want to walk with me to the clinic? I'm on my way there now. Don't you have an appointment? I think I saw you had an appointment."

I jingled the leash, remembering how Jeepers used to like it when I scratched him behind his ears. "Yeah," I said. "I guess I forgot about that appointment. My dog isn't up for a really long walk, anyway. Lucky I bumped into you."

Jillian picked up my hand and looked into my eyes, which made me uncomfortable. "What's wrong, Ellis?"

"Nothing. Shall we go?"

Holding hands, we walked to the clinic.

And so they took my eyes. My corneas, to be exact. In later years they discovered the corneas regenerated more perfectly when they took the entire eye. But these were the early days.

When I came to I was in my own familiar bed in my own cottage, and someone was puttering. I reached up and touched the thick gauze. Already the tingling of my re-gens had begun. My mouth was dry and sticky with the post-op crud.

"I'm thirsty," I said.

The puttering stopped (I think she'd been dusting). Brisk steps to the bedside. A hand gently lifting my head, a straw inserted between my lips. Cold apple juice, sweet.

"Please open the window," I said. "It's stuffy in here."

"It's cold outside," she said in a nursey voice.

"Please open the fucking window."

She opened the window.

"Sorry," I said. "Guess I'm cranky when I wake up blind."

"Mr. Ulin wanted to see you as soon as you were awake."

"Swell. As long as he doesn't expect *me* to see *him*. That was sort of a joke."

"I'll call," the nurse said.

"Do that."

She began to walk away.

"Nurse? I really am sorry. I shouldn't have said that about the window."

"It's all right, Mr. Herrick. I think it must be awful for you."

Something caught in my throat, but I kept it there and wouldn't let it out. The nurse left. She was right: it *was* awful. The eyes were only the latest in a seemingly endless season of harvest. Besides various organs, Ulin's medical team was particularly fond of my pituitary excretions. I mean, who wouldn't be? The process for harvesting those excretions was complicated, invasive, painful and recurrent. Ever recurrent. I was tired.

Langley Ulin showed up in my bedroom and sat heavily in the wicker chair. The chair made a dry straw cracking sound. Ulin's breathing was labored, as always. I couldn't see him but I pictured him in my mind: a walking cadaver "rejuvenated" by multiple transplant surgeries and the experimental hormonal, blood and pituitary treatments. Ulin's skin was deeply jaundiced and textured like bee's wax. There wasn't much they could do about that yet. My brain was the one organ they couldn't harvest. So they irrigated *Ulin's* brain with a chemical wash derived mostly from my pituitary gland. He should have left it alone. The treatments occasionally caused synaptic misfires.

"How's the world look to you now?" I asked.

He grunted. "They couldn't do the transplant. Your corneas degraded too rapidly."

"Sorry about that."

"It was an anomaly."

"Hmmm."

"We'll try again, as soon as your regenerations are complete."

I swallowed sticky spit.

"There's a concern that some regenerated organs are not adaptable to transplant."

"So maybe one set of eyes is all you get out of me."

He grunted again. "We'll beat the problem."

"Will we?"

"Inevitably, yes."

I pictured him slouched in the wicker chair, staring possessively at me with my own eyes—my original pair, which they'd taken almost ten years ago. None of my harvested organs lasted as long as they would have had they been left in my own body.

So it was horrible all right, but I'd stayed with the program. My dad's heart had failed. In many ways Langley Ulin had assumed the role of surrogate father, and I had no intention of letting him down and letting him die. That didn't mean I loved him like a father; far from it. Freud no doubt would have relished my cock-eyed contradictions.

It was dark under the thick gauze wrap, and a part of my mind clawed at the darkness, like something primitive and trapped. In a day or so the itch-tingle of regeneration would be driving me mad. Then, gradually, light would reenter my world, seeping in around the edges at first. In a few week's time I would be able to see in a blurry approximation of normal vision. A week after that I'd have regained full ocular function. At which point— Ulin had just proposed—my corneas would again be harvested.

"I wish I had my dog," I said.

"Your dog?"

"Jeepers, my dog."

"Don't you worry about that dog. My people take fine care of him, fine care."

I turned my head on the pillow, detecting a misfire.

"Jeepers wasn't ever lost, was he?"

"Jeepers creepers where'd you get them peepers!" Ulin said. "Remember that one?"

"Not really."

"Before your time."

"What about my dad?"

"What about him?" Ulin sounded distracted.

"What was your deal with him?"

"That's old news, ancient history."

"So I'm a history buff."

"You know something, Ellis?"

"What?"

"I've never felt better in my life, and I'm eighty-two years old. I've got you to thank for that."

"You're welcome as hell."

He stood up, the wicker chair crackling. His feet shuffled to my bedside. He smelled like something kept in a closet and brought out once a year for Christmas or Hanukkah. His fingers trembled over my eye bandages, touched them lightly. I flinched away.

"They're always blue," he said.

"I guess they would be."

"The clearest blue . . ."

"I hate it when you hover," I said.

He laughed dryly. The fucking Crypt Keeper. Suddenly I felt terrible loneliness.

"I miss my dog."

"That poor animal is dead," Ulin said.

After a day of depressive torpor I felt capable enough to do my own puttering. As soon as I woke up I suggested the nurse find something else to do with her day. She respectfully declined my suggestion and told me breakfast was ready.

"Thanks. I can find my way to the kitchen by myself. I can also

presented itself to me in soft cotton candy blurs of color and gray scale, painful if the light got too bright.

"Let's do it," I said.

October and unseasonably warm. The windows rolled down and the wind in my face, crisp and clean flowing behind the lenses of my very dark glasses. Eagles on the radio, cranked. *Hotel California.*

"How's it feel to get out?" Jill said.

"Scary."

We ate clam chowder on the pier. I dumped two packets of oyster crackers in my bowl and stirred them around with my plastic spoon. She hadn't commented on my "scary" remark but it hung between us just begging for elaboration.

"You know, this is my first time outside the village in ten years."

"*What*? Are you serious?"

"Not usually, but in this particular instance, yeah."

"That's amazing."

"Amazing plus other less appealing descriptors."

"Wow," Jill said. "I mean, I got the impression you didn't even *like* it there so much."

I slipped my glasses off and squinted at the blurry world then replaced them.

"I guess it has its virtues. It's confining but feels safe. Also, I signed a contract. Strictly speaking this little jaunt is illegal."

"Safe from what?" Jill asked.

"I dunno. The big bad world?"

"It's big, all right. But I don't think it's so bad. It can be a pretty nice place, really. Don't you like it here today?"

"I do. For one thing the chowder's great. Not to mention the company."

She placed her hand over mine and squeezed briefly.

"Would you categorize my last remark as a charming insincerity?" I asked.

"I don't think you meant it that way, but yes. I'm sorry. Don't be hurt. You want me to be honest, don't you?"

"Not really." I smiled to show her it was a joke, though it wasn't.

"I think your charm switches on automatically in certain situations," Jill said.

"You mean like during a clam chowder interlude?"

"Maybe."

I raised my glasses, but her face was a pink balloon framed in yellow soft-focus curls.

Back home I invited her to stay the night but she declined, which stung.

"I really want you to," I said.

She laughed. "I *know*. But I'm not ready for that again."

"It isn't auto pilot stuff," I said. "I promise."

"I'll come back tomorrow," she said.

"Okay."

"Unless you're mad at me."

"I'm not mad at you."

She kissed my cheek and gave me a soft, brief hug. I spent the night with myself and a recorded book. *For Whom The Bell Tolls.*

Pretty good but not Hem's best. To make it short, the damn bell tolls for thee and thee and *thee*.

But not for me.

The next day my eyesight was marginally improved. When Jill showed up I'd already made breakfast for both of us.

"They want you to come down to the clinic this morning," she said, accepting the cup of French roast I handed her.

"What if I don't go?"

She shrugged.

"What would happen?" I said.

"Mr. Paranoid. *Nothing* would happen. You're not a prisoner. You're not Number Seven."

"Six."

"Whatever," she said.

"I know, I know," I said. "I'm an employee with full benefits."

She sipped her coffee. "So don't go," Jill said. She grinned. "What do you want to do instead?"

"Can we go for another drive?"

"Sure. Where to?"

"I don't care. Anyplace outside the village."

Anyplace turned out to be Portland, a three hour drive. We had dinner in a Chinese restaurant. I got around okay. My eyesight had steadily improved but was still poor. The DMV would have declared me legally blind, but what do they know? In the restaurant I removed my dark glasses. The place was crowded, the whole city was crowded by Blue Heron standards.

"You look kind of nervous," Jill said.

"Yeah."

"So . . .?"

"It's just my Chinese restaurant look."

"I see."

"Okay—I *am* nervous. I feel truant. Two days in a row."

She giggled. "Do you want me to write you a note to get back into the village?"

"I think my mother has to do that."

"Right."

"Jill, you'd be honest with me, wouldn't you?"

"Honest about what?"

"About us. About why you want to spend so much time with me."

"Oh, brother. Don't go there, please don't. I thought you were getting over that."

"I'm trying to get over a lot of things. Let me ask you something. If I stood up right now and walked out of this place without telling you where I was going, what would you do?"

"Probably call an ambulance?"

"Why?"

"Because you can hardly see and you'd wind up getting yourself run over by a truck."

I laughed. "Good answer." I pushed my chair back and stood up, dropping my napkin on the table.

"Hey—"

"Relax, I'm just going to the men's room."

"Do you want me to—?"

"No, I can find it all right."

I negotiated my way between the tables. Things were pretty blurry. Each table had a little red lantern with a candle. To me they were like a fuzzy, pulsing star field. I put my dark glasses back on and asked a guy in a white coat which way to the restrooms. He steered me in the right direction. At the end of the corridor there was a green blur above a crash-bar door. EXIT. On impulse I walked to it, shoved the bar, and found myself outside in the cold night of Portland.

I picked my way around to the sidewalk. Traffic zoomed by. Towers of light all around, city cacophony. I took my glasses off and rubbed my eyes, blinked, rubbed them some more. Squinting, I could just make out the façade of the restaurant. The Jade Dragon. I moved down the sidewalk until I encountered a bus-stop shelter. I sat on the bench and waited, but not for a bus.

The minutes passed, maybe twenty of them. A vehicle pulled up in front of me, the door opened, and a man climbed out. I tensed, but it wasn't a UI goon come to round me up. The man sat on the bench next to me, the car drove away, and moments later a bus arrived. The man stepped into it but I declined to board.

After a while I stood up and wandered down the street, feeling lost. And then I *was* lost. Finally I asked a passerby to steer me towards The Jade Dragon. By the time I got there more than two hours had elapsed since I ducked out the back. Jill was gone, and I was alone, except for my deflated paranoia. Fear by any other name. I was my own goon, a depressing realization.

"Ellis!" It was Jillian, waving from her car. I got in and we drove away from there.

"I was so scared," she said. "I've been looking *everywhere* for you."

I made all the appropriate noises of apology and contrition and tried to keep the self-contempt at a minimum. It was a long drive back to Blue Heron.

"I want to renegotiate my contract."

"I see," Langely Ulin said.

We were alone in the kitchen of my cottage. My dark glasses lay on the Formica tabletop. So did a fresh ten year contract, virtually identical to the last one, and a Lacrosse pen. My eyes wouldn't stop watering, but that was okay; it was a good sign.

"You're unhappy with the current arrangement?"

"Maybe."

"I've mistreated you in some way?"

I wiped my Niagara eyes. "No."

"What new terms do you propose?"

"Simple. The truth. From your lips."

"The truth regarding what?"

"My father."

"You already know all that."

"I don't think so. My dad and I didn't have the greatest relationship, but it's never made sense that he would essentially sell me to you. I know he felt guilty about it, but why did he do it in the first place?"

Ulin sighed. "Back then I had my feelers out, my people watching everywhere for medical anomalies. Of course I funded—and continue to fund—life prolongation and rejuvenation research around the world. But my feelers have always been out. I believed in the possibility of you or someone like you appearing one day. Call it intuition, or a dream, if you like. Those Seattle doctors didn't know what they were dealing with, but my people recognized a green flag when they saw one. Preternaturally accelerated healing, and even the hint of organ regeneration. Fantastic."

Ulin coughed into his hand and picked up his red can of Coke, sipped, and put the can back down.

"Well," he continued, "you were a minor, so we needed your father's help. We required your exclusive cooperation. We couldn't afford to let the world find out about you."

"Yeah, I understand *your* motives," I said.

"Your father was a principled man," Ulin said. "But everyone can be moved. His lever, ironically, was surgery. Heart valve replacement. Congenital defect discovered later in life. He had no medical insurance, and besides: most insurance companies wouldn't have covered the procedure, not in 1974. Back then such a procedure was considered experimental."

"You promised him a valve replacement for signing me over to you."

"Roughly, yes."

"That's fairly slimy."

"A matter of business negotiation."

"He didn't last long. What did you give him, a lemon?"

"He never underwent the surgery."

"Why not?"

"He refused it after you ran away. He spent the final months of his life searching for you. I believe he intended to tell you everything and hope you would agree to cooperate of your own free will. If not he was prepared to accept the consequences and die. Some of this is conjecture. But the picture is clear enough, don't you think?"

I remembered that night in Long Beach, when I ran. And later a phone ringing endlessly in a lifeless house. The rest I shut out. Or tried to shut out. Flies.

That night I experienced something like a dream but not a dream. I was lying in bed. Claws scratched at the bedroom door. I got up in my boxers and T-shirt and opened the door. Jeepers stood there, his eyes like white marbles. *My* eyes were fine, the water works shut off, in crystalline focus. Now that he had my attention, Jeepers turned and padded away, and I followed him.

He waited at the front door. I opened it for us and we went out. The air was perfectly still. My bare feet whispered on the lawn. Then the sidewalk was cold and hard, and Jeepers was trotting, claws clicking jauntily on the cement, and I started jogging after him. The dog's nose was in the air. I looked up and saw a Glinda bubble drifting serenely above and ahead of us. Something moved inside that bubble but I don't think it was a good witch; it wasn't anything I could make out, just a shadow, like what you might see through the translucent skin of an insect egg.

The bubble led Jeepers, and Jeepers led me. We arrived at an open expanse of blue grass with an orderly copse of trees in the middle. Orderly? They formed a perfect ring. Each tree was between seven and nine feet tall and they stood close together.

As Jeepers and I approached, the two nearest trees opened up, or stepped aside. *Stepped* aside. In the middle of the circle a few people stood conversing quietly with one another. The night was so weirdly still that their whispery voices sounded like a sentient breeze.

Jeepers trotted right up to the group and they welcomed him. One man bent over and scratched the dog behind the ears, and Jeepers' tail started wagging.

The man was my father.

I stood apart from the group, just within the ring of trees, all of which had begun to sway gently side to side. The two that had parted for us now moved together again, closing the ring. I couldn't bring myself to look directly at these trees. I was frightened of them. A trunk pushed against me, urging me forward.

Only my father's face was distinct. The other people were silent now, their features not quite discernable. Above them the Glinda bubble hovered and pulsed with a ghost light of its own. The light fell upon the people, and I suddenly realized that was why I couldn't see them properly. The light did not illuminate but somehow obscured them. My father was recognizable because he had leaned out of the cone of light when he reached to scratch Jeepers.

"Dad—?" I said.

He smiled at me. It was a smile I'd never seen him wear in life. Easy and broad and loose, a happy and unselfconscious smile with parted teeth.

"That man lied to you," he said.

"What man?"

"Ulin."

Our voices were bell-clear within the circle of trees. My father's voice seemed to be right inside my head.

"What did he lie about?" I asked.

"That whole business with the valve. I would have taken the operation. Heck, I was dying. Of course I would have. But they told me I had to hunt you up first."

"You should have told me."

He shook his head. "Here's the deal, Ellis. Things happen the way they're meant to happen, and that's that. Everything has a reason and a purpose. That's what I'm told. Anyway, it's time for you to get out in the world. Past time. That's what this whole deal is about. You aren't supposed to hide out in Blue Heron anymore."

The others who remained under the cone of light nodded their heads. Dad sat down on the grass and roughhoused Jeepers a little. Jeepers licked his face and my dad laughed. He would never have let the dog do that in real life. He had loved Jeepers in his own taciturn way but wouldn't tolerate getting licked at like that. I laughed at the sight, and when I laughed it was a real sound, and I was walking clumsily, like a drunk or a somnambulist, in through the open door of my cottage.

An hour later I walked back out, leaving the contract on the kitchen table with the fancy Lacrosse pen lying on it, nib aimed at the empty signature line.

I thought about calling Jillian, waking her up, but knew I wouldn't have considered it if I hadn't needed a ride out of town. That was a little too mercenary even for me. Besides, I was no damn good at good-byes.

CHAPTER FIVE

I tried but couldn't find Nichole. Her father was dead. The wide lady in the purple housecoat who answered the door of Nichole's former house failed to enlighten me as to her whereabouts. I had left Blue Heron with only the cash on hand, about two hundred dollars. These resources were rapidly being depleted by bus fair and motel rent. There were no Nichole Roberts in any of the state's phone books available in the King County Public Library main branch. There was, however, one Adriel Roberts with a double listing, residence and business. I flipped to the yellow pages and found her ad. It had to be Nichole's mother. Fortunes, Tarot Readings, Past Life Regression.

She had set up shop on 15th Avenue in Seattle's funkiest community at the time, Capitol Hill. Third Eye Café was tucked between an East Indian restaurant and a counter-cultural cum revolutionary bookstore. The sign above the door of Adriel's place looked hand-painted but not amateurish. An eye burning over a pyramid. Yin/Yang symbols on either side. In black script a listing of services provided. Including "organic espresso." Under that, one word: *Evolve*.

I entered the shop. A young guy with cocoa skin wearing dreadlocks and a hemp coat turned toward me from a display of dreamcatchers. The coat was open. White letters on his black T-shirt read: EVOLVE. Was a theme emerging?

"Howdy," he said.

"Hi."

Adriel Roberts came through the beaded curtain behind a glass display case of Tarot decks and spirit stones. She wasn't dressed like a hippie gypsy or Stevie Nicks or anything. She wore a white blouse open at the neck and pearl gray pants. A thin silver chain lay against her throat, kind of classy.

"Hello, Ellis."

Like I'd been walking into her shop every Tuesday for the last ten years. In her mid-fifties now, she was still an attractive woman, and I could still see Nichole in her face. A stab of pure regret and loneliness pierced my heart.

"Hello," I said. "You remember me."

"I not only remember you, I've been waiting for you."

"Uh, sorry I'm late, then."

"You're *not* late; you're right on time."

The hemp guy was giving me a closer look, a speculative look. Still friendly but with a shadow of reservation.

"This is Herrick," Adriel Roberts said to him, gesturing to me. The guy's face instantly transformed, lit up with wonder, and he put his hand out.

"Holy God, are you kidding," he said.

"No, she's not," I said, taking his hand, which was big enough to engulf mine like a mitt. He didn't start a squeezy contest, though. His grip was light as feathers. He held my hand almost reverently, not shaking it.

"Is this the one?" he said.

"The one what?"

"The one that was severed." He lowered his eyes, suddenly sheepish, and released his grip.

"Actually it was my left hand," I said.

He peered at my left hand, which of course was as ordinary looking as anyone else's. I waggled it at him.

"Hey, it's just a hand. They reattached it after an accident and it healed up. No big deal."

He nodded politely, but the wonder didn't leave his eyes.

Adriel said, "Marvin, don't stare."

He looked flustered. "Sorry."

"I'm trying to find Nichole," I said to Adriel.

"She's married."

Take that first stab of lonely regret and try it again, but use a bigger knife this time. Use a fucking rapier. Might as well dip it in venom first.

"Who—"

"Somebody boring but stable. I think his name is Dan. Doesn't that sound about perfect for boring but stable?"

"Yeah, perfect."

"I think he's an engineer or something. He doesn't drink much. People like him. He buys her things. They go to baseball games. No kids. Are you all right?"

She said all this while staring directly into my eyes.

"I want to talk to her."

She nodded. "You should, of course."

"Do you think she wants to talk to me?"

"Maybe. Shall I call her and see?"

"Please."

"Marvin?" She turned to the Rasta man. "Be a doll and pick me up a gallon of soy milk." She opened the register, took out a ten dollar bill, and handed it to him. He folded the bill and stuffed it in his pocket. He had hardly taken his eyes off me since Adriel Roberts introduced me as "Herrick." By some inflective magic she had imbued my name with unwarranted significance. Now Marvin hesitated to leave. He looked from me to Adriel.

"What—" he started.

"Go ahead, Marvin," she said.

"What's going to happen now?" he asked.

Adriel smiled and placed her hand on his shoulder. She had to reach up pretty high to do it. "Everything is already happening," she said. "It has been for a long time. Now that Ellis is back with us the process may accelerate, but that isn't for us to decide."

"I know. I just— I'll get the milk."

"Thank you." She pulled him down and kissed him on the lips, tenderly.

As soon as he was gone, I asked, "What was that all about?"

Bestowing that sweet smile upon me, she replied: "Evolution."

Nichole agreed to meet me at Westlake Park in downtown Seattle at noon the following day. I was there early, like by an hour. The park consisted of an acre or so of Italian stone surfacing bordered by the Westlake Retail Center, a Seattle's Best Coffee franchise, and Nordstrom's. Pine Street cut through the middle of the park and there was a steady flow of traffic. Also, plenty of hungry pigeons and one steel drum band, but they were presentable. I sat on a bench with a latte and listened. They were pretty good, but after a while it got sort of repetitive. The band, not the pigeons. Well, the pigeons, too.

At about five past noon I saw Nichole cross Pine Street and

walk toward me. I stood up, leaving my cup of espresso on the bench. Nichole looked better than great, and very stylish in a black trench coat and beret.

"Nichole."

"I almost didn't come," she said. "And then I did come, but really early, and I waited around watching you. I wanted to leave but I couldn't. Now I don't know what I want for sure. A hug, I guess."

I put my arms around her and she crushed herself into me. In an instant my inner wall fell and my moat drained, and the poor little perinea fish were left gasping and flopping in the stinking mud. Also, as a bonus, Time was temporarily suspended.

"I'm sorry," I said. "You know about what."

"Don't talk about it yet," she said into my chest.

"I won't."

We held each other, held each other, and then we weren't holding each other, and Nichole had pulled back out of my embrace.

"Let's have lunch," she said. "If we do anything else we'll get ourselves in trouble."

"There's trouble and there's trouble," I said.

"Don't be charming. Just don't."

Shades of Jillian. Damn it.

She took me to The Palomino and we ordered a veggie thin crust pizza. She had a glass of Chablis and I ordered a Beck's Dark, which was pointless, considering my enhanced physiology.

After the timeless hug at Westlake, Nichole hadn't touched me once. I felt drawn to her by the same powerful magnetism that I'd experienced ten years ago, but if she felt anything similar she was playing it off.

"So you're married," I said.

She held up her left hand. A yellow gold wedding band and a fairly impressive diamond engagement ring.

"Yes," she said.

"Do you love him?"

"You're not going to start asking idiotic questions, are you?"

"Define idiotic."

She gulped her Chablis.

"Roadhouse pussy," she said, a little too loudly. It was her third glass of wine. The Palomino was crowded for lunch. *Roadhouse pussy* drew some stares.

"I was stupid."

"Yes."

"I don't know why I did it."

"I'm sure I don't know why, either."

"She didn't mean anything to me."

"I *know* that."

Our table was by the windows. The Palomino was four stories up. Nichole turned her face to the view. Her eyes were shiny.

"Then you just disappear," she said, to the window.

"My dad—"

"I know about your father. I was at the service. You didn't notice me. No, shut up. I didn't *want* you to notice me. That's not why I went. I just wanted to see if you were all right."

"I'm really sorry," I said.

"I never believed in magic," she said.

"What?"

"I never believed in that soulmate shit, that transcendental love shit. That 'meant to be' shit. Then in one night I changed inside. I had a dream, and it was like a new memory of who I was and who we were together. Who we were supposed to be. Right away I fought it but I couldn't, not really. It's like I could fight but what's the point? So I believed. And later I really liked running away with you. Those months when you didn't write or call me and I didn't even know where you were, it was like dying. Isn't that stupid, considering at that point we had like less than one full day to call ours? Then you did call, and you needed rescuing. Do you know what that was like, getting that damn call? Oh my God. Even when we were holed up in that cheesy no-tell motel, I didn't care. It's like the future didn't matter anymore, just the now, the now between you and me. Okay? So what if my parents were fuck-ups. So what if sometimes I felt like taking too many pills or cutting my stupid wrists. That didn't matter anymore. I *know* I was a pain-in-the-ass chick back then. But eventually I would have gotten over that. I just needed time, you know? I needed time to flush Roy Hathaway and his ilk out of my soul. I needed time to grow out of that. You think a person can be happy and healthy all of a sudden? You didn't give me enough time."

"Nichole."

"Shut up. Okay? Just shut up, I'm almost done."

I shut up.

She was still looking out the window. Her red lips pressed together, suppressing a tremble. I saw the momentum go out of her. She turned to me and daubed at her eyes with her napkin.

"Anyway," she said, "I'm married now. He's a real nice guy, too. He treats me nice. He hasn't got an ounce of charm, but he's steady and sane and he loves me. That's more than enough. You want soulmates and dreams, see my mother. She probably believes in that shit. I can't really afford to anymore, you know?"

She stood up.

"I'm sorry," she said. "I can't talk to you. I thought I could but I can't. Life really sucks, doesn't it?"

"Yes."

She touched my cheek with the back of her hand then walked away. Her eyeliner left black smudges on the white linen napkin. My moat flooded, but it was too late.

I was twenty-nine years old (now and forever?) and I possessed not one marketable skill with which to earn a living. I watched my meager funds dwindle, and I was too proud by half to contact Langley Ulin about the wages he'd supposedly been salting away for me those ten years I spent in the village. He had lied to me. The dream of my father and Jeepers had been more than a dream. I knew instinctively that what my dream-dad had told me was true. I was done with Ulin and he could keep his stinking blood money.

That left me without many options.

I decided to see what I could get on the open market for my miracle boy status.

What I got was laughed out of newsrooms of the *Seattle Times* and the *Seattle Post-Intelligencer*. Okay, I wasn't actually laughed at, not to my face. But I got the idea. Of course, I had no proof. I was better received at the editorial offices of the alternatives, *The Weekly*, *The Stranger*, but even they declined to present my story. Langly Ulin's status as a rich industrialist made him an attractive target, but again: I lacked proof. I lacked credibility. I was just some guy with a weird story and an ax to grind. In the end, I resorted to the lizard trick. Reluctantly. I knew in theory it would work. My eyes grew back with reliable predictability. So had my kidneys and a few other organs. The process would be the same for any other body part. Ulin's medical types had confirmed this. My whole body was a lizard tail. Chop a piece off and watch it grow back. Theories are nice. Chopping things off isn't.

I returned to the *Times*. There was a guy there who wrote a column called "Weird World." He did local stories about the unexplained. Haunts and Big Foot and Mysterious Sink Holes. The column appeared in the entertainment section.

I appeared at Joe Keegan's desk. He'd agreed to talk with me but made no promises about devoting any ink to my cause. I'd bypassed him on my first visit to the *Times*. I didn't want to appear in the entertainment section. I'd wanted a legitimate news story, national interest. Maybe a book deal? Why not.

Well, at least Mr. Keegan *worked* for a legitimate newspaper.

His desk was in the newsroom. I sat in a chair next to him and we talked over coffee. Keegan was a young guy, about twenty-five. He had a bushy orange mustache and wore a blue work shirt, sleeves rolled above his elbows, a burgundy tie pulled loose, and a red Kangol cap, Kangaroo forward. During the forty-five minutes or so that I spilled my guts he constantly tapped the eraser end of a yellow pencil on his thigh.

When I finished I said, "What do you think?"

"It's got a nifty local angle, and it's original, all right. But to tell you the truth it's a little outside my line. What we like to do is stuff where no one is going to come at the paper with a lawsuit in their hot little fist. That's why I don't pick on Mrs. Bill Gates and her secret seances, for instance."

"She has secret seances?"

"Who knows? That was just a for instance. Example given. Right?"

"Okay."

"Langley Ulin. It's not an immediately recognizable name, but that can be even trickier. Look. I don't want to blow you off. Your story is *cool*. I mean it. Otherwise am I going to sit here and listen to the whole thing? No, I'm not. But I'm the newbie around here. I get plenty of latitude for my attitude, but that's because my editors think I'm a joke. I'm *not* a joke, but perception is everything. The other thing is, I'm not Kolchak. I'm not on the Night Stalker beat. I'm not committed to Art Bell country. But it's an in? You know how tough it is to get your own column? At my age and experience level?"

"Pretty tough, I guess."

"Forget about it. So bottom line? I'm not pissing off my editors with any exposés on rich industrialists. I like you, man. But you know what? I wish you were sitting there telling me you were a werewolf or something, and telling it with the same level of sane sincerity that you told the re-gen story. *That* I could write up, post-haste. And it wouldn't hurt if you sprouted some bristles, right?"

He laughed, good natured as hell. I laughed, too, in the spirit of things. Then I reached into my coat pocket and withdrew the little butcher's hatchet I'd bought that morning at Kitchen Stuff. Keegan's eyes went big and round and his laugh dried up, but he kept smiling.

"Oh, man. What's that for?"

He looked around the newsroom, and I knew I had only seconds. Did newspaper columnists have "panic" buttons under their desks just like bank tellers and Seven-Eleven clerks?

"Take it easy," I said. "I'm not a maniac, and this isn't the ax I'm here to grind." I turned it in my hand. The fluorescent light gleamed on the flat, silky face of polished steel.

"So why don't you just put it down, huh?" Joe Keegan said.

"I'm not a maniac, and I'm not a werewolf, either," I said. "So I can't sprout bristly hair out of my forehead and grow fangs for you. But I am what I am, just like Popeye. And I can do the lizard trick."

"The lizard trick?"

I smiled. Queasily, I suppose. "Yeah," I said. "You know, you chop a lizard's tail off and it grows a new one."

"Oh, man. Don't do that, Mr. Herrick, okay? Really don't do that."

I put my left hand on the desk, pinky finger extended. The re-generated one that I'd already lost once.

"Oh, shit." Keegan's face drained of color. Probably it looked like my face. "Help," he said, but his voice came out squeaky and broken. A woman typing away on her computer a couple of desks to Keegan's left snorted without looking up from the yellow notepad from which she was transcribing.

"Trust me, Mr. Keegan," I said. "You're going to be glad I did this."

"*Shit.*"

I held my breath and brought the blade down with authority. Oh, man. Keegan got off a good hearty scream. Blood sprayed across his desk and speckled his computer's keyboard and his blue shirt and made black spots on his burgundy tie.

"You saw me do it," I said, then chopped at the severed digit until it was a ragged mess unsuitable for reattachment surgery. It was bloody Grand Guignol in the *Seattle Times* newsroom. By then Keegan wasn't the only one screaming. I dropped the little hatchet, and the clang of it hitting the floor was far away and dull down a swoony corridor, and I fell out of my chair, and fell and fell, the corridor now a bottomless elevator shaft.

My next fully cognitive moment occurred in a hospital emergency room. My hand was numb with local and a doctor was sewing the end of my stump. the anaesthetic lasted about half as long as I needed it to. Each needle poke became a brilliant flash of pain. I bit down on my tongue. There was a policeman standing by the privacy curtain.

Insert three days in the mental ward under observation, a mandatory psych evaluation, a couple of group sessions, some pretty bad meals, and release back into the world. I was deemed not a danger by an overburdened system. And I *wasn't* a danger. I had no desire to repeat the lizard trick.

I had the tingle.

When I walked out of the ward, Adriel Roberts and the Rasta man were waiting for me.

"I thought you might need a place to stay," she said.

I'd checked out of my no-star motel before my last visit to the *Times.*

"I guess I do," I said. "But—"

"No buts. I've plenty of room. Marvin will drive us. I don't drive."

Being mostly broke, I wasn't in a position to protest. She had a big two bedroom apartment on the top floor of a brick building a few blocks from her shop on Capitol Hill. It was loaded with dreamcatchers, surrealistic artwork, tasteful modern furniture by Dania, and cats. Too many damn cats. She shared her bedroom with Marvin, I discovered. My bedroom was really her business office. There was a desk with a gooseneck lamp, a wooden file cabinet, and an adding machine. There was also a comfy sofa, and Adriel made me feel more than welcome, despite the weirdness of the arrangement.

I holed up and watched my pinky grow back. It took about a week this time. I snipped the stitches out myself with a pair of nail clippers. The tingling sensation grew intense. The end of the stump began to elongate. It was very tender and I had to be careful of bumping it. The first knuckle formed almost over night. It was amazing.

"Holy God," Marvin said one morning at breakfast towards the end of the week. I'd been avoiding him as much as possible. I didn't like the way he seemed to regard me as some kind of Sign. Adriel was down at the magic shoppe or whatever it was.

"It's not much to do with God," I said, just to be contrary. I had no idea *what* it had to do with.

"Holy God is just an expression," Marvin said.

"Yeah, I know. What I'm saying is I don't have much to do with God, so I doubt my finger does, either."

"What's it feel like?" Marvin asked.

"Very tingly and kind of painful at first."

"You want to smoke a joint?"

"At nine o'clock in the morning?"

He shrugged. "Time isn't real, it's just something we make up and then build clocks to remind us of what we meant."

"*Mornings* are real."

"That's pretty true, yeah."

"Anyway, I'll pass on the joint for now, thanks.

"Okay."

"Marvin, can I ask you something?"

"Sure."

"Why do you look at me like that all the time?"

"Like what, Mr. Herrick?"

"I don't know. Never mind. What about the Evolution thing, tell me about that."

He smiled. "Consciousness evolution. I kind of understand it but probably not enough to really explain it to you? Plus it's weird me trying to tell you what it's about. You should ask Adriel. She's the expert."

"What's so weird about you explaining it to me?"

"Because you *are* it."

"I'm consciousness evolution?"

"You're like a pointer, the way Adriel says it. A compass needle aiming at true consciousness."

I flexed the fingers of my left hand. My pinky was almost back to normal. The only thing missing was the nail. I finished my toast and coffee.

"Can you drive me downtown, Marvin? I have to see a guy."

"Sure."

The guy was Keegan at the *Times*. Keegan and anyone else who had been there on chopping day. Security tried to stop me but

I dodged around and bolted into the newsroom and made it to Keegan before they could catch up and grab me. Keegan jumped out of his chair when he saw me. Two security types grabbed me by the arms, but I managed to slip my left one free and stretch it out for the columnist to look it.

"Keegan, you saw me do it!" I shouted.

"Keep that lunatic away from me!" he yelled at the guards.

I closed my fingers into a fist except for the pinky, which I left extended. The newsroom was in pandemonium. Then I saw it in Keegan's eyes. The guards got my arm pinned again and one of them snapped a pair of cuffs on me, but it didn't matter now.

"Wait wait wait," Keegan said as they started to drag me away. I'd ceased resisting.

"Let me see his hands," Keegan said.

I had a guard on each arm. They turned me around. Behind me, Keegan said, "What are you, some kind of magician?"

"I told you what I am."

"Which hand was it, it was this one, right?" He touched my left hand.

"The pinky finger," I said.

"Fuck me," Keegan said. A lot of other people came over and looked at my finger.

"It must be a prosthetic," somebody suggested.

"Bullshit," somebody else said. "That's flesh and blood."

"So they reattached the one he cut off."

"I don't think so," Keegan said. "He chopped that one to pieces. I *saw* him do it. Hey, Herrick." His hand was on my shoulder. "I've got the exclusive, right?"

"You're the man," I said, then the guards escorted me out. The SPD showed up and I was arrested, but I didn't put in much jail time. The *Times* made my bail, and the *Associated Press* made me famous. I gave Keegan more than an exclusive for the paper. I collaborated with him on a book. He turned out to be a competent enough writer. I gave him some good stuff to work with. "Regeneration Man" was a skinny little book in manuscript, and Keegan proceeded to shamelessly pad it. By the time the book was published I was already the subject of intensive medical research at the University Of Washington. In a way it was like being in Langely Ulin's clutches all over again. I put up with it because of the money from the book sales, mostly.

But all that happened later. Friday I was booked into jail and then processed out again within a matter of hours.

"I want to buy you a drink," Keegan said when we were on the sidewalk in front the Public Safety Building. "Then we can talk business."

"I don't drink much. I told you about the alcohol."

"Oh, yeah."

"We'll talk it through on Monday. Thanks for posting my bail."

He looked panic stricken. "You're not going to skip out, are you?"

"Keegan, I *want* my story told. Believe me. Why the hell do you think I chopped my own finger off right in front of you? I'll come in Monday, don't worry."

"Where are you staying? You need a place to crash?"

"I'm with friends, I'm okay."

"This is big," Keegan said. "If even half of what you told me last week—"

"It's all true. And there's more. But it'll keep over the weekend. Thanks again for bailing me out."

I shook his hand and started walking away. He called after me:

"Herrick!"

"Yeah?"

"This is *big*."

I laughed.

Friday night Adriel prepared a celebratory dinner of rice, tofu, hummus and pita bread. It was the sort of banquet Gandhi might have enjoyed looking at if not actually eating. Following dinner Marvelous Marvin put some Cat Stevens on the turntable and lit up a joint as fat and brown as his thumb. The three of us passed it around, and to my delighted astonishment I felt the vapors mellow my alpha waves in an agreeable fashion. Evidently my body metabolized dope the same way everybody else's did. Hallelujah!

"Your life is about to change," Adriel said, lotus-legged on the floor next to the sofa, her head haloed by candle light.

"It's already changed," I said. The dope was making me, well, dopey. I giggled.

"There's big change for everybody coming, and you're part of it, Ellis."

"Groovy."

Marvelous Marvin laughed. I did another dopey giggle, then all of us laughed.

"Hey," I said, suddenly remembering. "What's all this consciousness evolution malarkey about?" Except it took me three or four tries to get the word "consciousness" to come out with the right number of syllables in the right order.

"Yeah, tell him," Marvin said. "I know what it is but I couldn't say it right, you know?"

I laughed.

"Our planet is dying, Ellis," Adriel said. "And it's not a natural death. It's humans. And there's some really bad stuff coming up, because we can't get unstuck from our primitive, tribal thinking. Our monkey thinking, basically. The Harbingers are going to help us evolve to a higher stage of consciousness by filling the world with pointers, hints and clues. Impossible things for people who are ready to take notice and expand their minds with the possibilities of limitlessness. You're an important pointer, Ellis. You're crucial. The Harbingers told me."

"You're damn right I'm crucial," I said.

"Man, you are high," Marvin said.

"Very astute, Marvin. Very."

We all laughed some more. The beautiful mother of my lost soulmate, Rasta man, and miracle boy. Especially miracle boy. Smoke dat ganja!

Some time later I was lying on my sofa in the office bedroom, staring at the shadowed ceiling, my mind alternately crawling with visions and just plain crawling. It was one of those oatmeal ceilings they used to spray on. To me it looked like the surface of a hostile planet. Strangely I began to imagine an intricate network of graphite-colored tubes interconnecting with silver saucepan domes, a whole city network of these things planted on Oatmeal World. As a kid I used to play with my mother's sauce pan lids, and I loved science fiction, so I guess that's where it came from. At some point the image attained a greater reality. It became deeper, dimensional. I felt like I was above the ceiling in an orbiting vehicle, not lying on the sofa looking up. Lids and tubes focused into richly detailed structures. Specks of light moved across the surface of Oatmeal World, and I was drifting above it, drifting in free fall, zero-G. I felt vertiginous. It was all coming out of me and was me, wholly. I began to fall toward it, which was somehow like plummeting inward. I picked up velocity. The surface of Oatmeal World stood out in relief, a ravaged terrain ornamented by the complex works of man. A city of infinite meaning. Then Adriel Roberts touched my thigh and I tumbled out of my vision and back to the sofa.

"Ellis, are you all right?"

I swallowed and couldn't speak for a moment. She was sitting on the sofa beside me, wearing a shiny robe or Kimono thing, her hand still resting on my thigh, her hip against my leg. In the dark she *was* Nichole. But I couldn't move.

"I'm—" I croaked.

She tilted her head, that same way her daughter had, an expression of encouragement and curiosity and understanding. Her hand caressed my thigh, but I was mostly oblivious to it.

"I'm scared," I said.

Her hand paused. "There's nothing to be scared of."

She was wrong about that.

CHAPTER SIX

Twenty years later I was living in suburban Everett, Washington. My home was a tract house, a sixties-era rambler with gingerbread trim around the porch and a cute little satellite TV dish on the composition roof. I called myself Jack Ellis. Joe Keegan's book *Regeneration Man* had been a success back in 1984. A unique success, as it rode the *New York Times* best-seller list in both the fiction and nonfiction categories, for three weeks and nine months, respectively. Bona fide medical investigation out of the University of Washington is what bumped the book over to the nonfiction side of the list. Keegan had been covering his bases with his folksy "What if. . ." style. The book generated a lot of money, but I'd signed a wonky contract and wound up far from rich. Of course there had been plenty of people who wanted to buy various organs out of my theoretically inexhaustible supply. But I opted not to ramble down that particular path.

Eventually I withdrew from the world, changed my name, and went to ground. Every once in a while somebody managed to track me down. These people arrived in three types: those who wished to harvest me, those who wished to worship me, and those who wished to kill me. That last, I guess, just to prove it could be done. (I always *assumed* it could be done; all the would-be assassin had to do was deprive me of an organ I literally couldn't live without for even five minutes, say my brain for instance). Since I couldn't always tell the types apart at first glance (unless they happened to be wearing an "E" T-shirt), I kept a loaded 9mm Parabellum around.

I supplemented my income in a small way by working in a Mill Creek Starbucks. Plus it was nice to get out of the house and out of my head for a while each day. I liked my co-workers. They were all young. At twenty-nine I was the oldest employee at that particular café. And of course no one knew how old I *really* was.

I intuited someone was watching me before I saw who it was. My radar was always on. There was that vibe. I had started feeling it at work and at home, which was a bad sign. Someone had found me and he was being cagey about it. The Evolution-ites weren't cagey. They'd come right up to me and want to touch my hand, that kind of shit. The harvesters were usually desperate and you could spot them quick.

But I hadn't spotted anyone.

That left category three. Damn it.

Then one day I pulled a double-tall-skinny for this guy and I knew it was him. My stalker.

Just knew it.

He was a middle-aged man, hair receding to strand a ridiculous tuft. Incipient jowls. Eyes with luggage, like he lived on espresso. Off-the-rack sport coat. Clunky gold ring on the first finger of his right hand. A small paunch. He held a newspaper but studied me closely while I made his drink. I snapped a lid on the cup, called it out, and placed the drink on the pick-up counter, which was shaped like an oversized painter's pallet. The stalker reached for it and I caught his eyes and saw . . . something unhappy.

"Thanks," he said, which in this case was like code for: *I've got your number, asshole.*

He picked up his espresso and walked out of the store. I watched him cross the street and climb into a tobacco brown Taurus. I couldn't see the plate from where I stood.

But I saw the car again the next day, parked about three blocks from my house. I was out jogging in the morning and noticed it. Of course it didn't have to be the same car, but it would figure.

I looked around but the sidewalks were empty except for a German Shepherd that never seemed to be on a leash. She was nosing around in a hedge about a block away. Jeepers was my last dog. Their life-spans were too short, the grief factor too high.

I stood by the Taurus in my sweatshirt and Nike shorts, dripping, breathing hard. I'd been on the last leg of a six mile run when I spotted the car. The rear deck was pretty dirty. I wetted my finger tip and made a half moon about six inches wide, like a howdy grin. The plate was Washington State. I memorized the number, took a last look around, and started for home.

Then it struck me: Home is where the stalker is.

I stood on the front lawn and regarded my house warily. The 9mm was still in the drawer of my bedside table.

I started getting pissed off, which produced adrenaline, which is like rocket fuel. I slipped around to the back of the house and edged up to the slider. It was open, the cheap plastic latch snapped off. He was in there. My anger mounted. I exercised restraint, picked up a split of stove wood from the pile, and faded back to the side of the house to wait.

Less than three minutes elapsed and he came out, drawing the broken slider shut behind him. He would have to pass by me to get out of the back yard, unless he jumped the fence and crossed the neighbor's property.

I listened to him approach, and I tensed.

He swung around the side of the house, walking casually, tucking a pry bar under his coat. I lunged forward and cracked him across the knees with my stove wood. He howled and went down.

"Who the hell are you?" I demanded, standing over him in my jogging outfit, a mighty slayer of slow, paunchy interlopers.

"Motherfucker!" he said, hooked my ankle with his right hand and yanked me off my feet. I landed on my coccyx, otherwise known as the tailbone. Which is a painful thing. The man swarmed over me, slapped the stove wood out of my hand, knocked me flat on my back, and pinned me there with his forearm across my throat. He moved *fast*, and forget qualifiers such as: *For his age*. Physically I was probably twenty years younger and in ten times the condition. Yet here I was rendered helpless.

"My name's Ron Stone," he said, "to answer your question." His breath smelled like onions.

I made a strangled sound and he let up the pressure on my throat.

"Good to meet you, Ron. Would you mind getting off of me, please?"

He hesitated, forearm set to crush my windpipe. He searched my eyes, came to a decision and rolled off me and stood up, favoring his right leg. He offered me his hand. I looked at it a moment then took it and he pulled me up. He staggered a little, taking my weight.

"You coulda busted my knee, you know," he said.

"Hey, you're the burglar."

"I'm not a burglar."

"You came out of my house, and I don't recall inviting you over. Plus you broke my slider. That's B&E, right?"

"Yeah, well, I had to be sure you were who I thought you were."

"So am I? And why should I care what you think?"

"You're Ellis Herrick, the regeneration guy, and you should care because I'm representing somebody you'll be very interested in hearing from."

"You *represent* someone? What are you, a lawyer?"

"Private detective."

"Who's your client?"

"Not so fast. Confirm your identity."

"I'm Jack Ellis, just like it says on my driver's license."

He made a sour face. "There was nothing in your house to prove otherwise. But you're Herrick. You should have done plastic surgery, you were so concerned about being recognized. Hell, your face was on the cover of *Time* and *Newsweek*. It's easy to find those old magazines, not to mention the pictures on the internet, especially on that cockeyed Evolution website. A beard ain't going to cut it, not with all that stuff available. Besides. . ."

He was studying me closely again, and had that look.

"Besides," I finished for him, "I haven't aged."

"Yeah."

"Who's your client?"

"I can't reveal that without her permission, which I don't have."

"Her?"

"Nuts."

I'd thought it might be Ulin or his people. Twenty years ago, when I'd hurled feces into the fan, Langley had made no public statements, neither confirming not denying the veracity of my account. Of course reporters had invaded Blue Heron, Oregon. But the residents there had merely confirmed that I once lived among them, nothing more. Ulin himself had already withdrawn from public view even before I began my association with him, so there wasn't anything greatly unusual in his silence. Twenty years. Could Ulin even be alive? That would put him somewhere in his nineties. He had long been deprived of my genetic contribution to his rejuvenation efforts. Still. Who could say what the residual effects of the original protocol might have been? Anyway, it made no sense that Ulin would have hired a low-rent P.I. like Stone to hunt me up. Ulin

Industries had diversified into cutting edge computer chip development. If anything, Langely Ulin would be even richer than he had been when I knew him. If he wanted to flush me out of my half-assed retirement, he could probably have done it with one phone call.

"Listen," I said to Stone, "whoever your client is, tell her to locate herself a very deep lake and then go take a leap. I'm not interested. I'm retired from the regeneration business. I have nothing to donate, not even my time."

"She doesn't want a donation."

"Whatever she wants, I'm not interested. I'm out of the messiah business, too."

Stone was grinning. "Man, I don't see it."

"See what?"

"What *she* sees in you. You're just a whiny bastard with good genes."

I laughed. "You've got my number, Stone."

"I'll be sure to tell her not to bother with your sorry ass," he said.

He started walking away. I put my hand on his chest to stop him. He was a big son of a bitch. I could feel his beating heart.

"Hold up," I said. "You're forgetting the B&E."

"So what, you're going to press charges? Sue me? Things could get very public in a hurry, Herrick. That what you want?"

Without waiting for my reply, which I didn't have anyway, he pushed my hand off his chest and walked off. Whistling.

Two days later Nichole knocked on my door. I opened it and gaped at her.

"Close your mouth," she said. "Your tonsils are showing."

"They're the original pair, too," I said.

"They're cute. May I come in?"

Twenty years. And at least once a day for every one of those years my heart had ached open. Knowing she was out there someplace, living with her husband, growing older, retreating from me. Every day. Robert Bloch got it right: *Time wounds all heels*.

"I don't know," I said, "I'm kind of busy watching TV. Could you come back later?"

"I should slap you for that one."

"You really should," I said. "Come in. Please."

"Are you sure?"

I wanted to pull her into my arms. She was beautiful. Nichole. "Positive," I said and stood aside to let her pass then closed the door and turned. She was staring at me. Her eyes were too wet.

"Hey—"

I put my hand out awkwardly and patted her shoulder. This simple contact propelled us both through some invisible margin, and we fell into each other and held on tight for a long time. We cried. Eventually I said, "Come to bed."

It was mid-afternoon. My bedroom got plenty of western exposure. I closed the shades for privacy but it remained bright in the room. I stripped my shirt off. We kissed. I started pulling at Nichole's blouse. I noticed she had resumed crying, so I stopped what I was doing.

"What's wrong?" I gently touched her cheek, where a tear was slowly tracking down.

"I'm forty-eight years old, Ellis."

"Me, too."

She touched my face, my chest, with her fingertips. She shook her head.

"No," she said. "And you never will be."

"It doesn't matter."

"It does," she said. "But make me forget it for now, okay? You can do that."

I pulled her blouse loose and unbuttoned it. Her bra was sky blue, her nipples pink under the sheer fabric. She was wearing a short tartan skirt. My hand caressed sweetly up her thigh, my face in her breasts. Maybe she forgot it mattered, maybe not. I did. For a while.

Later, lying under the sheets, she said, "You didn't even ask me about Dan."

"I'm the type who asks questions later," I said. "Who's Dan?"

"My husband."

"Oh."

"Ex-husband."

"*Oh*. Good. I mean, I'm sorry. I think. Shit, what happened?"

"He left me three years ago for a younger woman."

"The idiot."

"She was very pretty."

"You're prettier, and smarter too, no doubt."

"Of course I am."

I kissed her mouth for a while.

"So you're Stone's mysterious client," I said.

"Yes, Ron's mine."

"Strange way to put it."

"I hired him right after Dan left me. It had been bad for years. I was loyal, even if he wasn't. What I'm saying is when he left he didn't break my heart, because he'd already done that and I was more or less over it. It was lonely in that marriage. Terrible. So I hired Ron to try to find you. I wanted to see you again. I can't really explain it. You hid yourself pretty well, didn't you."

"You've had Stone on the payroll for three years?"

"Not exactly. I couldn't afford that. But after a while he was sort of doing me a favor. I think just so he could stay in touch, you know. I'll be honest, we had a brief affair, early on, when things were at their worst for me. I knew it was a mistake and told him so right away. He was sweet about it."

"Right."

"He wanted to be my friend."

"It explains something," I said.

"What?"

"Just a vibe I got off him. I think he's in love with you, all right."

"Oh, I don't think so."

"You don't, but he does. If I had to parse it out I'd say he wanted to find me so he could show you what a worthless bastard I am. Like I'm the illusion that stands between you and him."

She laughed. "Jesus, where do you get all that?"

"I read too much."

"Is that even possible?"

"In theory."

Life resumed. I was so clueless that I hadn't even realized it had ceased in the first place. Now I shuddered inwardly when I recalled the desert years without Nichole.

Fast forward a few weeks: We were walking on the beach at Golden Gardens, holding hands. It was one of those sunsets where the sky is layered in pastels and sketched across with rafts of minted clouds. I chuckled.

"What?" Nichole asked.

"It's a Kodak *and* a Hallmark moment."

She smiled.

I had intended my usual variety of sarcasm but suddenly didn't feel that way. We stopped and kissed and became lost. I may have been immortal, but only Nichole could obliterate Time.

We turned around and walked back to the fish and chips stand. Sitting shoulder to shoulder at a picnic table I dipped a French fry into a blob of ketchup and said, "Without deep fat fryers western civilization couldn't exist."

"It could exist," Nichole said. "But it wouldn't be as fat."

"That's what I meant by not existing."

"Would you still love me if I were fat?"

"Sure."

"Would you still *make* love to me?"

"Naturally."

"Liar."

"I almost never lie."

"Are you going to eat all those fries?"

"Yes!"

She made a grab but I slid my cardboard tray out of her reach. So she went for the ribs, but in a tickle fight I would murder her, and she knew it and backed off, laughing. One of those seagulls that has learned the trick of hovering arrived above our table. I flipped a yellow fry with a red tip into the air. The bird caught it and immediately broadcast a telepathic message of feast to the rest of the local bird population. We left them the remains of our dinner and went home.

In bed our love-making was a blender, turning us into something like Nicholellis. At such moments we required only one soul between us. That was the meaning of the original Oz bubble dreams, I think. Afterwards we held each other like children.

I awoke alone in the dark. Hearing whispery voices and music, I got out of bed and pulled on a pair of boxers and a sweatshirt. Nichole had rolled my old television set out of the closet and plugged it in. She was curled up on the sofa with a glass of white wine, watching an old movie. Judy Garland in soft focus, the volume almost inaudible. The phone was on the cushion next to Nichole's foot.

"Oh, hi," she said. Her voice sounded a little choked.

"Sad movie?"

"Sappy."

"Mind if I join you?"

"Please."

I got a glass, moved the phone, and sat beside her.

"I was going to call my mother," she said, "but it seemed too late."

"Your mother?"

"Yeah." Nichole shrugged. "I had a bad dream. Probably I'm as kooky as she is."

"You're not that kooky."

She looked at me seriously. "Ellis, I love you."

"And I love you."

"I don't want to leave you again."

"I didn't know you were planning to."

"It's not up to me, is it?"

I caressed her cheek, but she just looked at me. After a moment she turned back to the movie and sipped her wine. It was very quiet in the house, and Judy Garland sounded a long way off, and Time was not obliterated.

One day Ron Stone paid us a visit. Nichole had moved right in. It was a natural inevitability. I quickly grew accustomed to finding her installed in my favorite chair with a book whenever I returned home from my espresso gig. She loved my chaotic library, otherwise known as the house. Books occupied every available space. I believed in the salubrious proximity of books. And even though I was a slow reader, I was one guy who would probably get to read everything.

I'd kept working at Starbucks because I enjoyed it and also because Nichole came to our soul-blender without many funds.

"No alimony?" I'd stupidly said.

"I never wanted his money." Curtly. And I apologized for asking and she forgave me.

Anyway I arrived home after working the morning shift and heard shouting while I was still on the sidewalk. I got through the front door fast, and the shouting ceased, like a switch thrown.

Ron Stone loomed over Nichole, his head turned in my direction. He was big and a pretty good loomer. He didn't look angry, though. It was more like anguish pulling his face down. I immediately recognized his torment, being well familiar with its source. He was in love with Nichole, and she was telling him to forget it.

Seeing me, his face underwent a rapid transformation. The slack went out of his jaw (it looked like he hadn't shaved in two days), his eyes narrowed, and he squared his shoulders and pointed at me.

"This is who you want? He's a freak, Nichole. What's he going to be to you in ten years? Twenty years?"

"Hey lighten up with that freak stuff," I said.

He ignored me.

"I'm sorry, Ron," Nichole said. "I really am."

"I'm saying think about what you're doing, that's all. Think about it."

"I have thought about it. You better go now."

The starch went out of him and he sagged again. A big man in his late forties with too many cheeseburgers haunting his gut and a ridiculous, wispy brush of stranded hair above his forehead. I felt for him but also experienced a zap of male dominance at his defeat. When he shouldered past me on his way out, shoving me a little, I said, unkindly:

"Better luck next time."

His head came around like a lion's, ferocious, closely followed by his fist. It was a fist in proportion to the rest of him: Big. It connected with my jaw, snapping me around and off my feet. Stars clouded up in my vision as I fell. A great many stars. And a rushing wind.

I opened my eyes, flat on my back on the faux Persian rug. My jaw hurt. My head throbbed dully. Some punch. The room was dim. Weird sunset light gilded the half-tilted Levelor blinds on the big living room window. Which was wrong, somehow. Where had the rest of the afternoon gone? Stone had clobbered me, and Nichole—

Nichole.

I sat up suddenly — which was a mistake. My head throbbed dreadfully. I groaned, cradled my forehead. Nichole was sitting on the sofa, shadowy, in the kind of light cooling embers produce.

"Are you all right?" I asked.

"I'm wonderful."

"Where's Stone?"

"Wherever Stones go, I suppose."

"I feel wonky."

"That's a funny word," she said.

"I just made it up, I think."

"What's it mean?" Nichole's voice sounded different, pitched too low. Everything felt off-pitch.

"It means the woozy feeling you get after a private detective conks you on the head. Wonky."

She laughed. "That's so *good*, Ellis!"

"Thanks."

I started to get up then had a better idea and remained on the rug. For the moment I was far too wonked to stand.

"Your boyfriend packs a hell of a wallop," I said.

"He wasn't my boyfriend."

"Sorry, I mean your detective."

"Not my detective, either. Ellis, I'm not Nichole. I'm Adriel."

"What?" I rubbed my temples, which did nothing to alleviate the throbbing. "I'm not really tracking you," I said. "What are you doing here?"

"First it might help if we clarify where 'here' is," she said.

"Here in my living room," I said. "Jesus I feel strange. What's going on?"

"I want you to remember a couple of things, Ellis."

"All right."

"Everything is simultaneous."

"What?"

"Everything is simultaneous."

The sunset light was extremely weird. Deep burnt orange with a smoky quality. Pumpkin light. I didn't like it one bit. It reminded me in an unpleasant way of Halloween.

I got up on my feet. It wasn't easy. I felt heavy. My legs were shaky. Adriel stood up from the sofa. She was beautiful. She looked about twenty-two years old, though I knew for a fact that she was past seventy and the matriarch of EC: Evolution Consciousness, a world-wide movement of those who believed the human race was on the brink of an evolutionary leap. *And she was at least seventy.* Oh, what the hell. Everything was simultaneous, right?

I felt drawn to the window. With the blinds tilted I couldn't see what lay outside in the pumpkin light, but I had a feeling it wasn't 22nd Place North East.

Adriel took my hand. "Let's have a look," she said, reading my thoughts.

Suddenly, I didn't want to.

"No," I said.

"It's all right if you don't want to."

"Good. Because I don't." I was afraid. "What's out there?"

"It's up to you, Ellis."

"That's a wonky thing to say."

"Just remember," she said and gave my hand a reassuring squeeze.

"Everything is simultaneous, and it's up to me," I said.

"Right."

"My head really hurts."

"Baby, I'll get you some ice."

I made a kind of strangled cry. Because it was Nichole who had spoken. And I was sitting on the rug again, and the room was filled with ordinary afternoon light.

A half hour later the phone rang. We were sitting at the kitchen table and I was holding a cold pack against my bruised jaw. She picked up the receiver, said hello, listened a moment, and started crying. I put the cold pack down and reached for her.

"What's wrong?"

"My mommy died."

CHAPTER SEVEN

Twenty-six years later I was sitting by myself in a Zingbar, looking out the window at the reflective copper towers of Bellevue, Washington. The bartender, a stunning redhead with fashionably flayed earlobes and the latest "mood irises," handed me a Zingcup with a sanitary disposable inhaler attached. I thanked her and held my left hand up so she could scan my debit nail.

"You're welcome," she said, her eyes coloring speculatively toward carmine.

The cup was cool in my hand. I fitted the inhaler over my nose and breathed deep. It was Taiwanese Zing and the real deal, no Republic of China adulterations. A junk wind blew through my head, clearing out the detritus of stress and fear.

A hand touched lightly on my shoulder. "Mr. Herrick?"

I turned. A woman of about fifty years with short razored iron gray hair and—believe it or not—glasses.

"I'm Herrick," I said.

"I'm Dale Posenjak."

We shook hands.

"You're the second private detective I've ever talked to."

She sat on a stool next to me. "Did the first one give you good results?"

"Depends on how you define results. He slugged me on the jaw and knocked me cold. That was a long time ago, however, and you don't look like much of a slugger."

She smiled. "You might be surprised."

"Can I buy you a Zing?"

"No thanks. How can I help you, Mr. Herrick?"

"I want you to find someone for me."

"Who and why?"

"My wife, Nichole. She's seventy-four years old. Until a month ago she was living here in Bellevue with me, in a condo we shared."

"And where do you think she might be now?"

"If I knew that I wouldn't need you, would I?"

The bartender touched my hand. "Another of the same?"

"Yes."

She brought me another Taiwan Zing. I inhaled and the junk wind blew. I felt *clear*.

Dale Posenjak said, "Aren't you supposed to wait a few minutes between those things?"

"I rarely do what I'm supposed to do," I said. "Besides it's non-addictive."

"That's what they say. Does Nichole want to be found?"

"Not by me."

"Why not?"

"She's being a martyr."

My detective nodded. She retrieved a stick of gum out of her breast pocket, stripped the foil off with her thumbnail, pushed the gum into her mouth and started chewing, thoughtfully.

"I don't think there's much time," I said. "Will you take the job?"

"What's the time factor?"

"She's dying."

Posenjak chewed her gum. She had very steady eyes and they never left my face. I wanted another Zing. My head kept filling with junk.

"You haven't said why you want to find her."

"I just want to talk to her again. She didn't say good-bye."

"She sounds old enough to do as she pleases."

"Jesus, do you always try this hard to avoid gainful employment?"

She chewed and smiled. "Not always."

"Then why now?"

"Just curious. According to EC lore you two are halves of a bifurcated soul."

I stared at her. Junk clattered in my head. "Oh, Christ, don't tell me you're an Evolution Consciousness type! You could have saved us both some trouble by—"

"I'm not an EC-er. I had a brief flirtation with the movement ten years ago, that's all. I'm a sensitive. I was one before it was acceptable to be one, so naturally I sought the like-minded wherever I could find them, even among the ranks of the Evolutionaries."

"How many Harbingers does it take to make a forest?" I asked.

She stopped chewing and grinned. "You can save the Harbinger jokes. I've never seen one and I don't believe anyone else has either. I told you: I'm not an EC-er."

"Okay. Will you help me find Nichole?"

"Yes."

"Thank you."

"It is funny, though, when you think about it."

"What is?" I asked.

"We live in a world Adriel Roberts predicted with fair accuracy. Look at us. The Regeneration Man and a psychic detective sitting here talking, and not too many folks would find that weird. The weird is *accepted*, it's as acknowledged as the periodic terrorist bombings and Quantum computer technology. People believe in things their parents would have scoffed at and their grandparents would have laughed at outright and maybe even had you locked up for espousing. The world has moved toward some kind of heightened consciousness."

I really wanted another Zing.

"Look, I thought you said you weren't an EC-er."

"I'm not. But I'm not blind, either. Everyone accepts my psychic abilities and I can even advertise them in the Yellow Pages. I've read all about you, Herrick. When you first made the national scene you were like some kind of miracle boy wonder. A lot of people flat out denied you were real. When the proof was produced it was like a *boost* or something. Some folks moved ahead and accepted a new paradigm, others closed themselves off. You were impossible. Now you could approach anybody in this bar and identify yourself and no one would doubt you for what you are. One generation back and that wouldn't have been the case, no matter how many fingers you hacked off. The terminator line for the impossible has moved."

"Ms. Posenjak, maybe this isn't going to work out."

I singled the bartender and pointed at my Zing cup. She nodded and brought me a fresh one, picked up my empty, detached the disposable inhaler from it and plugged the cup into a refill slot behind the bar. Above the slot were a few yellow slashes: a kanji character.

"I'm your best chance of finding Nichole," my detective said. "That's why you called me, right?"

I picked up the fresh Zingcup but didn't inhale it yet. "Listen," I said. "Whatever you believe, I don't care. I used to think all that stuff was true, about two souls in one. I never bought into the Harbingers, but I believed in Nichole and me. All I want to do now is find her and be with her, because I think she's dying and is trying to spare me that. I don't want to be spared. I don't need it. All right? So if you can do your job and find her, that's great. But there's nothing else here for you. Consciousness evolution is bullshit. Okay?"

"Sure." She pushed the used up gum out of her mouth and wadded the foil around it and put it in her pocket. She offered me her hand again and I shook it.

"Come by my office in the morning, bring everything you have, addresses, date of birth, history. And don't forget a personal item, something that belonged to Nichole. We'll sign the papers and make it official.

"Okay, Ms Posenjak."

"Call me Dale."

"Dale."

She left and I quickly fitted the inhaler to my nose. A junk wind blew. Then the bartender was there to take the empty, her eyes a tangerine invitation. As usual.

I showed up at Dale Posenjak's office in Pioneer Square at ten o'clock the following morning. She shared the fourth floor of the old Sloan building with two attorneys and a bail bondsman. A stylized eye, mystic and private, was painted on the frosted glass of her outer door. Under that: Dale Posenjak / Investigative Services. She could have added "Psychic Specialties" and no one would have blinked an eye, private or otherwise.

Inside, a young man with a crisp manner and a string tie announced me, and I was immediately invited into the Posenjac's inner office.

She had her feet up on the glass desktop and was filing her nails.

"Good morning," she said. "You look like shit."

"Thanks. I brought everything you wanted." I held up the leather folder containing all of Nichole's pertinent information.

"Rough night?" Dale asked.

"Not too."

"They say that Zing's not addictive."

"Can we stick to Nichole, please?"

She regarded me, appraised me, then swung her feet off the desk and sat up straight.

"Did you remember to bring the personal item?"

"Yes."

"Give it to me. We only need the other stuff if it fails to work."

"Does it often fail?"

"Sometimes. Psychometry isn't an exact science. It isn't a science at all. It's an 'impossible thing.' Don't look so sick, I just said that to irk you."

She held her hand out and wiggled her fingers. I opened the zippered folder and took out a precious item and dropped it into the detective's hand. A white gold ring on a chain. Just like the one on the third finger of my left hand.

"She cherished this," Dale said.

"Yes."

She closed her fingers over the ring. Her eyes stayed open but they grew distant. I shifted nervously in my chair. After a while Posenjak blinked. She reached into her pocket with her free hand and fished out a stick of gum, stripped the foil off with her thumbnail, and folded the stick into her mouth.

Now she handled the ring more casually, turning it so the light from her desk lamp slid silkily over the polished gold while she chewed her gum.

"Catch," she said and flipped the ring at me. I fumbled it out of the air, irritated.

"She loves you deep," Dale said.

"Yeah, so she took off her ring and disappeared."

"She left because she knew you weren't up to it."

"Do I have to pay extra for the relationship critique?"

"On the house. For what it's worth, you have the mind of a seventy-four-year-old man, the body of a twenty-nine-year-old, and the emotional maturity of a ten-year-old. Sorry. I'm compelled to say it. Next time bring something of personal significance only to the subject. Leave yourself out of it."

I waited, then said, "Where is she, do you know?"

"I have some impressions. It's clouded by all the gooey emotional stuff. Let's go for a drive."

She stood and grabbed her coat.

"Where are we going?"

"To find your lady, one hopes."

She drove a red Honda Voltage 900 model. We hummed through the city. The car seemed practically to drive itself. She kept two fingers on the wheel and stitched us through midtown traffic like a magic needle.

"Where are we going *exactly*?" I asked.

"I have no idea. Probably not too far. I can taste salt. Oops, left *here*. Damn it."

We cornered hard, drawing horn blare and at least one flipped bird. Under the viaduct. Traffic light, our noses pointed at Elliott Bay. She sighed.

"Over there," she said. "The island. Bainbridge."

The Winslow ferry took us across the bay. We rolled off the ramp. My detective nodded her head to some inner rhythm, humming.

"Okay, okay," she said.

"Okay what?"

But she wasn't talking to me. We drove in silence for a few minutes. She stopped where the road split in a Y, seemed to listen, then veered right. Then she visibly relaxed. She touched a button on the dash and Sarah Vaughn started crooning "You Must Remember This."

"We're almost there, aren't we?" I said.

"Almost." Then, two minutes later: "Here we are."

She stopped the car at the top of a private beach road overhung with shaggy pines.

"Down there. Probably there's more than one dwelling. Hers is the one with some kind of hideous wreath thing made out of shells glued together. It's hanging on the porch."

"She's there right now?"

"Yes."

I tapped my knee. "That was fast."

"Look. I'm not going to hold your hand. You paid me to find her and I found her. What you do with that is up to you."

I nodded. "Back at your office. . ."

"Yeah?"

"I'm wondering, did you pull that whole character critique of me off Nichole's ring?"

"I didn't pull any of it off the ring. Hardly any. Look. She goes off, what'd you say, two months ago? But you just get around to calling me yesterday, and even then it's half-assed, like you're in a Zingbar and you think of it. Guilt, whatever. Lucky for you I was in Bellevue, right? Then there's the redhead, but forget her. Where there's one there's another."

"You're fired," I said.

"Too late."

I got out of the car and started down the road. Nichole's ring was in my pocket. After a short distance the road opened up on a view of the water and a few houses strung out along the beach. If they had porches they would be facing the water. So I found a path and picked my way down to the rocky beach.

It was cold. I dug my hands in my pockets and hunched my shoulders. The wind was sharp and it stung my eyes and fluttered my pant legs. I noticed I was walking too slow and picked up my feet. Only grown-ups walk toward pain deliberately, and none of them want to.

A wreath of seashells dangled and spun on the porch of a weathered gray beach house with lots of bay-facing windows. Smoke tore from the brick chimney. A flight of crooked stairs ascended from the beach. I mounted them. Halfway up, I realized someone was watching me. A figure stood in the window almost lost among the reflections of cloud scud and water.

I kept climbing.

When I reached the porch a door in the glass opened and an old man stepped out. He was bear-like in a heavy Pendleton coat and watch cap. His face was pulled down by some significant pain. After a moment I recognized him, recognized his hangdog white-whiskered jowls.

"You," Stone said.

"Me."

"Betrayal's a bitch, ain't it?"

I wanted him to be twenty-five years younger so I could in good conscience pitch him over the porch rail head first. I was tempted to do it anyway. Then Stone did something unexpected. The grin slipped off his face and he said:

"I apologize. That was petty. She didn't betray you. She couldn't, she's not built that way. All she wanted to do is spare you some pain she knew you couldn't handle. You didn't deserve her. But hell, I probably didn't, either."

"Is she in there?" I nodded toward the house.

"Not really, not anymore. But go see for yourself. Straight down the hall, second door on the left."

The room smelled medicinal, even with the window open a crack. The sheer white curtains moved in the breeze, like beckoning ghosts. A table lamp glowed next to the bed. Nichole's head was sunk into the pillow, her gray hair spilled around. She was hollow-cheeked and pale. Her eyes were closed, her hands folded over her lap, and I was too late. She was dead.

That night I craved the junk wind but kept away from it. I wanted to sleep and dream. I wanted one of my special dreams. I wanted Nichole young and whole again, so I could say good-bye to her. A visitation from the dead, an enigmatic message, epiphany. But watching my love wither into old age, I had stopped believing in such things.

I didn't dream.

I did, however, receive a visitation.

First I was buried in sleep. Then I was awake again. I opened my eyes, the lids gummy. What was different? Well, the stink. Also: Rasping breath. Not my own.

I bolted up. A man sat in a chair in the predawn dimness of my bedroom. He was the one with the raspy breath and overripe smell. I rubbed my eyes.

"Who—"

"El-lis." A voice like rust scraping off an iron bar.

I fumbled for the switch on the table lamp.

"Don't," he said, raising a palsied hand. "The light hurts my eyes. Your eyes."

"My God. You're Langley Ulin, aren't you."

"Yes."

"What do you want?"

"To. . . live. More."

"*Why?*"

"Con-sider . . . the—Alternative."

In his case the alternative appeared infinitely preferable, but I didn't say so. I got out of bed and pulled on a pair of pants. Ulin was like a waxworks thing, a minor figure forgotten in Trousseau's storeroom where heat and neglect had softened him toward thin shapelessness. His hair was gone but for a few tenacious wisps. His face was too narrow, cheeks sunken together. His neck wobbled out of his shirt collar like a stick covered with chicken wattle.

"I'm out of the donation business," I said.

"Don't need. Your organs. We've worked the bugs out. Maybe just your eyes. These are no good anymore. So long. But your pit-oo-itary. That."

A whiff of rotten eggs. His body devouring itself from the inside, expelling gas.

"No," I said.

"Please, El-lis."

I looked out the window. A black Mercedes van with smoked windows was parked in front of my building. A goonish man stood next to the passenger door in a dark suit and white shirt. Five a.m. and the streets were otherwise empty.

"How'd you get in here?"

He made a distressed sound, coughing and spluttering, wheezing and gasping. I panicked a little until I realized he was laughing.

"You can't. Re-fuse. Me. It's in-human, El-lis."

I needed to clear the junk out of my head. There were a couple of Zingcups in the refrigerator. The bedroom door was ajar already. When I swung it wider I saw a man standing in my hallway. Big. Black suit, cool demeanor, hands folded in front of him. Goon two. I blinked at him then closed the door in his face, softly, and turned.

"You can't just come in here," I said to Ulin.

"Do you. Know. How old. I am, El-lis?"

"Roughly."

"One hundred and forty-six. Think. Of it."

"If you had a plug I'd recommend pulling it," I said. "I'd even do it myself."

"Nonsense. I am pre-pared. To offer you more. Money than you. Can imagine."

"Not interested."

He subsided into a long, gaseous wheeze. His head drooped, his long preying mantis arms dangled.

I opened the bedroom door again. Goon Two was still there. "Your boss is ready to leave," I said.

After a long unresponsive pause, he said, "Mr. Ulin will tell me that himself when he's ready."

"Mr. Ulin is in a coma."

"He's resting."

"Like a poleaxed dog."

Goon Two leaned to see around me then resumed his original stance. "He's okay."

I shut the door again.

After a few minutes, Ulin lifted his head, cleared his throat, and said, "I never bothered you. In all. These years. I've been good to. You. Now I need. Please. I. Won't grovel. Ellis. I'm afraid."

I was slightly tempted to surrender some of my precious bodily fluids. But only slightly. Looking at the thing in the chair I wondered how much more "life" it could endure under any circumstances. Besides, I'd made a bargain with myself many years previous. No more donations. The only one for whom I would have gladly made an exception was gone. Now I didn't feel charitable.

"I'm sorry," I said.

It had become incrementally lighter in the room. Ulin's eyes were like a pair of milky blue marbles. For the first time I noticed he was holding a device in his right hand. That and the goon in the hall gave me a bad vibe.

I opened my top dresser drawer and rummaged out my hand-gun. Old habits die hard. So do old industrialists. Really old ones. I lifted the gun out of the drawer. It was illegal as hell. Gun permits were a thing of the past. Like Ulin himself was a thing of the past.

"I'm sorry, too," Ulin said. "You can't. Be-gin to. Imagine." His thumb twitched over the device. A little green light blinked. I raised my weapon at the same time the bedroom door opened.

"Trust me," I said. "Mr. Ulin is more than ready to go."

Goon Two stared at my gun. "What's that for?"

"I'm the paranoid type."

He lifted Langley Ulin in his big arms, like a frail waxen baby.

When I was alone again I checked the door. The genetic lock was perfectly intact. It pissed me off. Ulin could do any damn thing he pleased by virtue of his wealth. Even defeat a security system that was supposedly undefeatable.

I yanked open the refer—and groaned. I'd been mistaken. There were no Zingcups left. I'd inhaled the last two and neglected to replenish my supply. *Damn* it.

I got on the cell. After a few rings a sleepy and highly feminine voice said:

"Bar's open, honey."

I dressed and went to her and lost myself in Zing and red hair and the comforts of young living flesh. Meaningless and repetitious, which was the whole point. The junk wind blew and blew, but it couldn't blow out Nichole's dead face or two of Langley Ulin's last words to me: *I'm afraid.*

PART TWO: INFINITY

"To Infinity...and beyond!"

—Buzz Lightyear

CHAPTER EIGHT

A dd a hundred and fifty years and see what you get.

It was visible even in the daylight sky; the thing was *big*. *Ulin's Folly*. Okay, its real name was *Infinity*. I sat smoking on the back porch of my little mountain retreat and watched it compete with the ghostly moon. My joint wasn't one of the packaged and heavily taxed brands. Call me old-fashioned, but I preferred growing my own and rolling it myself—which, weirdly, was *still* illegal.

Inhaling dope, I observed in the high blue sky a pin scratch of fire. Regular shuttle run returning from *Infinity*. They were prettier at night. I picked up my book (Dickens again) and lost myself in it until a keening penetrated my concentration. And I was hell on concentration, so that was some very intense keening.

I laid the book down. Up here in the Cascades it was mostly birds, wind in the trees, and other assorted natural occurrences that made noise. I'd learned to be wary of any *un*natural intrusions.

This unnatural intrusion came shrieking out of the sky, a silver needle riding a blue fire tail. It kept falling and falling then finally nosed up and slowed and the shrieking changed pitch, and it came to hover almost directly over my cabin. I hate that. I flipped it off, resisting the urge to plug my ears. I didn't want to give the bastards the satisfaction. There was no place to land. If they wanted me they'd have to return by some old-fashioned mode of transport.

I picked up my book and resumed *Bleak House*. I should have been more observant. With all the racket I failed to hear the canister drop into my yard and sprout antenna.

The ship withdrew. I didn't bother glancing up. My ears throbbed with its departure.

I finished the chapter then got up out of my chair to fetch a cold drink from the cabin, thumb in the middle of the book to mark my place. I noticed the broadcaster in the grass but my instinct to halt lagged about a step and a half, and I found myself within an interactive SuperQuantum Environment. Damn it.

I stood on a scaffolding about a kilometer high. Below, a verdant terrain spread out. I could see, at intervals, the organized sprawl of human habitations. It was like the view over Ohio from the Goodyear Blimp—a view I'd actually enjoyed once upon a time.

A man appeared on the scaffolding beside me.

"Hello, Ellis."

"Hello yourself, Laird. I don't appreciate this."

"Well, you're a difficult man to reach. I thought a little tour might persuade you to my point of view."

"You would think that. But don't count on it."

"What you're looking at is real time," Laird said. At age fifty he had begun to resemble the version of his great grandfather that I'd first become acquainted with back in 1974. Tall, projecting voice, gray templed. Distinguished in a soap opera-ish way.

He pointed a patrician finger. "The County. The living heart of *Infinity*. That's Bedford Falls almost directly below us. In the middle distance is Waukegan, and out on the horizon there is De Smet. Idealized small town communities, circa early twentieth century America."

"Yeah, I've read the brochures."

At this point I'm sure Laird would have enjoyed laying a fatherly hand on my shoulder. Fortunately, broadcast Environments didn't allow for that sort of thing.

"Consider the wonder of it," Laird said.

I guffawed.

He smiled indulgently, letting me enjoy my little outburst, then he looked up.

"Of course it's a little raw without the sky."

Above our narrow platform a vastly beamed interior ceiling was hung with great trunks of holographic projectors, still under construction.

"Here's what it will be like once we are outbound."

He shut his eyes theatrically. I kept mine open. In this place my eyes weren't real anyway. They were figments. What my subconscious allowed my eyes to be.

In a moment, the vast industrially beamed space above us vanished, and I was peering (squinting) into a cornflower blue sky adrift with puffy sheep clouds. One of them drifted right over us, momentarily shrouding us in damp white fog. I couldn't feel the dampness, of course, but I observed water droplets on the backs of my hands.

Grinning like a boy, Laird said, "That's right. This cloud is real. *Infinity* produces her own limited weather patterns in The County, as well as the holographic facsimiles. From the ground you can't tell the difference. Total environmental immersion for the population. We're talking three generations, Ellis."

"Three generations of sardines."

"That's not quite fair."

"Sure it is. What you've constructed is a larger than usual sardine tin."

I wouldn't let Laird know it, but I *was* impressed. Slightly. If nothing else, I was peering down upon a world that, after a generation or so, would forget I ever existed as a "Pointer." *Infinity* wasn't about consciousness evolution; it was about Laird's ego evolution. And it was also about spreading the human seed beyond our solar system. In a fundamental way it was about escape. And I was all about escape. Except not this time. The price was too high.

"Anyway," I said, "have a nice trip."

"Ellis—"

I did something that only looked brave if you happened to be weak-minded. Still, I was grateful for the cloud engulfing us. Heights tended to make me queasy.

I stepped forward off the scaffolding—

—and stumbled out of the broadcast environment and fetched up against the side of my cabin.

I worked my mouth, which was dry. The broadcaster squatted on my patch of lawn like a little robotic insect, filamentous antenna quivering in the mountain breeze. I glanced skyward. The shuttle was nowhere in sight. *Infinity* hung up there like a mirage. Big.

Carefully avoiding the insect's broadcast range, I made my way around the cabin to my wood pile. A big double-bladed ax was buried in a stump. I gripped the handle with both hands and jerked it out and carried it back to the front. The broadcaster squatted and quivered, cute as a bug. I hurled the ax at it and the thing shattered like a Christmas ornament. Inside, I made a glass of iced tea.

Then I started packing.

I had plenty of money. When Langley Ulin finally died, in 2144, I had been shortly thereafter visited by an attorney representing

Ulin Industries. The legal department had discovered an abnormality and wished to correct it. Legal departments and machines are like that. All my ten year's worth of fat wages which had accrued during my sojourn in Blue Heron had been invested in secure bonds on my behalf. After nearly seventy years I was a fairly rich man in my own right. Sign here, please. I did, time and distance having bleached the stench of blood off the money. At least that's how I justified it. Then I hired a long term investment brokerage of my own and gave them most of what Ulin Industries had transferred to me. The secret to retiring in style is practical immortality. Invest well and live forever. It should be on a t-shirt.

Add another eighty years or so, and even when they start calling money "cheets" (debit + chit) you've got yourself a nest egg bigger than the nest.

I rode my carbon-frame mountain bike down from the cabin, a few personal things in a backpack strapped over my shoulders. In Goldbar I picked up the solarpod that I'd paid to have garaged there. The cells were fully charged. I swiveled the joystick and rolled to the 90 where I let the magnetic pulse take over. And at one hundred and ten miles per hour I was on my way back to civilization, which is a place I'd had to relinquish years previous—thanks, inadvertently, to Laird Ulin's genius. At the time SuperQuantum had been in its nascent stages at some UI lab in Arizona. Laird had made me a proposal and I'd accepted, even without the flowers and ring. He wanted to use my memory engrams to create the first fully realized "Environment." He wanted me because I'd been alive longer than anyone else and, presumably, my memory stuff was that much richer. Beyond that, I believe even then Laird was nurturing his Young Frankensteinian ambitions and wanted to make contact with his granddaddy's former organ bank.

So, after years of blessed obscurity, the EC (Evolutionary Consciousness) movement had gotten hold of my SuperQuantum Environment and placed me squarely back in the public mind. People "experienced" my history, and the EC-ers provided context and the scientific proof. Millions visited the Environment. It created a sensation. Never mind that by the advent of the 22nd century the world was filled with impossible things that everyone more or less accepted. I rapidly became the object of religious fervor—and hatred.

I kept an apartment in Seattle, rented under a false name and unvisited by me in more than two years. I exited the magnetic 90, let the cells resume power, and guided my canary yellow solar pod through a rain squall to my building.

Which turned out to be a bad idea.

It was an old brick building with minimum security. I pressed my thumb over the smudged reader a couple of times before the door clicked open and allowed me into the damp-smelling lobby. Immediately I felt a bad vibe. A tired schefflera drooped in a terracotta pot. An old man slouched on a purple sofa, reading something on a flat display he'd unrolled on his lap. Now would have been a good time to leave, but I didn't.

In the hall outside my apartment on the fourth floor I paused, then thumbed the lockpad, stepped into a dark entry, reached for the light switch—and froze.

Deeper inside the apartment, a couch spring creaked. Before I could fully retreat, a voice in the dark said:

"Stop."

I stopped. Not because of the voice but because of the laser targeting dot that had appeared on my chest.

He approached me. I wanted him to. I wanted him to get real close. In the many decades following my scuffle with detective Stone I'd dedicated myself to learning various hand-to-hand defensive and offensive techniques. I was hell on pressure points. But none of that was any good against a gun.

The man in my apartment halted well out of my reach and directed me to turn around.

"We're going outside," he said.

"Okay."

"If you try to alert anyone, or if you try to run, I'll kill you. I *want* to kill you. So give me an excuse, please."

"Why would you want to kill me?" I already knew the answer, but it never hurts to ask.

"No questions. Move."

I moved. And I strove to provide him with no excuse to pull the trigger.

Outside I walked a few yards in front of him. The rain came down in dark curtains. The sidewalks were virtually empty of pedestrians. The rain plastered my hair to my head, saturated my clothes, made my shoes squelch. I looked over my shoulder a couple of times. The man behind me was dressed for the weather, with hood pulled up and both hands out of sight in his trench coat pockets, the right one presumably gripping the gun, business end pointed at my back. He could have been bluffing. Out here in the open I was tempted to break and run. But my instincts advised against it.

He started talking in a low voice — not to me but to his cellular implant. I walked by a door situated between a vintage CD store and a laundry, both closed. My abductor said: "Stop" in a voice loud enough to make it plain he was addressing me and not the party on his implant. Flaking gilt lettering on the glass paneled door read: *Arthur Murray Dance Studio.*

A steep and badly lit flight of stairs, the air close and stale. The man's heavy tread climbing the stairs behind me. Smell of our wet clothes. If I was going to make a move, now would be a good time, while I had the high ground. But he was still too far back.

We entered the studio at the top of the stairs. The hardwood dance floor was covered with unscuffed dust. Watery daylight filtered through a wall of dirty windows.

I turned. "Now what?"

"We wait for somebody."

"Okay. *Then* what?"

"I don't know," he said. "We'll see." He didn't look at me. Rain shadows flowed down his face like melting wax.

"I have to warn you," I said, "if you got me up here in order for me to teach you guys how to waltz you're going to be sorely disappointed. I'm hell on the foxtrot, but waltzing is beyond me."

"I own the lease on this property," he said. "It's not a froggin' dance studio anymore. It's going to be a meeting place."

"For your super secret club?"

"Never mind."

He had the gun leveled at me again. He didn't look like the type to actually pull the trigger, this chubby, soft-jawed guy of about thirty.

"When's your friend arrive?"

"Soon enough."

"You wouldn't really shoot me with that thing, would you?"

He pursed his lips. "Kill you? I thought you were supposed to be immortal. Isn't that the froggin' idea?"

"You tell me."

"I've experienced your stupid environment. So the Harbingers made you, is that it? Environments can be tricked up, no matter what they say."

I kept my mouth shut.

"I don't believe in the Harbingers," he said. "People say they can see them, but *I* don't see them. I don't see anything but some kind of Devil's trick. You call it consciousness evolution, but it's just plain blasphemy, Mr. Herrick."

"I don't call it anything at all," I said.

"Sure you don't. You're right about one thing. I couldn't kill you unless you made me. But there are others with purer faith than mine who will. The world is falling apart, Mr. Herrick. People are delusional. And you started it all. They think you can't die. They think you can't face judgment like an ordinary man. But we're going to prove them wrong. It won't end it. We know that. But it's a beginning. People will begin to wake up, and when they do they just might turn to the Lord. We're living in a Dark Age. But God's light everlasting will shine through."

"Amen."

"Mock all you want."

"Thanks, that one mock was enough to get it off my chest."

"Funny, funny man."

"Look," I said. "I'm not a devil or a portent. I'm an anomaly. You don't have to do this."

"What you think you are doesn't matter."

As I talked to him I inched closer, sliding my feet. He might have been capable of shooting me in the back, but I doubted he had the balls to do it face to face. So I kept talking and inching, because I couldn't afford to see the size of his friend's balls.

I was pretty close, and the gun began to waver. It was an old model Smith & Wesson "blaster," capable of incinerating my body with one discharge.

"What's your name?" I asked.

"Never mind my name."

"Come on. Just your first name. What's the big deal?"

"Bernard."

"Okay, Bernard, I want you to give this plan of yours a little extra thought."

"I bet you do."

Suddenly I pivoted on my left foot and kicked out with my right, a beautiful Jeet Kune Do move, executed with the fluid precision derived from countless repetitions. At the instant of contact, Bernard's finger twitched on the trigger of the blaster. The charge went wide, streaking meteorically across the big open space of the dance studio. It hit the bank of windows and exploded. Glass and flame coughed outward over the sidewalk and Second Avenue. The rain blew in.

My kick had knocked the blaster out of Bernard's hand, at least. Bernard stood holding his wrist. The gun lay on the floor. I scooped it up, dropped the load out of the pistol grip, and pitched the empty unit across the room.

I moved for the door. Bernard stood in my way.

"Bernard," I said. "Come on."

"I never saw them."

"Who?"

"They aren't there, they aren't really there. The Harbingers. People are crazy who say they are." He was practically in tears. "It's all a lie and people are delusional."

"I tend to agree."

"You've ruined the whole country," he added.

"I tend to *dis*agree."

I shot my arm out and found his carotid artery with two rigid fingers. Bernard collapsed.

Back on the street I found a lot of rain, a lot of broken glass, and one dead body. The body lay sprawled half in the gutter, eyes open and staring. A spear of window glass protruded from its throat. Blood pumped into a silver and black river, staining it red before it gurgled down the storm drain. The man's coat was open. He was wearing a holstered blaster, just like the one Bernard had discharged upstairs.

I stared at him, numb with shock. A siren started wailing in the distance and rapidly got louder. I looked up into the rain and opened my mouth. Someone shouted *He's the one*! and I quit my chicken-in-a-rainstorm act and looked in the direction of the voice. Two men were running toward me. Not policemen.

I bent over the dead man and ripped the blaster out of his holster, came up with it, but didn't fire. The two men, seeing the weapon, halted in the middle of the street, their hands up and open, palms out. Both men had shaved heads, except for skinny strips of hair—mini Mohawks bisecting their skulls. EC-ers. The hairline thing was supposed to symbolize something, I forget what. Right and left hemispheres?

"We're friends!" one of them said. He was the more dapper of the pair in a nehru jacket, slacks and shiny boots. Okay, it wasn't a "nehru" jacket, but it *looked* like one. In fashion everything that went around comes around. I ought to know.

His dumpier companion pointed at the body. "We were monitoring their cell implants. We got here just in time!"

"Actually you got here at least five minutes late. I could just as easily be a smelly pile of ashes right now."

They looked at each other.

"You are The Herrick?" the dapper one asked.

"I'm Herrick."

Relief relaxed the tenseness out of his face. They looked at each other again and smiled knowingly.

"Then that couldn't have happened," dumpy said.

"We have a vehicle," dapper said. "We can get you away before the police arrive."

The siren had become piercing. Blue light strobed through the rain.

"Let's go," I said.

They had a van. Dapper piloted us out of the city. We hooked a magnetic pulse line and the autodrive took over so the three of us could lounge in the back with cups of coffee and shortbread cookies. Dapper seemed generally more impressed with me than did his friend. He had the love light in his eyes.

"We knew you would return."

"It's nice to be back," I said. "Except for the assassins and all."

"They belonged to a Christian sect," Dumpy said. "They're mad."

I nodded. "They seemed that way. I've run into their ilk before, but this is the first time they actually tried to incinerate me for Christ. What a difference a couple of years can make."

"The world is changing," Dapper said. "Humanity is evolving. Some people can't tolerate that truth."

"It's only the truth if you believe it is," I said.

They looked at each other, significantly. Dumpy pushed another shortbread cookie into his mouth.

"Relax," I said. "That's just me being profound."

They stared at me.

"It's a *joke*," I said.

They smiled.

Dapper said, "You're different from The Herrick they tell us about."

"I'm bound to be," I said.

"You're . . . more human, I think."

"Yes," Dumpy said.

"But I'm still The Herrick," I said.

They both nodded enthusiastically.

Rain flooded the windshield. The wipers only functioned if someone was sitting in the front seat. It was getting dark outside. Oncoming traffic made yellow blurs on the rain-washed windshield. We were doing a hundred and ten, which meant we were on the Interstate pulse line, probably the 5 headed south.

"Where are you taking me?" I asked.

"A safe place," Dapper said.

"Safe from those Christ bastards," Dumpy said.

Dapper nudged his pal. "They aren't bastards. They simply haven't fully evolved."

"What about you two," I said.

They both looked question marks at me.

"Are you fully evolved?" I said.

"Oh, no," Dapper said. "We haven't even seen a Harbinger."

"I might have seen one," Dumpy said.

"You didn't," Dapper said.

"I *might* have."

Dapper sighed, exasperated. "You'd *know* if you saw a Harbinger."

"Maybe it's more subtle than that," Dumpy said.

Dapper rolled his eyes. "Please tell him," he said, appealing to me.

"You'd know," I said to Dumpy.

He looked at his hands, chastened by The Herrick.

"On the other hand," I said. "These things *can* be rather subtly expressed."

Dapper looked betrayed but tried not to show it.

"How much farther to this safe place?" I asked.

"An hour," Dapper said. "I've already notified everybody we're coming. There will be a gathering in preparation for your worldwide arrival."

I absorbed that information for a minute, then said, "I need to take a leak."

Dumpy pointed to a narrow closet in the back of the van.

"I prefer the great outdoors," I said.

Dumpy resumed the driver's seat. His hand moved over the auto-drive. At the next exit the van dropped off the pulse line and Dumpy took over manual control and steered us up a long, gradual loop of road.

"Anywhere is fine," I said.

"There'll be services a couple of miles up the road."

"Stop here," I said. "Now."

He pulled over to the shoulder. I was sick of them both. I was sick to death of everything. Sick at heart. I kept seeing that dead man in the gutter. A True Believer. Just like these two. On the opposite side, but otherwise exactly the same.

I climbed out of the van, and Dapper stepped down after me.

"You going to hold my hand," I said. "Or something else?"

"I—"

"Give me some privacy."

He stood by the van in the steady rain and I slogged off into a field of sucking mud. I had no idea where I thought I was going. Somewhere isolated. I wanted no part of humanity. Humans struck me as an ignoble lot, of which I was a prime example.

"Mr. Herrick!"

Feet mud-clopping up behind me. I kept moving. A hand fell on my shoulder. I halted, removed the hand, gripping it in a precise and painful fashion, turning it in an unnatural way that forced Dapper to his knees in the mud.

"If you come after me again," I said, "I'll hurt you for real. Believe it."

He looked up at me, injured—and not from my wrist twisting trick. Dumpy was watching us from the open door of the van. Unaccountably, my throat swelled closed with emotion and tears backed up in my eyes. This was some kind of good-bye. I turned and walked off into the field by myself. The Second Going.

The farther I walked, the darker, wetter and colder it got. My impatient revulsion at remaining with the EC-ers in their cozy van for another couple of miles began to appear, well, stupid. What I wouldn't give for a cup of joe and a nice shortbread cookie.

I looked back. The van was still parked by the side of the road, only now it was tiny and lost in a dark night of my soul. Maybe they knew what I was only beginning to acknowledge: I needed a lift.

A screaming came out of the sky. Sun-intense cones of light probed the muddy field, churning and boiling with needles of rain. I looked up, shielding my eyes with an open hand. An orbital shuttle hovered a hundred meters over my head.

"Go away," I said, but without much conviction.

The engine scream changed pitch, and the vehicle descended toward me, a port irising open in its belly.

CHAPTER NINE

Laird Ulin moved a knight and sat back, smugly. I regarded the chessboard, Onyx and teak with cut-glass pieces, and attempted to anticipate his strategy—a mostly futile ambition, even after a hundred and sixteen years.

We were sitting at a game table in Central Park, or at least a more-than-reasonable facsimile of Central Park. The physical real estate encompassed a pie wedge of about thirty meters at its widest end. Squirrel and pigeon society existed only in the holographic scrim that enclosed a few benches and tables, the real grass and one Japanese Maple, in the dappled shade of which we played our weekly game.

The sky was dialed down to near-gloaming, in consideration of my eye re-gens, which were at a sensitive stage.

I pushed my bishop into a weak counter position. Laird blew air out of his nose.

"Contrary to rational expectations," he said, "you're presenting *less* of a challenge over time."

"Maybe I'm bored."

"Ridiculous."

He took my bishop with his rook.

"Didn't you *see* that?" he demanded.

I shrugged. A dull headache persisted behind my neo-eyes. I wanted to take a nap. Another nap.

"You're becoming bad company, Ellis."

I looked up from the board. My own blue eyes peered back at me from a face of elongated waxiness. When Laird talked his mouth moved like a ventriloquist dummy's, stiffly, up and down, up and down. He had spent considerable time and resources building on his great grandfather's experiments in life-prolongation based on the use of my genetic material and transplant techniques. Looking at him, I had to think his efforts had failed to yield substantial improvements. Young Frankenstein.

"I didn't sign on to be good company," I said.

"Perhaps not, but things evolve."

That word.

"I suspect what you need is a vacation," Laird said.

I yawned.

"When was the last time you visited The County?" he asked.

"I don't know, but I didn't like it, whenever it was."

"I'll tell you precisely how long it's been," Laird said. "One hundred and twelve years."

"Gee, feels like yesterday."

At the wide end of the wedge where we were sitting, a biomechanical man stepped through the scrim and into the "real" portion of the park. He sat down on a nearby bench, unrolled a reader, and began perusing it. His name was Norm. I knew that because the name was printed in big block letters right on his breastplate. NORM. Sitting there, NORM sounded like a coffee percolator about halfway to a full brewed pot. Kind of a nostalgic sound.

"I'll arrange for a visa," Laird said to me.

"No, thanks."

"It will do you a world of good."

"I'd rather nap."

"And I'd rather you improve your disposition."

"You're so anxious to enjoy convivial conversation, why don't you talk to NORM?"

The Biomech looked up. His features and physique were designed to make him appear male. What he actually looked like was a department store mannequin with ambitions. Somewhere inside of him were the uploaded memories and dreams of somebody or other named "Norm." He gazed at me with his doll's eyes, and I intuited envious contempt. We were all trying to get to the promised land. In The County, only third generation inhabitants would live to see Ulin's World. On the Command Level Laird was gambling that he could survive the journey in his own body—with my help. The biomechs were uploaded puppets; they would make it to Ulin's World, all right. But the great unanswered question about biomechanical uploads was: Who, if anyone, was really in there?

I'd make it to Ulin's World, too. All I had to do was go on breathing.

"Your insults aren't appreciated," NORM said. When he spoke his mouth didn't move. Not even up and down, like a ventriloquist dummy's.

"Come on, you can only speak for yourself," I said. "I bet somebody more sensitive to the nuances of my delivery would appreciate my insults just fine. Besides, I didn't insult you. I merely suggested Mr. Ulin might like to converse with you. If you find that insulting I don't know what to make of it."

"Freak," NORM said and lowered his gaze to the unrolled device in his lap, which from my angle looked like a sheet of deflected blue light.

I wanted to return to my quarters and read, perchance to nap. But I couldn't seem to muster the necessary motivation even to stand up.

"You shouldn't taunt them," Laird whispered.

"Why not?"

"They used to be human beings. And even if they aren't anymore, they certainly remember being human. It's only decent to treat them with a certain amount of respect."

"So I'm not that decent."

"Shall we finish our game?"

"I guess not."

"Very well."

Laird sniffed and began collecting his chess pieces, returning them to the velvet lined box. I watched him, his corpse hands of sinew and bone and waxen flesh. NORM sat on his bench percolating. I experienced a simple urge toward human company.

"One hundred and twelve years is kind of a long time," I said.

Laird paused. "Shall I authorize the visa?"

"Yeah."

Strapped into a single passenger dropship, I fell out of a holographic lie and into real cloud cover. The vehicle piloted itself. I was engulfed, briefly, by a gray blanket. Droplets formed on the clear blister under which I sat. I watched the pretty display panels. Then the ship burst into clear air and banked steeply.

The County rolled out below me. Lots of green space, the big Oxygen Forest, a few lakes—shiny pocket mirrors on the landscape.

Three neatly laid-out town grids. Bedford Falls was almost directly below me. A wide main street cut through the middle. A pair of monorail lines threaded silver through the countryside, linking the towns. There was also a road winding in a leisurely fashion from Bedford Falls to distant De Smet, passing out of sight for a few kilometers in the Oxygen Forest.

The sky was amazing. It was raining lightly where my dropship banked and plummeted, but sun shafts pierced into the Oxygen Forest. And beyond, some kind of idyllic spring was occurring. All around me little eyebrow arches of rainbows shimmered.

The dropship picked up speed. The ground came up fast; so did my stomach. I skimmed the forest, the big poodle-puff tree tops engineered for maximum carbon dioxide to oxygen conversion. Then I was speeding like a ramjet at low altitude toward the town, engine noise ratcheting up. Without luck, I hunted for a manual override control.

The town shot forward and then was under me, and then was behind me. Glimpse of people in the streets looking up. The dropship racketed.

A steep bank, tightly controlled turn. Breaking vanes deployed. On the outskirts of the town I saw a landing pad bull's-eye. The ship scaled toward it, slowing, nose up, then settled gently to rest. Shutdown.

I unstrapped and popped the blister. The air was fresher than anything I'd breathed on the Command Level, even allowing for the scorched under-smell from the dropship's hot engine. I stood up and stretched in the misting rain.

Two guys on bicycles were pedaling toward me from the town. A third rider lagged some distance behind them. Mentally, I whipped the dust cloth off my people skills. When the two nearer riders coasted up to the landing pad and dismounted, letting their bikes fall, I said:

"Howdy."

"Just who the hell do you think you are," the first guy said. He was about fifty years old, fit, gray at the temples, his hairline in slow retreat. He was wearing an outfit that looked like a cross between nineteenth century business attire and a jumpsuit. The tie pulled it all together, I guess. His friend was much younger and dressed in similar fashion, and though he hadn't yet uttered a word, his vibe was even more hostile than the older man's.

"So you guys are the welcoming committee?"

They exchanged a look. Then the younger one stepped forward, chin out, glaring at me.

"You're human," he said.

"Usually."

"I don't know you," the older one said. "What town are you from?"

"I'm from the Command Level."

They looked at each other again.

"Come down from there. Let's see some identification."

"Are you always this friendly to strangers, or am I a special case?"

"There aren't any strangers," the young guy said. "And the only things that ever ride in these contraptions are mechanical men from overhead. You're different."

"I am that," I said, climbing down. I offered my hand first to the old man. "My name's Ellis Herrick."

He shook my hand tepidly. "Niels Bradshaw."

I turned to the younger guy, who ignored my proffered hand.

"Where's your identification?" he demanded.

I took a breathing moment, then said, "It's in my steamer trunk."

"What?"

"The porters will lug it out eventually. Which way to food?"

"You don't leave this pad until we see your paperwork, Mr. Herrick."

I nodded, then very deliberately stepped off the landing pad. "Uh oh," I said. "Now what are we going to do?"

His face tried to imitate plum skin. His hands balled into fists. He might as well have been sending me detailed telepathic messages: *Get ready, I am about to swing a cloddish right hook at your jaw.*

I waited for the move. It came. I stepped into it, caught his wrist, twisted his arm back and came up under it with my shoulder, hearing and feeling the satisfying pop of his ball and socket joint doing something it wasn't normally supposed to do. He cried out. Who wouldn't? And I pulled him around by his newly gimped arm, kicked his feet out from under him, and dumped him on the wet grass.

"My God," Niels Bradshaw said, "are you out of your mind?"

"No, just patience." Laird had been correct. This vacation was already doing me a world of good.

The third rider, whom I'd all but forgotten about, arrived on her bicycle. She wore a yellow form-fitting body suit, which was a good thing. Her hair was short and blonde, her eyes a striking violet. She could really straddle a bicycle. I'd never seen her before, but strangely something inside of me responded to her as to a familiar and cherished presence. Or maybe I was just horny.

"What's going on here?" she said. Then, addressing the guy moaning on the grass but barely taking her eyes off me, she said:

"Gerry, are you all right?"

I answered for him. "His shoulder is slightly dislocated. He'll live."

"They'll lock you up," Gerry snarled.

"I doubt that."

"Violence of any type is not tolerated," Bradshaw said.

"Why'd you do it?" the girl asked.

I said, "He wanted to see this, but he didn't know how to ask for it politely."

I slipped a wafer-thin card out of my breast pocket and started to hand it to her, but Bradshaw snatched it out of my hand and glowered at it first.

"You might have shown us this in the first place," he said.

"I might have."

The blonde took the card and looked at it. "Visa signed by Laird Ulin himself," she said. "Very impressive."

"No, not very," I said. "You haven't met Laird."

She smiled on one side of her mouth, half-dimpling. Then she flipped the card over and saw my name. That gave her an O mouth and eyes to match, briefly. I found all her facial expressions beautiful and charming.

"You're Ellis Herrick?"

"Yeah."

She handed the card back to me. I could almost see the electric spark jump between our fingers.

"Amazing," she said.

"What's amazing, you know him somehow?" Gerry said.

"Of course not," she said, swinging her leg off the bike frame. She let the bike tip over like the others and then crouched beside Gerry and said:

"Your poor arm."

He ate it up. To me he said, "I don't care who issued your visa, we don't appreciate you buzzing our town. We have children in school. They aren't used to that kind of noise. It frightens them."

"Gerry's the primary school principal for Bedford Falls," the girl said.

"Oh. Sorry about the buzzing thing," I said. "The dropship was preprogrammed and I couldn't override it. Probably Ulin's idea of a good time."

"Nobody's fault then," she said. "My name's Delilah, by the way."

"Nice to meet you, Delilah-by-the-way. Is it an Indian name?"

Nobody laughed, but Delilah dimpled on both sides.

"Delilah Greene," she said.

Gerry groaned a little, to bring the attention back where it belonged. Delilah was kind of propping him up, and he had his good arm around her and his naughty hand on her hip.

"Excuse me," I said. I hunkered behind him, crowding Delilah out of the way. Quickly, I hooked my left arm across Gerry's chest, to hold him still. Then, before he could figure out what I was up to and object, I pretzeled my right arm around his and popped his shoulder back the way God had intended it to be. Gerry only screamed a little, which was very manful of him.

I stood, offering to help him up, but he was pissy about it and refused.

"I have to get back to school," he said, martyrishly. He picked up his bicycle, wiped the seat with his sleeve, and mounted, making a good show of awkwardness because of his famously popped-unpopped shoulder. "Delilah?" he said.

"What?" she said, which I liked and Gerry didn't.

"We'll all be getting back," Niels Bradshaw said. "I hope you'll enjoy your visit, Mr. Herrick, but I also hope you will be able to restrain yourself from further acts of provocation. One thing you will notice about The County is that we have a very low tolerance for violence of any sort. This is an orderly place. It has to be, I'm sure you understand. And we are especially orderly here in Bedford Falls."

"I promise to be good," I said.

"In my opinion he should be detained," Gerry said. "Then expelled."

"You can't expel me," I said. "I don't go to your school."

"Niels?" Gerry said.

"Nobody's being detained," Bradshaw said. "I trust that Mr. Herrick will behave himself."

Gerry grunted unhappily.

"Stop by the mayor's office later," Bradshaw said to me. "I'd like to talk with you. I was unaware that any normal human beings lived on the Command Level. I think you've caught us all by surprise."

"I'll stop by. Mr. Mayor?"

"That's me," he said.

The three of them rode off. I retrieved my duffel bag out of the dropship. When I turned I saw Delilah Greene pedaling back to me. I stood on the grass and she rode around me, wobblingly.

"I wanted to apologize for Gerry," she said.

"He's a big boy, he could do it himself, if he was so inclined, which I doubt. He was about to punch me when I popped his arm."

"Oh, my. Gerry's a little high-strung, I'm afraid. He and I were having kind of an argument when you flew over. Also, he was supposed to be at the school and wasn't, so . . ."

"Let's just forget it."

She wobbled in close and charming in a dimplish way. "You'll need a place to stay," she said. "Try the Bedford Falls Hotel. You are staying overnight, aren't you?"

"I am and I will," I said.

The misting rain ceased abruptly, the sky clearing with remarkable rapidity, and false sunlight blossomed over us, gemming the grass and Delilah's violet eyes.

"Good," she said, and rode away.

I liked to watch her pedal.

I walked down the middle of Main Street with my bag slung over my back. It was a pedestrian and bicycle thoroughfare, and there were plenty of both. On either side of the street the building facades suggested quaint early twentieth century architecture. The three communities that comprised The County were modeled after idealized notions of small town America, circa 1920. Nice places to raise the kids. I was, of course, the one living man to have actually seen the real Waukegan and De Smet, having visited those towns on a quest for literary nostalgia; forget Bedford Falls, which existed only in the imagination of Frank Capra. But The County was more Main Street

Disneyland than an authentic reproduction. The settings were as artificial as the engineered PerfectWood out of which the towns were
mostly constructed. By which I don't mean to detract from the genu-
ine soothing effect. All I'm saying is I missed Mickey and Donald.

In the center of Bedford Falls there stood a gazebo. It was a
pretty thing, with lattice walls and a rooster weathervane on top.
There was a pretty thing *in* the gazebo, too, and her name was
Delilah Greene.

"Hi," she said, leaning above me on the white-painted rail.

"Hi yourself."

"We meet again."

"I guess we were bound to. The day sure cleared up fast, huh?"

"The weather is strictly controlled, you know," she said.

"I know."

"The Quantum Core makes sure everybody gets enough mois-
ture, but it occurs on a random cycle, so things don't get too God
awfully predictable."

"April randomly-dealt-moisturizing-cycles bring May flowers,"
I said. "Are we going to talk about the weather much longer?"

"Not much," she said.

"Good. Ah, this is going to sound dumb, but haven't we met
before? I mean prior to the ruckus out by the landing pad."

"You know we haven't," she said. "I've never been Overhead,
and I'm sure I've never seen you around here. I would have remembered."

"I *have* been here once before," I said. "About a hundred years
ago."

She took a few moments to appraise me, then said, "You really
are *The* Herrick, aren't you?"

It was my turn to groan.

"Please," I said. "Can we stick with plain old Ellis and dump the
'The?'"

"I experienced your Environment when I was a kid."

"Join the club. Promise me you're not a consciousness evolutionary type."

"I'm not. As far as I know there aren't any EC-er's in The
County. Laird Ulin's using you to live out the duration of the voyage,
isn't he?"

"Yep."

"Wow. I thought you were so familiar."

"That explains your side of it, but why do I feel I already know you?"

"Ellis, I can't say. And to be honest, I don't really think it's the Herrick Environment that makes me think I know you. It's deeper than that. Wanna go on a picnic?"

I laughed. "Right now?"

"Sure, why not? You got another girl in Bedford Falls?"

"Nope. Let's go."

"Wait here a minute, okay?"

She ran across the street and entered a building with the words BEDFORD FALLS HOTEL painted in large forest green letters over the porch. A few minutes later she came around the side of the building on a tandem bicycle with a picnic basket in the carrier attached to the handlebars.

"You County-ites really believe in people power, don't you?" I said.

"It would be wasteful to use anything else for local get-arounds, unless you're older generation. The monorails are good for distance travel, and there are a few electric transports."

"Hey, I'm not knocking it," I said, and I swung onto the backseat. We found our balance point and started pedaling. Up until the last year or so I'd kept myself in pretty good shape. Weights, Yoga, Jeet Kun Do workouts. But a year is a long time to sit idle, and the tandem bike demanded use of a different set of muscles.

"Where are we going?" I asked.

"Everybody heads for the Oxygen Forest. So it's more private out by the wall."

"The wall it is."

I got into the rhythm of it and began to enjoy the effort. The back of Delilah's neck acquired a sheen of perspiration. I felt a strong urge to kiss it but didn't. There was a cute little brown mole peeking above the scooped back of her bodysuit, and the finest silky hairs. About a kilometer outside of Bedford Falls I realized who she was and I almost fell off the bike.

We came to a point where the path began a wide loop back in the direction from which we'd come. Delilah kept us pointed straight and we whispered onto the grass and continued for another five minutes or so. When we finally stopped we were both slightly winded and sweaty.

Delilah grabbed the picnic basket and we dumped the bike on the grass. We had to be very close to the holographic scrim but it was impossible to tell where it began. The meadow seemed to roll off into distant haze.

"It's nice here, isn't it?" Delilah said, spreading the red and white blanket on the air and letting it float down.

"Lovely," I said.

She unpacked lunch: a baguette of French bread, synthetic cheese, real apple slices, a bottle of white wine and two stem glasses.

We sat on the blanket cross-legged, facing each other.

"What's the matter?" Delilah asked.

"Nothing."

"All of a sudden you look a million miles away."

"More like a couple of trillion plus two hundred or so years."

She made a quizzical face and uncorked the wine. "Explain," she said, pouring.

"I think I know who you are," I said.

"I'm Delilah Greene," she said and handed me my glass. Uncouthly, I drained off about half of it in a single draft.

"I should have said I know who you were."

She half dimpled. "And who were I?"

"Never mind, it's crazy."

"Come on."

"It's just a resemblance, but a striking one."

"A resemblance to who? Whom."

"Once upon a very long time ago there was a girl."

She lit up. "Nichole!"

That damn Environment. "Yeah," I said.

"You think I'm Nichole reincarnated."

"I didn't say that," I said, though I had and regretted it. "And you're still thinking of the Environment."

"It really bothers you, that everybody knows your life, doesn't it."

"Everybody *doesn't* know my life. What bothers me is that they think they know it."

"Isn't the Environment constructed out of your own unconscious memory patterns?"

"That's what they claim."

"And you willingly participated, or did you? I thought you had to be willing or the environment wouldn't work."

"I was willing, but I had no idea the thing would wind up on the open market."

"So. . . the tech is no good?"

I drank the rest of my wine and held my glass out for a refill. Sometimes if I drank fast enough I could attain a fleeting buzz.

"The tech is good," I said.

"Then it's kind of accurate, isn't it?" she said. "I mean on your first night with Nichole she brought up the whole past life thing. And you and I have this, I don't know, *frisson*. So it's kind of what you think is going on. Or is that not right?"

"How far are we from the scrim?" I said.

"Oh, I don't know. I mean I'm not sure. It's pretty close, though. Don't you want to talk about Nichole?"

"Nichole has been dead a long time."

"And dead is dead?"

"Probably."

"What about all your visions?"

"I never trusted them, and I wouldn't characterize them as visions, exactly. I don't know what they were, and I haven't had one in more than a hundred years. Do you mind if we talk about something else?"

"I don't mind, Mr. Cranky."

"This is good wine," I said. An ephemeral bee inhabited my mind then vanished, leaving behind a dull ache.

"It's passable," she said.

"Should we go back to the weather?"

"Whatever you feel would be interesting."

"What about Gerry?" I said.

"What about him?"

"He likes you."

"He likes the idea of having me," Delilah said. "But he can't, so he's pretty unhappy about it. This is a generation ship. Lovers are matched up by genetic compatibility. What pairings will produce the brightest, healthiest offspring with the best chance of enriching the population. That's what counts."

"And you're not matched up with Gerry."

She shook her head and poured herself more wine. We'd just about killed the bottle already. "Nor do I wish to be," she said. "Gerry's a nice guy, but on the level of bed buddies, he's creepy."

"He's a nice guy, huh?"

"Not really."

We laughed.

"Sorry about getting touchy about the Environment thing."

"That's all right," she said.

"I'd pretty much slipped into blessed obscurity back on Earth. Then Laird came up with SuperQuantum. People all over the world entered my Environment. There was a resurgence of the Evolutionary Consciousness shit. I became 'The Herrick.' It's like a bad joke; at least to me it is. It didn't help that people in general seemed to be going slightly crazy. The Harbingers were *my* delusion, I thought. You wouldn't believe the polarization, in America at least, between the EC-ers and the Jesus contingent."

"I wish I could have seen it. At least I would have been on Earth. Sometimes it's hard to accept my whole life will begin and end on *Infinity*."

"It's not so bad," I said, then wished I hadn't.

Delilah sipped her wine. My two glasses had gone to my head in a melancholy way. Except it wasn't the wine and couldn't be. I rolled onto my back and looked at the sky, false and true. A fluffy white cloud drifted, and I wondered whether it was real or projection. Then it did something funny. There occurred a brief flicker along its leading edge, and the scrim produced a rudimentary duplicate so it would appear to go on drifting.

I sat up, then stood. I cocked my arm back with the empty wine glass in hand. It wasn't exactly Waterford crystal, just some plastic polymer.

"Make a wish," I said.

And Delilah was up like a shot, grabbing my arm.

"Don't," she said.

I lowered my arm. "Sure, but why not?"

"I don't like to . . . spoil it. I don't like to think of a bunch of junk on the other side of the scrim. I don't like to think of it as a scrim at all."

"All right, Delilah. I understand."

"No, you don't. And don't be smug about it, either. I know this isn't your world. You were born in a real place, and you'll still be alive when *Infinity* reaches Ulin's World. But this is all I've got and all I'll ever have."

I dropped my empty wine glass and started to hug her, but she stiffened up and said, "I don't need sympathy."

"I'm not offering any. I just find you highly huggable."

She dimpled on the left cheek. "Huggable, huh?"

"Highly."

"Well, that's different."

We hugged and it was a good fit, her head snuggled under my chin. After a while she said:

"Is that part about you being, you know, sterile, is that true?"

"Yeah. Ironic as hell, wouldn't you say?"

"As hell."

"Hey," I said. "If you're not matched up with Gerry, then who are you matched up with?"

"It isn't just one person, of course, though there is usually only one *perfect* genetic match."

"Who's yours?"

In my arms, she shuddered. "The Mayor of Waukegan."

"What's he like?"

"Old."

"How old?"

"Almost wizened. Why, are you jealous?"

"Naw, I'm above that sort of thing. Besides, we just met. And also, he's wizened."

"Almost wizened. Anyway, when I get pregnant it'll be in vitro. Ellis, do you really think we just met, or do you think the other thing's possible?"

"Anything's possible," I said, then I kissed her pretty mouth.

CHAPTER TEN

We parked the tandem bicycle behind the Bedford Falls Hotel, crossed the promenade, and entered the hotel by the rear entrance. A middle-aged woman was behind the front desk. Delilah took my hand and led me up the stairs, passing through diamond-paned light on every landing.

"You have a room here?" I asked.

"I have every room here. My mom and I run the place. That was her at the check-in desk."

"So you know which rooms are empty."

"Naturally."

We came to a room on the second floor. Everything from the rug runner to the wainscoting to the paneled doors was mock period accurate. But the locks, which resembled yellowed ivory doorbell buttons, were actually thumbprint readers. Delilah pressed her thumb to the reader by our door and the lock snicked open.

I followed her in and shut the door. She turned to me. I slid my finger along the collar of her bodysuit, felt the slightly raised nub, inserted the edge of my fingernail and drew the finger down, smoothly parting the clever static seal. The suit fell off her like a yellow shadow. Beneath it she was naked. She unzipped me then undid me, and we went on from there, wonderfully.

Much later, I said, "So is recreational sex discouraged?"

"Is that what this was," Delilah said.

"Not as far as we're concerned, but I'm wondering if the PTB might have other ideas."

We were lying on the bed, damp among the rumpled sheets and pillows. It reminded me of a similar situation a long, long time in the past.

"PTB?" Delilah said.

"Powers That Be."

"There aren't any PTBs in The County. That's all on the Command Level. We all know what's at stake and what can and cannot be tolerated in the interests of the overall mission. The County power structure is minimal. And are you sure this isn't just recreational for you?"

"Delilah—"

"What?"

Something disarming and charming came to my lips, but I recognized it for what it was and wouldn't let it out. Instead I said, "You're not Nichole."

Uncomfortable beat. Then: "I know that."

"I mean, this isn't anything mystical."

"Okay, Ellis. I know. I was kidding about the reincarnation idea. Don't worry."

"I'm not worried."

"Good. I'm not worried either."

"We're on the same page, then."

"Sure, of course."

More uncomfortable beats.

"Well," she said, "I've got a hotel to run."

"Come on," I said.

"What?"

"You're mad."

"I'm not mad. What makes you think you know so much about me, anyway?"

"Hubris?"

She laughed, which was better. "Really, though. I've got work I'm supposed to be doing. The whole day can't be picnics and sex, can it?"

"Can't it?"

"It can't. At least not *recreational* sex."

"Ouch."

She got out of bed and clothed herself. "Are you still planning to stay a while?" she asked.

"Hell, yeah, the room service here is phenomenal."

"Very funny."

She was all sealed up again, like a pretty yellow banana with curves and bumps and a sexy musk. If only there were a bunch of her, but that might have been more than I could have peeled.

"Do you like this room, sir?" she asked. "It's one of the nicest ones. If you look out this lovely bay window you can see Main Street. You might as well keep it. I'll log you into the register."

"Okay."

I started to get up but before I could she was already halfway out the door.

"See you later?" I said.

"You'll see me, Ellis."

She shut the door.

I got up from of the bed, suddenly in a non-recreational mood. I rummaged a loose-fitting suit out of my bag and put it on.

The view from the bay window was as Delilah had described it, but I wasn't in the mood for quaint vistas. Way off in the direction of the Oxygen Forest, a dark streaking haze indicated somewhat heavier precipitation than we'd experienced here in Bedford Falls at the time of my arrival. It made me wonder how much livelier the weather could get. It also made me think of that other time with that other girl. Nichole. That spontaneous eroticism that seemed to transcend itself, that *frisson* (as Delilah would put it), and Nature's accompanying storm, as if to underscore the event.

But what were my memories? A normal man might accumulate seventy years of accessible recollections, but I'd already survived more than four times a normal life-span. Distance and imagination reshaped memory. That happened to everyone. In my case wasn't it reasonable to assume my brain's storage capacity was exceeded? The truth was still in there, perhaps, but the versions I was able to call up were undoubtedly corrupted by my conscious and unconscious desires and expectations.

Maybe it was time I had a look at my own Environment. For decades I'd assumed everyone who read it was getting a jaundiced view of my past. But perhaps I was the one not seeing straight. Perhaps.

I'd started to turn away from the window when I noticed a man standing in the street by the gazebo, looking up at me. It was Gerry. Didn't he have urchins to herd? I waved at him, friendly as hell. But he didn't wave back.

Downstairs, Delilah was working the front desk.

"Hi," she said, "Where are you off to?"

"The Mayor's office. He invited me to drop in, so I thought I'd take him up on it."

"Watch out for Gerry," she said. "He was just here."

"Aw, he's a pussy cat."

"With claws."

"Gerry? Come on." I laughed. "Anyway, I can take care of myself and him too."

She looked doubtful.

"Something you're not telling me?" I asked.

"No. Not really."

"Dinner tonight?"

"Sure. Anyway, tell Niels I said hi."

I promised I would, then exited the building. It was a lovely day, and Gerry was gone—which made it even lovelier.

I knew enough about The County to remember that the Mayor's office in each of the towns had its own Core Access Interface. In fact, these were the only CAIs outside of the Command Level.

Twenty minutes later I was looking at the one in Niels Bradshaw's office. It was kind of like an old-fashioned barber chair with an equally old-fashioned hair dryer attached. I knew from the CAIs on the Command Level that the interface apparatus needn't be so clunky.

"May I?" I said, nodding at the barber chair.

"You want to interface?" He sounded a little put out. After all, wasn't I there to talk with wonderful *him*?

"If you don't mind," I said. "I need to check something out."

"Be my guest, Mr. Herrick."

I sat down and performed a soft interface. The Super Quantum Core read me and produced a cloud. You never know what you're going to get when you interface. It's part of the charm, I guess.

My cloud was all puffy and white, and it drifted serenely in a blue sky. Probably it was the one I'd watched sail into the Scrim earlier.

You can see anything in a cloud. Dragons, whales, castles. I lay on my back and watched this one drift and subtly shift shapes. I felt sleepy and *there*, at the same time. My Rorschach cloud began to look a little like a two story house, circa 1970, with gables.

Come up here, Romeo.

It was like shuffling through indexed memory files. I knew what I wanted, and now the SuperQuantum Core knew, as well. The desired Environment already existed, and if I was anybody else, that was the Environment that would now manifest. But since it was *my* consciousness that had provided the original memory materials, the computer now had a choice between dropping me into the old Environment or drawing out a new one from the original source: me.

I wanted to see the existent Environment. It was older and had been produced at a time when I had no particular expectations of the technology, and was less likely, therefore, to corrupt the process with an agenda. On the other hand it wasn't necessarily a good idea to enter one's own Environment. In fact, it was strongly discouraged, which is why I'd never done it. There had been cases of psychotic dislocations resulting in some very quirky mental rubbering. That happened rarely, though, and I was feeling reckless.

I came forward, *pushing* at the Rorschach cloud, making my preference known.

SuperQuantum accommodated my choice.

The cloud lost its white puffiness, flattened out, darkened, retreated into the distance, joined a night time overcast. Lightning flickered inside of it, and then I heard the rumble and felt it, and I was viewing the spring storm through the window of Nichole's bedroom, post-coital.

She snuggled against me under loose sheets. Elton John's gap-toothed grin on the poster over the Gerard turntable. I was inside of myself and outside at the same time, and that wasn't altogether the quantum effect; it was true experiential recollection. Being myself remembering myself within a previously constructed personal Environment, I *knew* it was a true thing.

—what did you mean about knowing me before—

—like in a past life—

. . . .

I stopped listening to what we were saying. I tried to turn up the gain on the feel of Nichole's presence. It struck me forcibly, and I pulled abruptly out of the Environment.

The computer placed me under the drifty cloud again. I hovered a few moments. The cloud shifted subtly, suggesting various objects, various hooks into my memory pond.

When I was ready I came forward, *pushing* again. This time I rejected the existent Environment and let the computer resurrect it all out of my present conscious/unconscious paradigm. The cloud resolved itself into a house shape. I stood on a dew-damp lawn, looking up at Nichole in the window of her bedroom. Only it wasn't Nichole but Delilah Greene leaning on the window sill/ gazebo rail.

—we meet again—

—we were bound to—

—come on climb up here romeo—

I withdrew from the interface, shaking and strangely enervated.

My visa had a one week expiration stamp. I ignored it. I not only ignored it, I buried it. Scooped a hole in the soil of somebody's window box a couple of blocks from the hotel and pressed into the hole the wafer with it's tiny blinking red expiration dot, and covered it over. Then I picked up my new overnight bag and Delilah and I strolled down to the monorail station.

Slipping along at a leisurely speed in the silver train I was again struck by the theme park ambience. *We are now departing Tomorrowland. Next stop: Frontierland.*

Actually the next stop was Waukegan, but Delilah didn't want to go to that town where her "perfect" genetic match was doddering around the Mayor's residence. So after another short ride we found ourselves standing on the platform in De Smet, watching a handful of passengers board the train heading back to Bedford Falls.

The object was to disappear for a while. Not an easy thing to accomplish inside the closed world of an interstellar vehicle, even one of the immense proportions of *Infinity*. Nichole knew the manager of the De Smet Hotel, Amy Granger, and she agreed to put us up as unregistered guests. That would do for the short term.

Delilah was a sport about it, but she did ask, "What's the big deal? Won't Ulin just extend your visa?"

"He might. But I don't feel like asking him."

"Why not?"

"It irks me."

She laughed. "You're easily irked."

"Am I ever."

I felt the way I'd felt during my final months in Blue Heron. I was weary of being Ulin's personal organ bank. I was sick past the coping point of the invasive procedures and extractions. I knew it was the price of my ticket to another world (any other world, please) but I was still sick of it.

And then there was Delilah. I wasn't a True Believer, not even after my experience with the Core interface. My unconscious mind could and probably did have an agenda. But I had an agenda of my own *conscious* devising. I'd enjoyed the comfort of girls on the Command Level. They were volunteers, carefully chosen by Laird based on psychological profiles, approached quietly and offered various inducements to be of . . . service. My presence on board *Infinity*, more than a hundred years out, was still largely unknown by the general population. (Laird feared a repeat of the situation that had eventually occurred back on Earth, with my known status causing division and desperation). So I'd had girls, some of them very nice. But I hadn't had *a* girl. As in girlfriend. Not even on Earth, not for uncounted decades. Lots of girls but no companion.

A human being (and I was still that) requires more than occasional sex to complete the male/female equation. He needs relationship. Like air or water. Even I needed relationship, as much as I tended to resist it.

A couple of days after our arrival in De Smet I decided to give Delilah a present. We were in the dining room of the hotel. I watched her unwrap it. She was at half-dimple then went to a full double when she saw what it was.

"Ellis, my *gosh*!"

A white gold ring on a fine link chain.

"It isn't really gold, is it?" she asked.

"Bite it and see."

"Huh?"

"Just a joke. Yeah, it's really gold."

"But where in the world did you get it? There's nothing like this on *Infinity*."

I brought it with me from Earth," I said. "I guess you could say it has sentimental value. It used to belong to someone important to me."

Nichole hung between us like an exhaled breath, but neither of us said her name.

"Well, it's beautiful," Delilah said. "I mean, if you're sure you want me to have it?"

"I'm sure."

She ducked her head and slipped the chain around her neck. She held the ring for a moment, admiring it, then tucked it under her tunic where I generally wanted to be—in the warm and breastful place. Man.

"Come here," she said.

I half stood, leaning over the table, and she kissed my lips.

Then Gerry walked in and more or less spoiled things. I saw him weaving through the tables of the sparsely populated dining room, zeroing in on us.

I broke the kiss and said, "Uh oh."

"What?"

"The principal's here and he doesn't look like our pal."

"Gerry?"

She turned and saw him. He appeared a little on the haggard side. Like he needed more sleep and less of whatever he had been drinking. Also a shave. He swaggered up to our table and, rather sneeringly, said:

"Mind if I join you two?"

"Did we forget to turn in an assignment?" I said. He ignored me, which was reasonable from his perspective.

"Dee?"

Dee?

"Gerry, what are you doing here?"

He pulled a chair out noisily and dropped into it. "What I'm doing here is bringing you back to your senses, hopefully."

"That sentence needs to be re-thunk," I said. "It don't parse. You did everything but dangle your participle, and for all I know you even did that."

"You *shut up*," he said, his face momentarily furious. Then to "Dee" he went on. And on.

"I could tolerate it with your gene match. That's the way it has to be. But this man isn't anybody's gene match. He's a genetic freak. I've been reading up on him. He can't even impregnate you."

"Gerry, do you want to keep your voice down, please?" Delilah said.

"Why should I? Are you so ashamed of your dirty affair with this—person?"

"Gerry," I said. "Shut up."

"Because otherwise," he continued, "why would you run off in secret? Why would you want to hide?"

"We prefer to think of it as a romantic getaway," I said.

"And I prefer for you to shut the hell up while I'm talking to my friend, *whom* you didn't even know existed a week ago."

"Whom yet."

"Dee, I love you. That has to count for something. I know you don't accept it but you have to believe me. Love matters, even here."

He had a point.

"Gerry?" I said. "Go away now, okay?"

"Dee?"

No dimples for Gerry. Delilah closed her eyes and cradled her head in her hand.

"Dee, *please*."

Delilah didn't look up. Very softly, she said, "No, Gerry."

Something collapsed behind Gerry's face. Without visibly moving, he slumped. Delilah could collapse men as easily as Nichole used to. Gerry stood up, turned, and walked out.

"You okay?" I asked Delilah, touching her arm.

She nodded, then raised her head and wiped her red eyes.

"He's really in love with me," she said. "And I made the mistake of sleeping with him."

"Oh." A surprisingly robust current of jealously surged through me.

"How does that work," I asked, "if you're supposed to have somebody else's baby?"

"It can work, just not with Gerry and me. Love isn't outlawed. We're talking about two parent homes, but they don't have to be the biological parents. I'll have Ben Roos' baby, but that's just the genetics. Obviously it can get complicated. Harmonious couplings are important, for a stabilizing family group. But sometimes somebody's not so happy."

"Or stable," I said. "Who's Ben Roos, by the way?"

"The mayor of Waukegan."

"Oh, yeah."

"Love does matter, doesn't it, Ellis?"

"Yes."

She touched her chest, the ring under her tunic. For one craven instant I regretted giving it to her.

"Well," I said, "if Gerry can find us I suppose anybody can."

"You're not going back already?"

"Not if I can help it."

"But even if you do we could still see each other. Like I said, it's not outlawed. It wouldn't be every day, I know that. But sometimes. You could come back, and I could even visit you Overhead."

"Sure," I said. "But I don't want to go back. I'm not ready. I—"

"What is it?"

"They do things to me. It's not that far off from rape, what they do. I agreed to it. I signed aboard, just like I did with Langley all those years ago. But I hate it. I thought it wouldn't be so bad, but it is. In a few days Laird will need me. I don't want to be there."

"What will happen if you're not?"

"Nothing good, as far as he's concerned. If his great grandfather's experience is any indicator he'll persist for a long time anyway, but there will be progressive degeneration. Then he'll die, like everybody else. Almost everybody else."

"But if he dies what happens to *Infinity*?"

"It goes on," I said. "Laird's one man. His wealth and vision got this ball rolling, but we're on the downhill slope now. Whether Laird's with us or not, this vessel will reach Ulin's World."

"Ellis, do you know what you're saying? It's like killing him on purpose, isn't it?"

"No. His natural death would have occurred decades ago. He's on borrowed time. Time borrowed from *me*. It's more like pulling the plug."

"Pulling the plug?"

"Old expression. It meant disconnecting a hopeless case from life supporting machines. It meant allowing a brain dead person's body to die, too."

"But Laird Ulin isn't brain dead."

"You'd be surprised," I said.

We went upstairs to grab a few things before departing. There weren't a lot of places we could go, but Delilah did have friends in Waukegan and she thought we could stay with them a short while. After that, we'd play it by ear. Maybe do some camping in the Oxygen Forest. I wanted to stay ahead of Laird for as long as possible; it didn't have to be forever.

"Things could get dicey," I said, "once Laird figures out what I'm up to. You might want to consider cutting me loose right now."

Delilah kissed me. "We're together," she said.

"Yes, we are," I said, and meant it, but a piece of me started rattling his tin cup against the bars of the door before it was even shut all the way. The trouble with practical immortality is that it necessitates serial grieving. Nichole had figured I wasn't up to it, and I'd spent a lot of years proving she was right. Was that going to change now?

A high, spiraling whine over De Smet interrupted my thoughts and our packing. Delilah at the window said:

"Dropships."

"Your friend called the truant officer," I said, and believed it was true. Years later I discovered Ulin had other more reliable ways of keeping track of me.

They were in the town square when we bolted from the lobby of the hotel. Biomechs. A half dozen of them, their dropships squatting on scorched rings in the middle of the street. One of them had crushed and partially melted somebody's bicycle.

"Oops," I said. Back door would have been a smarter choice.

One of the biomechs approached us. He was a seven-footer (they were all outsized; you needed room in which to cram all the gizmos that gave them "life"). His name was TONY B. He was holding a stun gun in his right hand. His perpetual smile was like a men's wear sale at Nordstrom's. He and the others were far from stylish, however, in their Nazi black body suits and caps.

"It appears you've lost track of time, Mr. Herrick," he said.

"Nothing like it," I said.

"We have a ship waiting to take you up."

"I'm extending my stay in The County."

"You'll have to discuss that with Mr. Ulin."

"I'll call him next week. Or the week after, or something."

TONY B started to raise the stun gun. I shoved Delilah out of harm's way and dove back into the hotel. I made it all the way to the rear entrance before it hit me. The stun blast felt like a gust of hot wind blowing *through* me. My insides joggled, which was weird, and the blast carried me forward, stumbling out the door and down steps on rubber legs. Then I went sprawling.

I struggled to drag myself forward, but I was the Rubber Man of Borneo and had no strength in my arms. I stopped struggling and lay with my face in the grass. Then Delilah was there, her voice close.

"Ellis—"

Abruptly she was gone, and something was lifting me up as if I were stuffed with feathers. My silly head dangled all woozy. I vomited and saw the nice lunch I'd just eaten with my girl splattered on the green grass. I couldn't raise my head to see what had happened to Delilah.

They strapped me into a dropship. By then the effects of the stun blast were wearing off. My whole body ached.

The engine wound up. I felt the vibration through my bones. Then we reared off the ground and accelerated toward the blameless deception of a summer sky.

CHAPTER ELEVEN

Time is a process, a wheel, an illusion, an invention, a vapor in the mind of Man.

Time just *is*.

Everywhere except the Command Level of the starship *Infinity*, where a society of puppets stalked around wondering if they were who they thought they were, and Laird Ulin had acquired a habit of obesity.

I lived in a gilded prison in a world above the sky. Mostly I read (I was back onto Hemingway), smoked herb (I cultivated the plants under special grow lights and harvested the leaves as my needs moved me, which was all too frequently), practiced Tai Chi and plotted sabotage. In between these activities I endured Laird Ulin's invasive medical procedures, not to mention his lugubrious presence.

One day nine years after my unceremonious removal from The County it occurred to me that I missed Delilah Greene. I came to this realization while reclining in my quarters smoking a fat joint of my home grown and reading that passage in *A Farewell To Arms* in which the American Tenente is blown up and discovers himself rushing bodily out of himself and out and out and out, and all the time bodily out, and it was all a mistake to think that you just died, etc.

My mind followed this image out and out and out, the way a mind will when it's floating in a fog of dope, and I was reminded of my visions of Oz bubbles and the dead and the Harbingers. Ironic that about the time that a significant portion of the human race began claiming to see them I *stopped* seeing Harbingers. If I'd ever seen them in the first place. It's a lonely feeling when your visions abandon you. And it becomes easy to abandon *them*, in return. By the way, that goes for people, too. You abandon them, or let them abandon you. It hurts, then it fades, then you stay high and remote—and safe.

Time is also an escape hatch. Especially for someone like me.

But it wasn't the existential dilemma that really appealed to me about *A Farewell To Arms*. I went for the love story, which should have been mawkish but wasn't.

I went for Catherine.

All this, lying back, the novel open in my lap (I'd insisted on real books made out of real paper when I signed on for the voyage), the room hazed with smoke—like my mind. And I conjured up Nichole, whom I could never entirely un-conjure, and that first night in her bedroom. And visions, and Fate, and, well, the love story.

And I thought perhaps it was time I stopped getting high and started getting serious. But it was hard to uphold the love story of my own life, especially with the latest volunteer lying naked on our recently shared bed. She was nineteen, with hair so black it was almost blue, and cut boyishly short. The dim lighting in my quarters fell softly on the swell and curve of her hips and bottom, which weren't in the least bit boyish. In my case dope generally inflamed desire while inhibiting function, however, and I had become mostly a window shopper since my return to the Command Level.

Nine years. I dragged on my joint—the one with the hot coal on the tip. Time's clock spring unwound up here on the Command Level and floated by like a pretty ribbon discarded from the package of immortality. It was easy to remain floating. All I had to do was wait and eventually the long voyage would be over. And by then the entire population of The County would have cycled into a new generation. The lovely girl now purring through sleep on my bed would be either a very old woman or a very dead one.

Nineteen.

And I was twenty-nine. Two hundred and fourteen in Herrick years.

I thought about that, and my jaded armor slipped a little. Damn it. I ground the joint out and sat up. I reached over and touched the girl's ankle. She stirred, stretched, rolled over, smiled. I must have touched the right spot. I started to say her name, then realized I'd forgotten it. My armor slipped a little more, and something like shame moved sluggishly inside my heart. It was an unusual name, I remembered that much. It had reminded me of something, but what? Pumpkins?

"Hi," the girl said, in just the right way. "Are you ready to try again?"

I hoped I was, but not for what this child had in mind.

"Uh, I thought we'd go have a drink or something."

She came off the bed in one sinuous movement and was kneeling by my chair.

"That sounds fun," she said. "Unless you want to do something else."

I did. I wanted to shoot myself. But that would have been rude.

"Let's try Paris," I said. "Ever tasted Pernod?"

The Seine was blue, like the hour. Naturally. And the Pernod was synth, but you can't have everything. We sat under an awning on a sidewalk café. The other tables were empty. Holographic scrims suggested a City of Light bustling with romantic humanity, but really there was nothing out there but the horror of the biomechs puttering around. Okay, they weren't all that horrible. But creepy, definitely creepy.

"How's your drink?" I asked The Girl With No Name.

"It's wet but tastes dry."

"It isn't too much like the real thing," I said.

"Have you tasted the real thing?"

"Back on Earth, sure. On the other hand I never tried it until after my body changed, so for all I know my taste buds were mutated along with my biochemistry and I have no idea what it's 'supposed' to taste like."

She smiled and sipped, very self-possessed for a kid. Then she said, "My name's Autumn. Autumn Janklow. You forgot it, didn't you?"

"Sort of. I'm sorry." Shit, I knew it was seasonal.

We returned to my quarters. She picked up her few things, and I escorted her to the dropship bay. She presented her visitor's pass and visa, and a biomech strapped her in.

"Good-bye, Autumn," I said into a speaker grill on the other side of a thick window. I wasn't allowed in the dropship bay. Ever.

She twiddled her fingers as the blister closed over her. The biomech retreated to an enclosure, and moments later the dropship fell out of the bay and was gone.

When I turned, Laird was standing there.

"She didn't last long," he observed.

"Time is relative."

"Your eyes," he said.

"My eyes?"

"Yes."

Laird was not fun to look at. Not that he'd ever been a movie star. But in the last decade, perhaps driven by the cadaverous specter that used to peer back out at him from his shaving mirror, he had been indulging in a high-caloric diet and bulking on fat at a feverish pace. His skin still appeared shiny and waxen, but now his jowls sagged and his neck was bulging and seamed. Also, like his great grandfather before him, he suffered mental lapses, stutters in cognitive organization that pointed toward eventual madness.

"Didn't you just take my eyes ten years ago?" I said.

"They're worn out. All your third and fourth re-gen organs wear out too quickly."

He coughed and wheezed, and clapped a sausage-fingered hand on my shoulder. I thought of his (my!) heart lugging away under layers of blubber in his great chest cavity. We were still almost a hundred years from Ulin's World.

"See you in surgical prep tomorrow at nine," he said. "And as long as you're coming in anyway, we'll do a pituitary extraction, too. Kill two birds."

God.

I nodded dully and watched him waddle off. Pituitary extractions were bad. But eyes were the worst.

I walked the Grand Promenade, trying to shake off the residue of dope. My mouth felt sticky. Biomechs strode stiffly by me. Their bodies were partly organic, maybe fourteen percent. Enough to allow them a limited range of human sensation. Exercise was good for their fluid circulation.

The overhead Scrim presented a mackerel sky dyed rose with sunset. I walked the length of the promenade, three point one kilometers. My mind felt marginally sharper. Probably fear-bursts of adrenaline had replaced the vapors of herb. I made a decision and allowed my thoughts to crystallize around it.

It was time to revisit George.

Sabotage? George was the name of the virus I'd been tinkering with for years. When I'd first been dragged back to the Command Level and forbidden from ever leaving again, I'd immediately begun plotting. Over time my plot grew diffuse and became more of a hobby. A "some day I'm gonna—" And then I didn't.

Now I departed the Grand Promenade and made my way circuitously, by ladder and maintenance corridors, to the Orbital Flight

Operations Center. The Oh Fuck wasn't suppose to be online until that far-flung day when *Infinity* would establish itself in orbit over Ulin's World. It was a fairly small deck space, packed with equipment of exactly zero usefulness while the ship was in deep space transit.

Except for one item: a Quantum Interface Terminal.

I'd figured out a way to fool the power use monitors by making it appear as though insignificant energy surges were occurring throughout the holo projection system, when in fact the additional drain was caused by my occasional use of the quantum interface. Stealthy as hell.

The Oh Fuck was dark, except for a few panel lights. I seated myself in an operations couch and fitted the transdermal leads to my temples, performing a limited interface with the quantum core.

I touched a green pad and a data Environment sprang up around me. I shuffled through it, seeking my disguised entry point, found it, and opened a gate into my partially constructed virus.

I'd named it "George" after a junior high school geography teacher whose class I'd had to endure once upon a distant time. He had been an eminently fair and eminently dull teacher. Probably the last person you would have suspected of any devious acts.

I remained installed in the operations couch for hours, meticulously completing George. I didn't want to cripple *Infinity*, merely disrupt a few routines, make it possible for me to escape back to The County and create the kind of minor havoc that would make Laird's efforts to retrieve my ass an exercise in futility—at least for a while.

I was going all the way this time, determined to elude Ulin for as long as it took. My harvest days were over. I was pulling the plug.

I set George on a short timer and then withdrew from the interface. A few white lights blinked in the dark of the Oh Fuck. I started to get up from the couch, and a panicky impulse seized me. I could still go back in and stop the timer, dismantle George. I hesitated a moment longer, then levered myself out of the couch and returned to my quarters.

It was safe in there with my books and barriers. Barriers against emotional involvement. Barriers around that most vulnerable organ— my heart.

I had an hour to kill before George began screwing with *Infinity* in a noticeable way. Whenever there was an open space I tended to fill it with dope. So I started preparing my usual answer to any uncomfortable possibility. Standing before my plant collection I picked up the little shears and started snipping likely buds. My hands moved slowly, then stopped, and I thought: The hell with it. I dropped the shears and switched off the grow lights. That closed my most reliable escape hatch. I could still feel the heat on the backs of my hands.

So when Laird Ulin came for my eyes, I wasn't there. Around the time he was expecting me in surgical prep, I was strolling through Venice. Someone had turned the canal water periwinkle. Since no real water was involved, such a transformation was easily accomplished and did no harm, except to the verisimilitude.

Two biomechs sat in front of a café façade (which was real) sipping from demitasses of espresso (which was synth). They were supposed to resemble a man and a woman. And they did, too, if the light was sufficiently dim and you squinted and were perhaps drunk or a little blind. BUZZ and ROCHELLE. A cute couple. I wished they would go away. Venice usually was unpopulated at this hour.

I sat at a nearby table under the shade of a Cinzano umbrella. The biomechs glanced over by turning their necks in little jerks and auto-focusing their doll's eyes. I smiled and waved, and they turned away again, no doubt conversing on a closed channel.

I said "Espresso" and a thing like a traffic light with four erector set legs clickety-clacked out of the café and placed a thick, white saucer with a demitasse of black synth on my table. You didn't need periwinkle canal water to spoil verisimilitude.

I sat sipping synth (not out of a seashell by the sea shore, thank goodness), pinky extended at the proper angle, and directed my strongest *Get Lost!* vibe at BUZZ and ROCHELLE. They ignored me. And their bodies made percolating sounds, as if they were brewing the wretched synth in whatever passed for their intestinal tracks—which is how the stuff tasted.

"Lovely day," I remarked.

They didn't like me, and showed it by not deigning to acknowledge my presence beyond their initial glance. None of the biomech population liked me, though, so I wasn't offended. I inhaled deeply and said:

"It feels good to be alive!"

BUZZ jerked his mannequin head in my direction again. His range of facial expression was nil, so who knows what he intended to convey. Without speaking, he and ROCHELLE stood up together and, holding hands, walked toward the Scrim. They could *remember* being alive, but that didn't count. Their fourteen percent organics allowed them to ingest synthetic espresso and even taste it. They could hold hands if they wanted to, but coitus was a technical conundrum beyond their design.

It *was* good to be alive. And perhaps not so good to be BUZZ and ROCHELLE. From now on I was all for life.

After a short distance they passed through the Scrim that presented the illusion of a street continuing in diminishing perspective. The street scene shivered, and two instantly created figures strolled in place of the biomechanical couple.

I put my demitasse down.

The street scene continued to shiver and wobble. Then the canal turned black, which gave the parked gondolas the appearance of projecting over a Stygian abyss.

After that, the whole damn thing crashed.

Presently there came the sharp *clack* of magnetic locks releasing. A panel opened in the velvet blackness before which the image of the canal had resided moments ago.

I moved quickly. My perusal of the ship's design database had informed me that from this point I would be very near the port to a kilometers-long access tube running from the Command Level to the floor of The County. Picture *Infinity* as a giant armadillo, twenty kilometers long, half again as tall and five wide. In between the Command Level and The County was a middle section devoted to farms and resource reclamation. The access tube pierced all three levels. It was *long*.

Orienting myself, I turned right and followed the corridor between bulkheads until I came to a wider place and a hatch recessed into the deck.

I knelt on the deck and retracted the hatch by turning a hand-operated wheel. The purpose of this tube, as well as several others located along the outer hull of *Infinity* was to provide direct access between deck levels in the event of a catastrophic systems failure. At such a time one might also assume a loss of gravity, which would make traveling the tubes a somewhat less harrowing experience than it was likely to be now, with full gravity—full gravity on *Infinity* being roughly eighty-eight percent Earth normal. It was a very long way to The County.

The tube was three meters in diameter. As soon as the hatch was fully retracted, three linked platforms, each large enough to accommodate a single passenger, rose out of the opening. The platforms were attached to pairs of skinny rails on the side of the tube. They were powerless contraptions operated on an elaborate arrangement of counter weights and had been built with no very great expectation of ever being utilized.

I stepped onto one, secured myself with a strap, released the lock, gripped the handrails and began utilizing the hell out of it.

I dropped at a moderate rate. Amber light illuminated the tube. Looking up made me feel like I was inside a giant straw, slipping back after the big suck.

As I slowly descended, my stomach fluttered with anticipation. Images of Delilah inhabited my mind. Even at this point a long-frightened child inside me clamored to get off this ride before it was too late. Below me lay a world that had moved on only a short number of years. But if I stopped, went back to my quarters, back to my books and dope and timeless retreat, that world below would eventually cycle all its present population, including Delilah, into the next generation. And I could go on and dwell in semi-blissful numbness until *Infinity* completed her long journey.

I shook off the fear and stayed with the ride.

After ten minutes or so the lights began to flicker up and down the endless tube. I gripped the handrails tighter. Was George making his broader acquaintance with *Infinity*'s intimate architecture?

The lights stuttered a final time and went out. It wasn't too bad at first, but after a while a flashlight would have been nice. The long black fall gave me an uneasy feeling. I hadn't planned on any lights going out. Perhaps George had some plans of his own. Perhaps "plan" was the wrong word altogether. All I'd wanted to do was unlock some doors and disrupt a few nonessential functions. But I was no genius when it came to tampering with SuperQuantum Core technology. Perhaps no one was. Not even Laird himself. There was something a little magical and unpredictable about SuperQuantum.

Eventually the platform encountered a pneumatic brake and shushed to an uneventful halt. I locked it down, fumbled my safety strap loose, and began groping for the exit.

I emerged behind one of the giant holographic Scrims that provided The County with a portion of horizon. It was like standing behind an old-fashioned cinema screen. I craned my neck but could not see the top, which curved almost imperceptibly with the hull.

I stepped forward, through the Scrim, and stumbled slightly with the disorientation of a sudden transition in perspective. I found myself a few miles "east" of Bedford Falls. Grassland spread out in all directions. It felt too warm. Generally The County maintained a climate not unlike that which used to be found in suburban shopping malls of the late twentieth century.

I gazed skyward. Clouds were already beginning to gather, and some of them might have been real. Down here *Infinity* generated her own limited weather phenomenon; the rest was vivid illusion. However, embedded in my virus was a tutorial on stormcraft, which I hoped to see manifested shortly after my arrival and—fingers crossed—reunion. Just a mild thunderstorm, a little sound, not much fury. It was the romantic in me. Tinkering around with the idea, I'd felt positively Byronesqe.

I started walking faster.

CHAPTER TWELVE

The little girl with choppy yellow hair pointed and said, "The sky's broken."

Infinity was a ship full of skies. And sometimes they 'broke.' But this was of a different magnitude. A large rectangular section had turned black. Even though I knew it only indicated that a Scrim projection grid had gone offline, it was still vaguely disturbing. And much more so to this child, of course.

It was hot. I had come upon the girl in the Town Square of Bedford Falls, sitting on a bench in a red jumpsuit eating a vanilla ice-cream cone. I guessed she was about six. She made such a pretty picture that I approached her and said hi. It had been quite a while since I'd last talked to a child. Up close this one looked familiar. As soon as I greeted her she got a look on her face and started pointing at the sky, pale lips puckered worriedly.

"Don't worry about it," I said. "It's probably just a minor malfunction. Hey, watch out, you're melting all over the place." I sat beside her. She wouldn't stop staring at the black section above us. Those eyes.

"The *sky's* wrong," she said.

"What flavor's your cone?"

"Huh?"

"I said what flavor's your cone?"

"What flavor does it look like?" she asked.

"Strawberry?"

"It's vanilla."

"That was going to be my next guess. What's your name?"

"Alice Greene."

I nodded. "I bet I know your mom's name."

"Bet you don't."

"Delilah."

She licked her cone. "Everybody knows everybody."

"Yeah? You don't know me."

She shrugged, then shouted: "Mommy!"

A woman had stepped out of the Bedford Falls Hotel and was crossing quickly in our direction. The resemblance was obvious, the hair, especially the violet eyes.

"There's my girl," she said, picking Alice up and holding her.

"Something's wrong with the *sky*," Alice said.

"Don't look at it, Honey."

"Why not? Will it unbreak if I don't look?"

"I'm sure it's just a minor glitch," I said. "Hello, Delilah."

She stared, bestowing upon me the same stupefied gawk her daughter had given the broken sky.

"Ellis—"

"I was on my way over when I bumped into your daughter."

"On your way over. It's been *ten years*, Ellis."

"Nine, actually. But it feels like ten to me, too."

"Mommy I wanna go inside now," Alice said.

"Just a minute, baby."

"Cute kid," I said.

Delilah gave me a measuring look. "Ellis, what are you doing here?

"Hey, I thought absence was supposed to cause various internal organs to grow fonder."

"You haven't changed a bit."

"Neither have you. Beautiful as ever."

She smiled, but said: "Yes, I have. Changed." She didn't mean the crow's feet, which I hated myself for noticing.

A hot breeze scurried through the square. Since I had arrived the ambient temperature had risen by at least five degrees. That was at ground level. I estimated it was a lot cooler a kilometer or so above, where George was playing with alterations in the atmosphere, orchestrating temperature and pressures changes. Real clouds formed rapidly. There was something disturbingly aggressive about it. I thought of dark tubes and black wounds slashed into the sky.

"It might not be a bad idea for you to get inside," I said to Delilah.

"Go inside, Mom!"

"What's happening, Ellis?"

"I'm not sure. All I had in mind was a little wind and a rumble or two. This feels bigger."

She regarded me strangely, her fair brow was misted with sweat. "Come inside with us."

"I think I'll sit and watch for a while."

Delilah hesitated a moment longer, glanced at the sky, then turned and walked swiftly toward the hotel. Alice hung over her shoulder and dripped a trail of creamy yellow-white spots, in case she wanted to find her way back to Uncle Ellis.

The square was filling with people. They emerged from storefronts and restaurants and work centers. They halted on the sidewalks, stood straddling bicycles. They pointed. Now the sky hung low and threatening, pregnant with storm. The wind picked up. Everyone appeared uneasy. I wanted to pull a Jimmy Stewart, quell the citizenry's incipient panic. But I didn't have it in me. Perhaps I needed somebody to quell *my* incipient panic first.

More than a few (Bedford Fallsians?) noticed me sitting on the bench looking at them. I was a stranger, so that was to be expected. What made me nervous were the flashes of recognition some of them threw at me. And it wasn't happy let-me-shake-your-hand recognition, either.

I got up and followed the drippy trail to the hotel, keeping my head down.

Somebody gasped. There were some oh-my-Gods. I looked up from the steps of the hotel. The sky was tinted green. In the distance a narrow funnel cloud probed downward. Jesus.

I went inside.

"You'd better see this," Delilah said. She handed me a unrolled Palmscroll. "The alert is running continuously. You seem to be a wanted man."

I activated the device. Laird Ulin's face swam into focus. What lovely eyes!

"This man—" Ulin said, and an image insert of yours truly opened in the lower right corner of the scroll. "—is Ellis Herrick. He is an unauthorized person at large in The County, and is personally and solely responsible for the disruptions now occurring. If you encounter Mr. Herrick you must detain him and immediately alert Command Level authorities."

I handed the device back. "Feel like turning me in?"

"Should I?" Delilah said.

A gust of wind buffeted the building.

"It might be more useful to point me in the direction of the nearest Core Access Interface. I think I need to turn the weather off."

"God makes the weather," Alice said, shaking her head seriously.

Perhaps she was mocking me? I reached down and wiped a daub of ice-cream off her chin.

"Can you do that?" Delilah asked. "Turn the storm off?"

"Maybe. By the way, where's *Mr.* Delilah?"

She wrinkled her nose. If you mean Alice's father, he's in Waukegan. And his name is Ben Roos."

"The name I remember."

"Ellis. You went away. Remember? For a long time. Besides, you knew I had to get pregnant."

"Ben's my gene dad," Alice piped up. "He's old."

Kids say the darndest things.

"I bet I'm older than your gene daddy," I said to Alice.

"He's the mayor," she said back, not sounding too impressed.

"What a guy."

"He's a water farmer, too."

"Now I'm getting all tingly."

Alice giggled.

We were in the apartment behind the front desk of the hotel. A window looked out on the promenade. The light through that window suddenly dimmed, as if a giant shroud had been drawn over the town. There was a roaring. I closed the shades.

"Hang on!"

Something monstrous moved over us. The building shuddered. A woman screamed in the next room. My ears popped. Delilah's face was tense and frightened. She hugged Alice against her breast, and I couldn't see the child's face. Then the window exploded. Sucked out the opening, the shade rattled and danced. I felt the breath drawn from my lungs. Outside in the weird purple-green light, a raggedy man swept by, arms and legs flailing like the limbs of a boneless doll. *Son of a bitch!*

In a minute or two it was over.

The light turned buttery, and shadows fled across the courtyard. I stepped to the window and ripped down what remained of the shade. The sky was blowing clear. Above the shredded clouds a holographic lie of serenity persisted. My hands were trembling, and I made them into fists. There had been nothing in my virus that could have given birth to this. *Nothing.*

I climbed through the window frame and went to the man. He lay sprawled and twisted. The grass was as vividly green as his blood was red. My hand unsteady, I touched the place on his neck that should have been pulsing and found it wasn't.

Behind me, Delilah said, "Ellis—?"

"This is my fault," I said.

Then the man's eyes fluttered, and I jerked my hand back. Hearts can be tricky things.

What a nice day for a bicycle ride. Delilah Greene (with Alice riding tandem) pedaled ahead of me on the winding, swooping path through the Oxygen Forest. With George running amok and the monorails dependent on the centralized computer system, it seemed best to take the scenic route. Also, I wanted to avoid being observed.

It was an odd-looking forest, the trees engineered for maximum carbon dioxide-to-oxygen conversion, bulgy on top like big green cartoon poodle puffs. Whimsical. But I wasn't feeling too whimsical myself. Not like the way I'd felt when I concocted a harmless little thunderstorm.

We were on our way to Waukegan. There was an old water farmer in town who also happened to be mayor—and in the office of the mayor was a Core Access Interface. The one in Bedford Falls had exploded, unfortunately (Core interface, not water farmer/mayor). A lot of other things had, too. We left behind us a debris field of PerfectWood flinders but—luckily—no bodies. A black pillar of smoke, wind-smudged, climbed over the roofs of Bedford Falls. Whimsy.

And George was already busy rearranging the atmosphere for round two. Before entering the forest we saw an impressive cell of mini thunderheads, gorgeously mauve and dimly aflicker from within, standing on the phony horizon like purple-robed clerics of doom.

Suddenly darkness fell. Like a guillotine. One moment it was afternoon, the next deepest midnight. We stopped riding. I didn't even bother holding my hand in front of my face, because I already knew I wouldn't be able to see it. Riding was too dangerous, and even walking was problematical. We left the bicycles and blundered around until we found a soft spot to sit and wait.

Eventually the stars come on, erratically, in clusters, through the branch tangle and cloud tatter. Then the clouds thickened, and the stars were lost. Above the clouds, the moon dialed up, preternaturally bright. Moonlight shot through the clouds like milk poured through India ink. It wasn't enough light to ride by, but we could see well enough to walk. For safety's sake we held hands. I let it feel good, Delilah's hand in mine. The first time I let Delilah feel good to me she had been twenty and I had been twenty-nine (two hundred and seventy-four). Now she was pushing thirty. This knowledge tweaked my urge towards isolation, but I held on tight to that hand.

There was a distant roll of thunder, and Delilah said, "Why a storm? I know you didn't intend for it to be violent. But why a storm at all?"

I felt embarrassed but said the truth anyway: "My first night with Nichole, there was a thunderstorm."

"I remember from the Environment," Delilah said. "But—"

"Listen," I said. "The way around serial grieving is to stop living fully. Withdraw. Which I did, back on Earth. Then I came out here so I could do it even better. Then I slipped up and got involved with you. And ten years ago, when Laird Ulin sent his henchmen to take me away I didn't even *try* to come back—not for a long while did I try. Because it was safer to hang out with a bunch of ageless mechanical men and one waxy bastard who could play chess. Then it occurred to me that I missed you, and everybody grieves. Maybe it had something to do with being locked up in the Command Level, having my choice denied. Whatever. So now I'm the Dr. Manette of the stars, recalled to life. And, for me, *you* equal life. Capital L. I wanted to whip something up for you, to show you how I feel. I can't bake worth a damn, but I'm evidently hell on storms."

"I thought it was nine years," Delilah said, and squeezed my hand. Some people just aren't equipped to appreciate a beautiful speech rife with Dickensian allusions.

Alice said, "I have to pee."

So she squatted in the bushes while Delilah held her hand and I held Delilah's hand. That's how it gets when you don't want to lose anybody in the dark.

Delilah said, "I'm glad you came back." And she leaned over and kissed me.

"I'm glad I did, too," I said and kissed her mouth.

A breeze freshened through the forest, rustling things. The atmosphere felt charged and smelled wet. Then it *was* wet. Very. Lightning forked across the sky, followed closely by a big rolling boom of thunder.

Suddenly Delilah collapsed. I was still holding her hand, and her weight pulled me off-balance as she went down. A brilliant beam of light fell on us, churning with silver rain. The shiny tranq dart in Delilah's neck flashed. Her hand was loose in mine. Her other hand was empty; Alice was gone.

I squinted into the light, held my free hand up, and felt the second dart punch into my shoulder. Instantly I snatched it out, but my legs turned to rubber anyway and dumped me on my ass. My body's super metabolism immediately began rushing the tranquilizer through my system.

Cold rain pounded down. I felt woozy and wanted to lie back but resisted. When I put my hands down to prop myself up I felt the smooth shape of a rock under my fingers. I pried it out of the mud as the drone approached.

It was Laird Ulin—his proxy, anyway. The drone was shaped like a big watermelon, with a small but powerful searchlight attached to a gimbal on its bottom, skeletal manipulator arms, and a ten inch screen that displayed Laird's mug behind a haze of static.

"Ready to come home, Ellis?"

The inside of my mouth was cottony. I worked up some juice and replied, "How'd you find me?"

Laird winked grotesquely (everything about him was grotesque, as far as I could tell). "I've always got an eye on you, Ellis," he said, and laughed. Grotesquely. "Come along now."

One of the manipulator arms extended towards me. I shoved away from it, sliding in the mud.

"I think I'll stay," I said.

"But they hate you down here now," Laird said. "Everybody knows you're the bringer of storms. You aren't *ever* going to want to come back."

"Now I get it," I said.

The wooziness had passed out of me. A locus of pain throbbed behind my eyes. I tightened my grip on the rock. The wind and rain intensified. There was a lurid light under the clouds. Fire?

The drone swayed closer.

A giant spider leg of sizzling blue lightning stomped down, missing us by only a few meters. My skin suddenly felt too tight. Fried ozone crisped the little hairs in my nostrils. An oxygen tree erupted in flame. Laird's face disappeared in a surge of static. The drone wobbled, and I came up under it with the rock and smashed at it. The drone's manipulator arms flailed around me. I jerked out of its reach, and it bobbled erratically, undirected. Which probably had more to do with the proximity of the lightning strike than it did with my caveman routine.

Delilah wouldn't wake up. I hunkered beside her. In the firelight I saw Alice huddled under a tree not fifty meters away. I shouted over the wind and rain, and she ran to me.

Alice was scared, but she knew something important and was able to tell me. Having previously traveled the forest path, she remembered that midway along there was a rest-stop shelter.

We proceeded there. I carried Delilah fireman style, and held onto Alice's little hand, which was clammy and wet and soft. The wind tore at our sopping clothes. The air smelled of ozone and smoke. For now I was *glad* of the rain, since it was keeping who knew how many fires under control.

By the time we reached the rest-stop the only unquenched blaze I was aware of was the one in my lower back. I lay Delilah down on a bench and pushed her eyelids open one at a time with my thumb. She had nice pupils. I checked her pulse, too, which was slow but steady. The storm rattled on the roof like a shower of bones. There were PerfectWood benches, a lavatory, fresh water, a rack of personal traveler's packs and first-aid kits.

Alice stood in a corner, shivering. I gave her a hug and advised her not to be scared.

"I'm not scared," she said. "Why doesn't my mom wake up?"

"She will," I said. "But probably not for a while. You're going to sit here with her and make sure *she's* not scared when she does wake up."

"All by myself?" Alice said.

"Sure. You're a big girl, aren't you?"

"I want you to stay, too."

"I can't, honey. But I'll come back, then we'll all three be together, okay?"

She looked at her feet. "Okay."

"Good girl."

There was one more thing to do before I left. The traveler's kits contained, among other things, a vacuum sealed "fruit" paste snack and a little spoon. I told Alice not to freak out if I got loud. She made her worried mouth, that sour pucker of pale lips. I kissed the top of her wet head, then took my spoon into the lavatory and locked the door.

My eye offended me, but I sure as hell didn't want to pluck out the wrong one. To be on the safe side I could have done both, but that would have left me blind for a week or so. Not a good idea. I did eenie-meeny, but my intuition suggested one more miney after the final mo. Left eye.

I did some Zen rigmarole, breathing myself into a kind of auto-hypnotic trance while I sat on the jakes. Then I waited for a particularly loud thunder clap and scooped my left eye out with the spoon. Zen breathing techniques are wonderful; I barely screamed at all before fainting.

When I came to on the floor, the eye was staring at me, trailing a spaghetti string of optic nerve. My left orbit throbbed like mad but had already filled in with a damp membrane that signaled the beginning of regeneration.

I brought my hand down flat on the severed eye. I'd miney-moed wisely. Threaded into the goo was an organic transponder with, I'd bet, about a ten year life span. Laird must have been seeding these things into my eye re-gens for decades. That bastard.

I used the little scissors from one of the first-aid kits to cut an oval of black fabric from my shirt. A fastidious traveler had left a partial roll of dental floss on the shelf over the sink. I poked holes on two sides of the patch and used a length of the floss to hold the patch in place.

When I emerged from the lavatory Alice stared at the eye patch and said, "I don't like it here."

The light was stark. Delilah looked like a wet corpse on the bench. Rain blew against the shelter's walls. I checked Delilah's pulse again and found it steady. I'm hell on pulse-checking, I thought, remembering the not-dead man behind the Bedford Falls Hotel.

"Is my mom okay?" the kid said.

"She's doing fine."

Alice chewed on her lip, waiting for the only conscious adult in the vicinity to make the next decision. So I did that.

"You want to come along with me?"

She nodded. "But what about Mom?"

"She's going to sleep for a long time," I said. "And when she wakes up we'll probably be back. You don't have to worry about her."

She still looked doubtful, so I told her we'd write Delilah a note, letting her know where we went. That seemed to relieve some of the tension in the kid's face.

"Okay," she said. Her face lit up with a smile, and I recognized her for what she was: an anchoring strand in the web of human attachments I'd recklessly begun to spin from my guts.

CHAPTER THIRTEEN

D aytime dialed up hot after the brief and violent night. Steam rose off everything, even our clothes. An exploded curbside terminal burned merrily on a Waukegan street corner, the flames nearly invisible in the glare of the false sun. Broken glass glittered in the street, trash hustled around in hot little whirlwinds. The air had thickened, and I almost had to swallow every breath like thin soup. Alice had taken hold of my hand again and was squeezing it hard. A couple of times during the long walk from the Oxygen Forest my stomach had moved in queasy undulations. Which could have been guilt, or—much worse—an indication George had begun to tamper with The County's gravity field.

"Here," Alice said, tugging me toward the double doors of a chalk-white and very official-looking building, like maybe the place where Mickey Mouse planned all the parades and stuff. On our way to the stairs I drew some unfriendly looks from people who appeared wrung out and pissed off. One guy did more than look. He seized my arm and spun me around to face him. "You bastard," he said. Bared teeth, blood crusted on flared nostril. I braced myself for a blow I probably deserved. But a couple of other men pulled him off, and Alice pulled urgently at my hand. I didn't bother telling her not to be scared.

"This one," she said, once we'd attained the second floor, and she pushed her finger against a door marked by a simple plaque: "Mayor."

I knocked.

The old man who answered was short and stooped. What little hair remaining on his pate was wispy as cobwebs. The wrinkly face brightened slightly at the sight of Alice. He kissed her cheek, then rubbed her head with a palsied hand. She put up with it.

When he turned his attention to me all he said was, "You're Herrick." And his eyes were like a pair of peeled grapes staring moistly from nests of papyrus skin. I didn't hold my breath for a kiss.

"And you're—"

"Ben Roos. Alice's father."

"Gene father," Alice said.

Roos scowled at her. "Where's Delilah?"

Alice looked at me. Delilah had called Roos before we departed Bedford Falls. She had assured him that I could put things right if given a chance.

"We had to split up," I said.

He grunted. "You can fix this mess?"

"Possibly."

He grunted again, eloquently, and turned his back. We followed him into the office. He pointed at the Core Access Interface, another big barber chair version, like the one I'd once used in Bedford Falls. At the sight of it a queer sensation passed through me. Something like fear. Then it was gone.

"There you go," Roos said. "People could die, Mr. Herrick. I hope when you say 'possibly' you're just being coy."

"Me, too."

I sat down and performed a soft interface with the CAI. The old man and Alice and the room and the world slipped away. The SuperQuantum environment read me and produced an analog. George. Mr. George, my seventh grade history teacher was an Ichabod Crane knock-off, only not as handsome. I'd left him in an empty classroom "correcting" student papers with a liar's red pen, disbursing a stickman army of D's and F's to papers deserving of better. This was my unconscious symbolic language for the smidgen of chaos I'd intended to introduce and which, apparently, had morphed into something much more serious.

I looked over George's shoulder. He was drawing smiley faces on the endlessly replenishing stack of papers. Huh?

"You can't outfox me with my own toys," Laird Ulin said, speaking through the mouth of Ichabod George, not looking up from his endless scribble of smilies.

I backed away. The room lacked windows and doors. Laird had isolated my virus and was letting me know as much. I pressed into a corner and found myself folded over to my parent's bedroom, the way it had looked when I was an eight-year-old boy. There was another analog: Me, this time. I was rummaging through my mother's purse. I came up with Mom's wallet and started plucking bills out while sneaking looks over my shoulder. Sneaky. Repeat.

I fled from that scene and passed through a complex chain of interconnected vandalisms. My various analog selves set fires, kicked some kid in the balls, tortured insects and small animals, etc. Anyone else seeking problems in the SuperQuantum environment would witness their own versions of various malicious acts—but *my* individual stamp would be on every single one.

"It's quite out of control," Laird Ulin said.

I turned. He was sitting behind a free-floating ebony slab the thickness of a sheet of paper, fiddling with cut glass chess pieces.

"I thought George would catch you off guard," I said.

"You forgot about shadows," Laird said. "Or gambled one wouldn't occur."

"Shit. I gambled."

Ulin grinned.

A quirk of SuperQuantum technology is the occasional quantum shadow—a future ghost in the machine. Laird must have seen my tampering before I even did it, which gave him time to do a little tampering of his own and stamp it with my personal signature—conferring upon me instant persona non grata status in The County.

I felt a weird combination of relief and resignation.

"So now I'll come back to surgery and you'll make things right," I said.

Laird smiled.

The chessboard turned into a crystal display of complex quantum language: the reality behind the dramatic analogs.

"The errors are self-perpetuating," Laird said, pointing. "I constructed it that way. Couldn't help myself, Ellis. You made me mad this time." He waved his hand and the chessboard returned.

"Definitely mad," I said, picking up a knight. It was slightly tempting. Retreat was my fatal flaw and I knew it. Besides, there was nothing I could do about the quantum errors Laird had unleashed. Only he could spare The County. Hell, returning to my emotionally remote cocoon on the Command Level was practically an act of noble self-sacrifice.

"Maybe we should skip the game for now," I said.

"Nonsense," Laird said, taking the knight from my fingers and replacing it in its proper position on the chessboard.

"Shouldn't you be getting busy? I nodded toward my delinquent analogs.

"There's plenty of time," he said. "All the time in the world. Besides, correcting these errors will be very difficult, and I'm not inclined to do it. The more miserable life is in The County, the less likely you will be to find safe haven. Ever. There will be *no more running away*, Ellis. Now why don't we relax and have a game while the Environment sustains?"

I quoted Ben Roos: "People could die."

Laird shrugged. He tapped a pawn on the chessboard. "Shall we play?"

"We shall not."

Laird scowled. I inhaled deeply, withdrew from the interface, and leaned forward in the chair, rubbing my good eye. The patch had slipped a little on the other one, and I adjusted it.

Alice was gone. Ben Roos sat on the small sofa by himself with a cup of tea or something that he didn't appear inclined to drink.

Two men flanked me. They didn't look friendly. Something ticked against the window. The ticking increased and subsided, in waves. Rain. Wind. I looked up at the man on my right and said, "Not guilty." He pulled a frown.

Ben Roos was staring daggers at me from the sofa. He was a pretty good dagger starer, too. Welcome back to the land of the living. Actually, I was glad to be there. *No more running away.*

"Where's Alice?" I asked.

"She's gone off," he said. "And if anything happens to her it will be on your head, like the rest of this mess."

"I can explain some things," I said.

Roos snorted. "Save your explanations." He stood. "I'll check the uplink. Keep Herrick here until they arrive."

He went out.

I got up but my flankers crowded me.

"I'll just be on my way," I said. "I have uplinks to check, and miles to go before I sleep."

The slightly older man shook his head. "You're staying right here until the Command Authority comes for you."

"Hmmm," I said.

When I started for the door, the younger guy stood in front of me, rather beefishly.

"Have a seat, Mr. Herrick." He grinned. "What are you supposed to be, anyway, a pirate?"

"Yo ho ho," I said. "And what are you supposed to be, an idiot?"

He scowled impressively, and I moved into his space, held the back of his head as if I intended to kiss him, found his carotid artery with two rigid fingers, and invited him to unconsciousness. He looked surprised, then slack, then he fell.

His friend said, "Hey—" and started to reach for something in his pocket. I punched him once, hard, on the point of his chin, and he dropped.

I guess they hadn't been expecting a fight. There were two sets of hooded raingear hanging in the corner, dripping on the carpet. I appropriated the larger set, put it on, and exited by the window. In eighty-eight percent gravity, one story is doable if you're fussy about landing.

On the sidewalk, I pulled the hood up and kept my head down. There were dropships smoking in the street. A pair of biomechanical men with sidearms drawn entered the building I'd just exited. How long could I elude them and their ilk? I was counting on Laird correcting the quantum errors in the interest of keeping me alive until he could recover me, which is the only way *he* could remain alive. But it was a gamble. There had been more than a touch of madness in his eyes.

On the path beyond the suburbs of Waukegan a small girl's voice squealed after me.

I turned around and smiled. "Hey, kid."

"Hi," Alice said. "I ran away."

"What a coincidence."

"Are you going to see my mom?"

"Yeah."

"Me, too."

I thought of Delilah out there, certainly awake by now, perhaps on the path to meet us. I thought of hugs and tears, and the tightening web of relationship. I thought of letting her in through the open door in my heart which was really an unsutured wound.

The top-heavy oxygen trees tossed wildly in the wind. Dark clouds scudded overhead, dumping rain below a holographic flicker of summer. The great black gash in the sky was visible, and Alice stared upward, her lips puckered tensely.

"Don't be afraid," I said.

"I'm not afraid.

I picked up her little hand. "Me neither, kid," I said. But I was a liar.

We did not encounter Delilah on the path, which was strewn with leaves and wind-ripped branches. I experienced a sinking feeling the deeper into the forest we hiked. Suppose after we left Delilah her body had manifested an allergic reaction to the tranquilizer? She had appeared so . . . *lifeless* on that bench. I began to dread what we might find at the rest-stop. Cold dread: it's what you get for caring.

Alice became tired of walking, and besides she couldn't keep up with me very well.

"We'll piggyback you," I said.

"What's that?"

I shook my head. "Poor ignorant child." I explained what a piggyback ride was, and she quickly grasped the idea and climbed aboard.

Finally I saw the domed roof of the shelter, like a landed saucer among the wildly thrashing trees. I put Alice down and she immediately started for the shelter, but I grabbed her little arm and said, "Hold up."

She looked at me and read my anxiety and borrowed some for herself.

"What's the matter?" she asked.

"Probably nothing, but you wait here for a minute."

I led her to a young tree and told her to hug it. "So you don't blow away." I was genuinely worried about it; some of those gusts were *big*.

Then I approached the shelter. I didn't allow myself to hesitate, because I didn't want Alice to know I was scared. Grab the handle, turn it down, and enter. The lights came up automatically, revealing the empty bench. I breathed out but didn't relax. The bathroom was empty, too. I tried the com-line but heard only hissing static. Whom did I think I was calling, anyway?

Alice was hugging the tree like a long-lost sister when I came back outside, her face a little white oval with hectic red spots on the cheeks.

"Looks like she flew the coop, kid," I said, all lighthearted.

"Flew it *where*?" she said.

I squinted into the relentless wind. *Flew it into the dark and wild forest where we'll never be able to find her*, I thought. But that was just me being pessimistic.

"Come on and we'll find out," I said.

I crouched for her, but she said, "I can walk now."

"I know, but I can go faster if I'm carrying you."

"Okay."

She hoisted herself onto my back and I stood up. I moved away from the shelter and stood upon the windy path for a moment, which didn't diverge in the wood and was about equally traveled in both directions. The question was, which direction had Delilah chosen? We certainly would have bumped into her on our way out of Waukegan, if she'd gone that way. Unless she'd wandered from the path and was blundering lost in the forest. My mind threw up the frightening image of her coming awake by herself in the shelter, listening to the wind and rain battering at the walls, maybe the lights flickering in her face, and Delilah all dopey with the drug and fear. In such a state what might she *not* have done?

But such speculations got me nowhere. I turned toward Bedford Falls and started walking. Fast. After a while I saw the bicycles we'd abandoned when the lights went out. I put Alice down and we climbed on the tandem cycle and took off, making good time at last.

At about the moment we emerged from the Oxygen Forest, George dialed up the sun again. Rainbows occurred in the blowing rain. I leaned over the handlebars and pedaled for town.

Men and women in raingear humped it across the town square. We coasted up to the front of the Bedford Falls Hotel and dismounted and dumped the bike.

Inside it was warm and noisy and smelled like wet clothes. A hearth fire blazed in the lobby. I shouldered some people out of the way and installed Alice by it to warm up and dry out.

A woman about sixty years old was behind the check-in counter. I'd never met her before, but I knew who she was.

"You're Delilah's mother," I said.

"Birth mother, yes," she said, distracted. Her hair was pulled back in a tight bun, but some gray wisps had escaped and floated around her face. It gave her a scattered look. Her eyes kept moving over the milling crowd.

"Business is booming," I observed.

"Half the power grid's down. People are cold and wet. And frightened. Every room is full, but you're welcome to huddle in the lobby until things get running again. Are you a friend of Delilah's?"

"Yes. Have you seen her?"

"Not for a day. She said she was going away with someone. Are you the someone?"

"I was, but now she's gone away from me, too."

She looked at me closely for the first time.

"You're familiar," she said.

"I've got one of those faces."

"No, you don't."

"Alice is with me, she's over by the fire. Can you keep an eye on her while I go look for Delilah?"

"Alice *lives* here, Mr. Herrick. Of course I'll keep her."

"Mr. Who?"

She tilted her head sideways and smiled. "Don't worry about me turning you in," she said. "I believe in you. I've studied your Environment."

Inwardly I groaned and sighed with relief at the same time.

"It's nice to be believed in," I said.

"Yes, but remember there are many who don't believe in you. They believe in Laird Ulin and the Command Authority. And they *will* turn you in. Happily."

A swarm of children invaded the lobby, squealing and chasing through the crowd.

"God," Delilah's mother said. "I can't wait till things return to normal and we can stuff these kids back in school. I guess they can't all be little angels, like Alice."

School. A light bulb appeared over my head, for anyone who could see such things.

"Speaking of school," I said, "Do you know where I can find the principal?"

"Gerry Rozsonits? I have no idea. He has living quarters attached to the school itself, of course. But I doubt if he's there with no electricity. You're not thinking Delilah's with him?"

"Why not?"

She pushed the errant hair out of her face. "Gerry is a little extreme when it comes to my daughter."

"Extreme in what way?"

"In unacceptable ways, Mr. Herrick. Delilah plays it down, but

I know Gerry is obsessed with her. I've thought about bringing it up with the town council. It's the kind of thing that can't really be tolerated. It happens, of course. We're all human on *Infinity*. At least in The County we are."

"What could the Council do?"

"Encourage him to move to a different town, probably do a direct swap."

"Suppose he didn't want to move?"

"In an extreme case the Council could compel him to swap."

"Tell me how to find the school," I said.

She did. I thanked her and started to turn, and two guys grabbed me, one on each arm.

"Relax," one of them said.

I did that. I let my body slump, totally nonresistant. It caught them off-guard and off-balance. Which is something good to take advantage of. I twisted loose of their equivocal grips, elbowed a solar-plexus here, stomped an instep there, and bolted for the door.

Dodging around the back streets of Bedford Falls, I made my way to the elementary school. It was a low-slung building, somewhat out of keeping with the ancient Americana ambience of the town in general.

As I regarded the structure from the playground a strange rippling sensation passed through my stomach. I felt light and dizzy momentarily, then it passed. Definitely George playing with The County's gravity field. I hooked my arm around the monkey bars, anchoring myself, and waited to see what would happen. But there was nothing but the continual, gusty wind.

I walked toward the school. The windows were polarized to black. A kid's backpack lay abandoned near the front entrance. I felt like I was being watched, and I very well might have been.

I tracked around the building and saw the principal's residence, a kind of bungalow thing, with black windows, same as the school. I walked up to it and knocked on the door. No answer. I tried the knob, but it was locked.

"Gerry!"

Nothing.

But I knew he was in there. I could practically feel his vibe emanating out of the walls. And Delilah's, too.

I made my way to the back of the residence and wasted time with another locked door, twisting the knob, pounding on it a little.

I kept scanning the sky for dropships.

Gerry's electric cart was parked half in and half out of the driveway, suggesting a hasty maybe even panicked arrival. As I was looking at it, fat drops of rain began showering down, and I pulled my hood up.

It was a schizophrenic sky, dumping rain and splitting open with sun bursts at the same time. Clouds scudded like runaway galleons. Maybe Laird couldn't launch any dropships, until the weather cleared. That was an optimistic thought, but transitory.

I needed to get into the bungalow and find out whether or not Delilah was there.

So I ran at the door and kicked it in.

I sprawled into the kitchen, and came up on my feet, and fell down again. My door-kicking right foot was now attached to a sprained ankle. Damn it.

Footsteps came pounding through the house.

I got up, despite the pain. Gerry appeared in the kitchen. He didn't look happy. And he was armed.

"Get out!" His face was brick red.

"Where's Delilah?"

He leveled the weapon at me.

"Get out," he said, "or I'll kill you."

"*Kill* me? Have you ever killed anyone before, Gerry?"

"I'll do it."

"I doubt that." I'm hell on bluffing. I didn't know *what* he'd do. I was focused on Delilah and the time factor.

I stepped toward Gerry, and he backed up a step. The whole thing reminded me of a dance I'd once done with a potentially homicidal Christer back on Earth.

"I'm warning you," he said.

"I know, I know."

I took another step. The weapon was trembling in his hand. In the next moments he'd either kill me or start crying. I decided to help him make his decision.

I shuffled incrementally closer. He was backed up against the wall.

"You bastard," he said.

"Come on, Gerry."

Suddenly murder appeared in his eyes. Clear as a red light warning.

I struck out with a reverse kick, balancing on my good left foot and making contact with my gimpy right one. The weapon went flying, and a bolt of pain shot up my leg and started a campfire in my groin.

If Gerry had gone for the weapon right then he would have had me; I was doing a flamingo routine on my left foot, holding my right foot and injured ankle off the floor. But Gerry *didn't* go for the weapon. He started to cry, and then he slid down to the floor, right hand cradled in his lap, left hand covering his face. I felt sorry for him, almost.

"Where is she?" I asked again.

"She's sleeping," he said, and that's all I could get out of him. She was sleeping.

I went limping through the residence, calling Delilah's name and receiving silence for an answer. After I checked every room, I began to wonder how whacked Gerry might be. Then I heard a muffled thump directly overhead.

The attic space.

I located a set of pull-down stairs in a back hallway and hauled them down. Someone moaned. I climbed the stairs with maddening slowness, hopping and balancing and hopping again.

Delilah was there.

Tied and gagged: portrait of Gerry's heartfelt love and devotion. I untied her and held her while she cried, which didn't go on for long.

"I guess he followed us into the forest then got lost when the sun went out. Later on he found me in the shelter. He kept saying he was going to take care of me and everything was going to be all right. This right after I started coming out of the drug. By then he already had me here. I was too weak to make much of a fuss. I thought he was being nice, or trying to be. Then I remembered things. I started asking him about Alice and you, and he said I didn't understand. Understand *what?* I said. It's just us now he told me. The two of us, the way it was meant to be. That's when it really hit me. I told him to think again, and that was so dumb of me. I know it was dumb. I should have gone along with what he was saying. He would have calmed down eventually. Don't you think he would have calmed down, Ellis?"

"Sure."

"But I got scared," Delilah said. "Can you believe I got scared of Gerry Rozonits? But there was something in his eyes. Or not in them. And all of a sudden I got so *scared*."

The tears came again, welling up from some place deeper. Reaction tears of someone who had been in the grip of a primitive fear.

I gave her as much time as I thought we could afford, then I said, "We better get out of here, Delilah. They'll be coming for me."

I stood up awkwardly.

"What happened to your eye and your poor foot?" she asked.

"It's my poor ankle, actually. And it was a couple of things. First I used it for a battering ram, then it didn't hurt enough, so I used it to disarm Gerry. Now it hurts plenty. The eye's a slightly longer story. Let's save it."

She helped me hobble downstairs. Gerry was gone, which I took for a good sign. However, the weapon was gone, too, which I took for a bad one.

We paused there at the entry to the kitchen, where I'd left Gerry. I had my left arm around Delilah's shoulders, and she was supporting quite a bit of my weight. Wind blew through the broken back door. Rain pelted the window, which looked out on a scrap of lawn continually blooming and darkening with rapid shifts of sun and shadow. The rain spots on the floor where I'd kicked my way in gleamed like fish scales in the peekaboo sunshine.

"What's the matter?" Delilah said.

"Gerry's the matter," I said.

There was a weird pressure in my ears. A handful of spaghetti worms squiggled queasily around in my stomach, and my eyes seemed to flip over like lead weights. For a moment, I'd blacked out. Then I felt light and drifty. Then, suddenly, my full body weight resumed, and Delilah and I shuffled off-balance.

She said, "What was *that*?"

"George," I replied. "My virus. Ulin mutated it and now it's out of control. What you just felt was, I think, the gravity field going wonky."

"Dear God."

"Yeah."

Outside, we climbed into the electric cart. Delilah took the driver's seat. She started the motor and swung us out from behind the residence and rolled us at a sedate fifteen kilometers per hour across the playground. We were approaching the swings and monkey bars and stuff when there was a crackling sound followed instantly by a

FAAARUMPH! and the cart bucked us out of our seats and flipped over on its side, burning.

I looked frantically for Delilah, saw her, and crawled over. She had a cut on her forehead that looked bad enough for stitches, but she got right up on her feet and appeared otherwise unhurt. I struggled up, too, using the monkey bars.

Gerry stalked toward us, leveling the weapon.

"She doesn't want you!" he shouted. "She doesn't want you!"

I tried to shove Delilah away from me but she wouldn't budge.

"He won't shoot me," she said, and wrapped her arms protectively around me.

"He just *did* shoot you," I pointed out.

Then the queasy-wormy sensation was back in my guts, only ten times worse. Sweat popped out all over my body. My vision blurred, cleared.

Gerry wavered, then fired, and a very strange thing occurred. The discharge burst into the ground a little in front of him, and he went tumbling into the sky, end-for-end, tumbling up and away into a wild sky of broken black clouds and shimmering rainbows.

CHAPTER FOURTEEN

Turn the wheel. I'll stand over here and watch. Time is a process, brutal, relentless, etc. Blah.

Delilah's face was deeply etched by pain and age. Her hair was short, iron gray, and the texture of straw. She lay unconscious on our bed, dying, gradually. Alice and I stood over her and conversed in low voices.

"I think it's foolish," she said. Alice had grown into a beautiful, strong and tirelessly upright woman of middle years. Unlike her mother, she didn't have a romantic bone in her body. Above all else, Alice was *practical*.

"Your mother always wanted it back," I said, "and I'm going to get it for her."

We were talking about the white gold wedding band on a chain which I had presented to Delilah forty years ago. The same ring I had first presented to Nichole several lifetimes previous. Delilah had accidentally left it behind when we evacuated The County. She had realized almost immediately that it was missing. But at that point there had been no going back for bobbles; the calamity in The County had been well underway.

"Mom needs you here," Alice pointed out.

"I know that. I'll only be gone a couple of hours. Alice, this is my last chance to get that ring for her. I want her to have it in her hand. I want her to know I got it for *her*.

"It's more important for you to be here when—" She looked down at her mother.

"When what?"

She looked up again into my face. "When she passes."

"There's plenty of time," I said.

"No," she said. "There isn't."

She was right. And that was why I had to go.

Accessing The County level was easy. Basically open a hatch and vomit. The gravity well was fucked up beyond redemption. At least George hadn't infected the middle decks where we now lived. What had occurred on the Command Level was anyone's guess. The overhead was sealed tight. No communication. No egress. It had been that way for decades.

Alice and her husband Josh saw me to the emergency access tube. Josh was tall, blonde and capable. He was also a fair poet. Every once in a while he let me have a peek in his red-covered composition book, a precious thing he'd made himself.

"Dad," Alice said, "please don't go."

"I could go with you," Josh suggested. "It would be safer. I've always wanted to go back down and . . . see how things are."

"Thanks, but I'll go alone."

"Well." He shook my hand. "I think you're making a mistake."

Alice hugged me, which felt nice. We held on tight for a long while, then I broke the embrace and picked up my backpack.

"Honey, I have to hurry for Mom."

"Take this." She pressed a com button into my hand.

"You know it won't work," I said. "No one's ever been able to send a signal out of The County since the Calamity."

"Take it anyway, just in case."

They stood back while I cranked the hatch aside. Invisible waves undulated up the tube. It gave me a queasy feeling even to stand next to the opening. I checked the straps on my back pack, pulled the flashlight out of its loop.

"See you soon," I said. Then I turned, bent at the waist, and went head-first into the tube.

Hoping for whatever brief effect, I'd taken a kind of super-Dramamine, but I still threw up when the gravity fluctuations wobbled through my guts. At first I dropped pretty fast, then it was like plunging into warm water, and I drifted downward, nearly weight-less.

All this in utter darkness.

I thumbed my flashlight on. A brilliant bar of light preceded me but faded to a vague blur without touching bottom. It was a long descent. Every once in a while I reached out and pulled myself forward by one of the platform rails. Even though the gravity field in The County had been approximately one fifth that of *Infinity* normal for decades, I knew it didn't necessarily have to remain that way. It had fluctuated wildly during the great Calamity, at one point acquiring crushing intensity and killing thousands.

The farther I descended the warmer it got. I wiped sweat out of my eyes and referred to my chronometer. It was twenty minutes before my flashlight beam revealed the bottom of the tube. By then my weightless condition had adjusted up again to a lunar approximation. I reached out for a rail and slowed myself. My sweaty hand slipped on the polished metal. I drew my knees up and rolled around, reorienting myself so I came in feet-first, letting the big muscles in my thighs absorb the minor shock.

Touchdown.

Of course I wasn't the first person to visit The County in forty years. But I hoped to be the one who returned safely. Out of fifteen thousand County population at the time of the Great Calamity, only some six hundred had successfully fled to the reclamation deck, where life was a bit on the industrial side but *good*, by virtue of the fact that it was possible at all. And over the decades twenty people had tried returning to The County, mostly on missions of retrieval— just like mine. Twenty went down and none came back. What befell them no one knew.

At the bottom of the emergency access tube I worked the hatch open. Light burst upon me. I dropped the flashlight and covered my eyes, turning away.

I let my eyes gradually adjust. It took a while after the long tube dark. When I could see without tearing up I slipped out onto the dead plain "east" of Bedford Falls.

What had been a green expanse of grassland was now a blasted desert place. The air was thin and hot. Not thin enough to require an oxygen supplement, but thin. And the sky was white.

Here at the bottom of the gravity well my body had some weight. I experimented with long strides and settled on a variation of the old moon bunny hop. Moving thus, in long bounds, I attained the wreck of Bedford falls in a matter of minutes.

Much of the town lay in ruins. Lightning strikes, fire, hurricane force winds, pernicious whirlwinds, and the coup de gras: a sudden increase in gravity, had taken their considerable toll. Buildings tumbled, sewers erupted, power grids ignited.

The Bedford Falls Hotel had abruptly converted from three stories to one story. Jagged fingers of PerfectWood pointed at the white sky.

I unshouldered my backpack, took out the modules of the laser-cutter, quickly assembled them. An eerie silence prevailed. I interrupted it with the sizzle and spark of laser-assisted excavation.

I swung the cutter in surgical arcs, slicing away debris and half-standing walls. Delilah had left the ring in the first floor bathroom of the hotel. The odds of locating it within this mess were low, to say the least.

As I worked, my stomach kept gurgling and roiling around, and it worried me. But I kept my concentration on the job. I cut my way through, reducing big rubble to smaller chunks that I could fling aside manually in the low G. But after a while I noticed it wasn't as low G as it had been.

Soon I'd worked my way into the lobby. I saw bones and stopped. Of course The County was a vast graveyard of bones. Knowing that didn't make discovering some underfoot any more pleasant. I stepped around the partial female skeleton (I knew it was female by the tattered remains of clothing still clinging to it) and activated the laser again.

Abruptly the lights went out, leaving only the ruby cutting beam of the laser.

I turned the laser off and groped for my flashlight. In the darkness the air seemed even thinner. I thumbed the flashlight on at the same moment that I caught the heel of my right foot on something and fell backward, landing hard, striking the back of my head a stunning blow.

Landing *hard*; the gravity had increased dramatically.

Stars throbbed in my vision. They kept throbbing even after I'd opened my eyes again. Damn it. I waited, and the throbbing subsided.

My flashlight lay a few feet away, its beam striking a bright track across the filthy lobby rug and terminating at the crushed skull of the skeleton. Something shiny and white gleamed in the skeleton's ribcage. I rolled onto my knees and crawled over to it, squinted, and reached in. It was the white gold ring. Of all the bizarre luck! I lifted the chain over the skull and held it up in the flashlight. The ring winked and turned before my eyes. Here was a story that would never be told. Who was this nameless person? Had she stolen the ring before we ever left The County? Or had she come across it in the bathroom, right where Delilah thought she remembered leaving it, and hung it around her neck as the most convenient place to keep it until she could evacuate up to the resource reclamation deck and find its rightful owner?

I stood up and hung it around my own neck.

In my heart, I'd never really expected to find the thing, but I would have gone on slicing and poking around the rubble of the hotel for as long as it took to avoid Delilah's "passing" as Alice put it. A coward's impulse. From Zingbars to potent hand-rolled dope, to simply doing a fade when it was time to grieve; my escape hatches were many. Forty years ago I'd told myself no more running away, and I'd almost accomplished that. Crapping out at the end was ignoble.

Fuck it.

I swung my flashlight around, hunting for the direction back to the emergency access tube. In darkness and full gravity, it wasn't going to be easy returning to Delilah. Is this what had happened to the twenty who never returned?

Although I knew it wouldn't work I tried my com button. Static hissed into my ear, and I put it away. I guess I'd had my one stroke of luck when I found the ring.

I followed my flashlight beam out of the hotel and into the Main Street. From there I could get my bearings. I pointed myself at the eastern plain and started hoofing it. Was it harder slogging than it should have been for a man of my size? Would the gravity come up and crush me as it had so many others?

I was out on the blasted plain when I noticed I could see again. I switched the flashlight off.

Starlight.

I looked up. A huge moon slowly emerged. It had a face. Laird Ulin's.

I stumbled, feeling high and disconnected from reality. It must have been the thin air. Ulin's moon face leered down upon me. As I stared, it dimmed away. The sky turned pearlescent then dialed up throbbing bright. I plodded toward the Scrim, panting for breath. The holographic projection still showed a grassy green expanse rolling away into afternoon haze. A stark contrast to the desert place The County had become.

Something about the light from above changed. I looked up again—and almost screamed. Laird's face stretched across the heavens, mugging and clenching.

I looked away from it and saw a figure approaching towards me across the plain. It appeared to be a man but moved haltingly, with stiff jerks of its limbs. It moved like an old time movie zombie.

The sky went black.

In the dark again, I slung the backpack off and dragged out the laser-cutter, reassembled it by flashlight, fumbled over it and found the power switch. The battery pack was about half depleted.

Once more moonlight flooded the blasted plain. I could see the figure. It was only a couple of dozen meters away. I leveled the laser-cutter and rested my finger on the trigger.

The thing stopped. It raised one arm, palm out, and waved jerkily. It spoke my name, bell-clear in the unnatural quiet of The County.

I moved closer to it, still holding the laser up. "Who are you?"

"It's me. Laird."

I craned my head back to see the Ulin moon. It was grinning, though the voice had issued from the biomech standing before me.

"Where are you really?" I asked.

"I'm all over The County," the biomech said. It's breastplate name plate identified it as RODNEY.

"Who's RODNEY?" I said.

"He doesn't matter. I use him. All the biomechs are tied into the SuperQuantum Core. This one happened to be in The County when it all went to hell. And I own everything in The County. Including RODNEY."

"I meant where are *you*?" I said. "Right now, where are you speaking from?"

"That's what I wanted to talk to you about," Laird said. "I need a little help. Nobody else wanted to help me, so I crushed them. You want to help me, don't you?"

"Absolutely. Ah, help you what?"

"*Help extricate me from this god damn fucking viral environment, that's what!*"

Reluctantly, I followed Ulin/RODNEY back to Bedford Falls. On the outskirts a dropship squatted like a big insect. I looked from it to the biomech.

"Fly the ship back up to the Command Level," Ulin/RODNEY said. "And unhook me from the interface. You *can* fly the ship can't you?"

"Sure."

"The others couldn't and I crushed them."

"Laird, why don't you just withdraw from the interface yourself?"

"Because I *can't*! I went in to correct the errors, and the errors swallowed me up. Now I *am* the virus, part of it, integrated. And I'm stuck in The County systems, and I'm sick to death of it. I'm— I'm a little bit lonely, Ellis. I don't mind telling you that. I'm lonely. Do you want to have a game? Let's have a nice game together after you unhook me from the interface. *Let's fucking do it!*"

"Laird, I—"

"Do it, do it now or I'll crush you, you little fucker."

I climbed up and opened the blister. The interior smelled musty. "This thing's been sitting here forty *years?*" I said to the biomech.

"Fly it, Ellis."

"It probably won't—"

"No excuses!"

I lowered myself into the pilot's seat and tried the power-up button. Nothing happened. Big surprise.

"It's dead," I told Ulin.

"Fix it."

"You should have had RODNEY fly it up decades ago. He could have pulled you off the interface, too. For that matter, why couldn't any of the biomechs already up there do it?"

RODNEY/Ulin stood stock still, making little percolating sounds.

"Laird?"

"Never mind," he said. "They aren't trustworthy. You have to do it."

I clambered out of the dropship, picked up my backpack and laser, and started walking towards the Scrim and the emergency access tube. I hoped to God the counterweighted platform would function.

"Where are you going?" RODNEY/Ulin said, and the biomech began stumping after me.

"The dropship's dead. I have to get back to Delilah before she's the same way."

"What about me! You're forgetting about me!"

I kept walking until I suddenly weighed around three hundred pounds and found myself flattened to the ground on my back. The white sky turned into a stretchy faced Ulin again. The RODNEY biomech creaked and percolated up to me, struggling with the increased gravity.

"I'll *crush* you," Ulin said, and the pressure increased until I could not breath, then it let up slowly, until I felt normal again, except for maybe a cracked rib.

"Let's have a game!" RODNEY/Ulin said, and Laird's stupendous sky-face winked at me.

So I used the laser-cutter's battery to jumpstart the dropship. It took me a while to figure out how to do it. RODNEY/Ulin kept pestering and threatening me. Finally the console displays lit up. I held my breath and tried the engine. A miracle occurred and it lit.

"Good job!" RODNEY/Ulin squawked.

"Yeah, whatever."

I worked the joystick and watched the control surfaces to be sure they tilted and swung the way they were supposed to.

"Come on, come on! Hurry up!"

"Okay," I said. "Jesus."

I throttled up and pulled back on the joystick. The vehicle lifted sluggishly and began climbing. My piloting skills were pretty rusty. I tried to line up on the directional beacon that indicated the chute in the ceiling of the world. At least I couldn't hear Laird anymore. But, peering up out of the dropship's blister, I saw his sky-face reduce in size and morph into a gigantic hand with a finger pointing at a slot in the overhead Scrim: The chute.

The Command Level appeared unaltered since the time I'd lived there. I walked down the Grand Promenade among strolling biomechanical puppets, who ignored me utterly. The Scrim presented a lovely river scene, complete with the murmuring purl of water. It felt surreal, after all that had transpired in The County and the after-math of the Great Calamity.

I found Laird's quarters locked. A biomech walked by. GEORGE, his breast plate said.

"Hey," I said.

He stopped.

"I need to get in here."

GEORGE turned and faced me, blank-faced—but he couldn't help it.

After a while he said: "So?"

"So . . . what do you know about it? Is Laird in there?"

GEORGE percolated a moment or two, then said, "One doesn't know or care."

Then he turned and proceeded on his way.

I went to stores, got a pry bar, and levered the door open. So many years. It was like entering a room of dried leaves. That was the only discernable odor. Laird's remains reclined in the interface couch, an undisturbed skeleton with a fat body suit collapsed over it like a tent.

All access points to the resource reclamation decks had been sealed, welded. I stopped the first biomech I encountered and de-manded why.

"It was deemed prudent," ANDREA said.

"By whom?'

"All of us. We couldn't risk the biologicals swarming over the Command Level, throwing all order into chaos."

"I need to get down there," I said. "Now."

ANDREA looked at me with her doll's eyes, evaluating. "We couldn't risk opening up," she said. "The disturbances in The County constitute a serious threat to the mission. The chaos must be contained."

"You wouldn't be risking anything. No one wants to come up here. I want to go *down*. Seal it up again, after me."

"There won't be any further contamination," ANDREA said. "Even the dropship bay has been properly deactivated, as it should have been years ago. Since you're here, you may remain. But don't interfere. That won't be tolerated. The mission is all that matters."

"Who's in charge, now that Laird's gone? I want to speak to the authority."

"No one is in charge. We all function for the mutual benefit of successfully completing the mission."

"My wife is dying," I said. "I need to get *down* there."

"Dying, Mr. Herrick? That's what biologicals do. All except you. Aren't you used to it yet? We are."

She strode away.

Okay.

I retrieved my laser-cutter and a fresh battery and went to work. I'd only had time to slice a single glowing arc in one of the titanium plates sealing the hatch, when I heard them coming. Their heavy footfalls, dozens of them. I swung the cutter in their direction.

"Stop," I said.

They didn't.

I triggered the laser and burned a hole in BURT 2's right thigh. A whiff of gray smoke puffed out. He acquired a limp but kept coming. So did the others.

"Don't you understand?" I shouted. "I have to get down there. I have to!"

I resumed cutting the plate, and then they overwhelmed me, took the cutter away, and carried me off.

They isolated me on a quarter deck of my own. I had adequate supplies, a view port, San Francisco (a faux chunk of it, anyway, where I could lounge on a bench by myself in the Presidio without even mad Laird Ulin to play chess with), and a stasis module. The stasis module looked like a black lacquer coffin with a window in the lid and a Medusa's tangle of pipes and tubes springing from it. My option, should I grow bored.

So this is how I learned that something human did indeed survive the uploading process. How else could the biomechs exercise such cruelty?

I had all I needed but communication. Sometime during my initial days in this new captivity, Delilah must have died. I remember sitting in the afternoon sun of the Presidio and feeling an emptiness open within me. The white swans floated by, and I didn't bother to wipe my tears. I was alone.

Fuck San Francisco. I got up and walked through the Scrim.

My view port was small. I pressed my nose to it, making fog ghosts. All the stars in the universe seemed to be gathered in a ball.

I disrobed entirely, except for the white gold ring and chain around my neck, and climbed into the stasis module. *Infinity* had a number of these things, but probably mine was the only one about to be put into use. Revival odds were in the low percentile. Stasis tubes were a last resort option.

I began to control my breathing. Gradually the world misted over, and my consciousness sought the peace of oblivion. On the way there I experienced a vision.

A ring of trees in a moonlit meadow. Two of them stepped aside and allowed me to enter the ring. There were some dead people in there. My mother, my father, my brother. Nichole, too. She turned and looked at me. The others were pale, painted in moonlight, ghostly. But Nichole was vibrantly alive. Energy burst from her in a nimbus of colors. There was no sound in this vision, but Nichole clearly mouthed the words "Welcome home, Ellis."

I shook my head. This wasn't any home I knew.

She smiled and took my hand. The others all touched me and tried to draw me in with them, into their embrace. But I was afraid and resisted. Then it all became vague and I went to sleep for a long, long time.

PART THREE:
EVOLUTION

"Thou art God."

—Michael Valentine Smith

CHAPTER FIFTEEN

M r. Herrick?"
    I heard him but preferred not to.
"Mr. Herrick, can you hear me?"
Yes. Now go away.
A thumb pushed up my left eyelid. Bright light, stabbing. I tried to bat it away, but my arm wouldn't obey me. It lay inert, a dead thing at my side.
So thumb the other lid up.
"Dilation is reactive and even."
Another voice, female: "He's looking very good, considering."
I blinked.
"*There* you are," the female voice said.
"Yep, here I am," I said. Only it came out sounding like I had a gym sock crammed in my mouth.
"Welcome back," the first voice said, the male voice. "You're a very lucky man."
Funny, I didn't feel lucky. All I could see was the ceiling, which was white. I closed my eyes again and went back to sleep.

I woke up in some kind of hospital room. There was a chair, a door opening onto a bathroom, and two beds, one of which I occupied. A heavily bandaged woman lay in the other. Her breathing was noisy and ragged. Most of her face was wrapped in bandages that appeared damp. Her arms lay on top of the covers. A needle was inserted into a vein on the back of her left hand and an IV bottle dripped something down a tube and into her. I could see part of her neck, and it looked burned and shiny wet. There was something about her. I almost felt as though I should know her.

I was thirsty and weak. A door stood open to the corridor, and I thought I heard distant voices. I looked around but there was no call button.

"Hey," I said, my voice too weak to be heard outside the room.

I tried to sit up and couldn't manage it. My arms were like meatless bones sticking out of the short sleeves of the gown thing they had me in. Slipping my hand under the shirt, I could feel my ribs. The skin sagged between them. No wonder I felt so weak. My body was starved down to the point of emaciation. Strangely, though, I didn't feel hungry.

The woman in the next bed made sounds of distress. I looked over. She thrashed weakly. The IV needle pulled out of her vein and started dripping on the floor. The woman's eyes were bright with fear. She was looking at the door.

So I did, too.

A figure with a red devil's face loomed in the doorway, so tall it had begun to duck in order to enter the room. It's chin was about a foot long. Its eyes were round and black with yellow pin-point pupils.

Fear injected me with a kick-ass dose of adrenaline, and I sat up. The thing immediately hunched away. My heart thudded. I took advantage of the adrenaline rush and threw the covers back and swung my matchstick legs off the mattress. I looked down at my Dachau body and wanted to weep.

The woman was watching me.

"It's all right," I said, "I'll get help."

She nodded, her eyes grateful.

I placed my bare feet on the cold floor and tried to stand. It worked, sort of. Using the bed frame to assist me, I shuffled around toward the door. I would have to let go to make any further progress. I did—and fell. From my new vantage point, the corridor appeared empty. The IV tube dangled between the beds, dripping, dripping, making a clear puddle on the floor.

"Help," I said, but the word emerged as little more than a dry rasp.

Okay. I started dragging myself forward. Eventually I got my head and shoulders past the doorway. At the end of the corridor—oh, twenty kilometers away—two women were talking animatedly. I said "Help" again, to no effect. So I waited for them to notice me. After a while, they did.

They were young. The first girl who knelt beside me solicitously could have been no more than twenty years old. She had the loveliest eyes. Her friend got on the other side of me. They hooked their arms under mine and hauled me up to my knees and then my feet and walked me back to bed.

"What's your name?" I asked the girl with the eyes.

"Tamara," she said, and smiled.

The other girl reattached my roommate's IV. Amazingly, the burned woman appeared to be sound asleep. I assumed the nurse had given her something.

"There was a monster," I said. "It scared her badly."

The two nurses, or whatever they were, looked at each other.

"Well," Tamara said. "Can I get you anything for now?"

"I'm thirsty."

"Of course you are. I'll bring you a cold drink."

"Thank you."

They went away, and Tamara returned shortly with a glass of something carbonated and lemony with a straw sticking out of it. I sipped at it gratefully, and she watched me.

"You really are Herrick, aren't you," she said.

"Yes, I really am."

"Then why did you ever climb into that stasis module? You would have survived the remainder of the trip easily without it."

"I know that."

"But the module might have killed even you."

"That was sort of my half-assed idea."

"Then it was a dumb idea."

"Agreed," I said, though I didn't. Then I yawned deeply, which was a more sincere expression; I felt exhausted.

"Sleep now," Tamara said. "I'm sure you'll have a lot of questions when you wake up."

"I'm sure I will."

She adjusted my blanket and started to leave. I stopped her at the door.

"Hey," I said. "What about the Devil?"

"The—"

"The monster that scared my roommate." I nodded at the other bed.

"Mrs. James was in an accident," Tamara said. "A very serious one, as you can see. She and her son were operating a high-speed overland vehicle and collided with a vehicle occupied by members of the indigenous population. What you saw wasn't a monster or a devil. It was a Trau'dorian. And it was here to apologize to Mrs. James. Her son was killed, you see."

"Indigenous population?" I said. "Where am I, exactly? There was never any indication of an indigenous species on Ulin's World."

"This isn't Ulin's World. Very far from it. You're on a planet orbiting a star in the Vega system."

"Excuse me. But that doesn't make sense."

"You mean, it makes no sense according to your preconceived ideas of what is possible and what isn't. Don't forget: You've been away from Earth a very long time."

"Nurse—"

"I'm not a nurse. I'm . . . kind of a doctor, I suppose you would call me."

"Kind of a doctor?"

She smiled. "I'm here to see to your psyche and help you through a difficult transition, I hope."

"What kind of transition?"

"As I said: a difficult one."

"That's fairly vague."

"Fairly. Rest now, Mr. Herrick. You need it."

"Ellis," I said. "Call me Ellis."

She smiled again, lighting up. "All right, Ellis, I'd be delighted to."

There was something damned familiar about Dr. Tamara. After she left I tried to figure out what it could be. The odd thing about it—the *exceedingly* odd thing—was that the moment she walked out the door I was unable to call up in my mind exactly what she looked like.

"That woman lied," Mrs. James said.

"I'm sorry," I said. "I thought you were sleeping. You looked like you were sleeping."

"I don't talk to them," she said. "There's no point. They don't believe me. They treat me like a crazy person, but I'm not a crazy person. I know what I saw. Those Trau'dorians took my son away, and now they want to come here and take me away, too."

I experienced an immediate empathy for Mrs. James. She didn't sound crazy to me.

"Tell me what happened," I said.

"There *was* an accident, if you want to call it that. My son and I were traveling one of the new roads outside the Dome. An excursion, that's all. Perhaps we were foolish. Then we were struck, our vehicle disabled. We were both hurt. Our oxygen was venting. I couldn't move, but Jeremy managed to reach our emergency masks and helped me into mine.

"Then *they* came.

"The Trau'dorians. They don't want us on their planet, transforming it. So what if they live underground and have long abandoned the surface of their world? They regard us as trespassers, no matter what they say openly. I believe they deliberately crashed us. And when we were disabled and helpless, they came and dragged Jeremy away. They left me but they took him, God only knows why. They have no human feelings. No morality as we understand it."

"Mrs. James, maybe you better try to rest now."

"What's your name again, young man?"

"Ellis."

"I'm afraid of them, Ellis."

"Don't worry. I'll stay awake while you rest. I promise I will."

But I didn't.

I woke up feeling terrifically enervated and heavy. Someone was weeping. Mrs. James. With an effort, I turned my head on the pillow.

The monster—the Trau'dorian—was bent over Mrs. James. Each of its hands possessed three very long, triple-jointed fingers and one opposable digit. The fingertips of its left hand were planted on Mrs. James's temple and forehead. It didn't seem to be hurting her physically, but it was obviously causing her a great deal of mental anguish. The Trau'dorian's face was very close to hers, and the thing was wickedly hideous.

The light in the room had not altered from the last time I was awake, and I could see all this very plainly. Especially the fear in Mrs. James's eyes.

I swallowed a couple of times and said, "Stop that, whatever you're doing."

I was too weak to even sit up.

The Trau'dorian turned its devil's face to me. Whatever guts I thought I had turned into hot liquid and spilled into my bed. I'd

never been so scared before in the whole of my incredibly long
life.

"Leave her *alone*," I said.

The Trau'dorian reached out toward me with its other hand,
the fingers spread. The rice paper skin on the tips of the fingers
was pulsing. I couldn't breath. The creature was so big it was able
to easily reach across the gap between the beds. Before it touched
me, I blacked out.

Sometime later, the cold wet sheets woke me. I'd pissed myself. I felt ashamed. Then I looked over at Mrs. James's bed.

She was gone.

No one came to help me. I waited a long time. I had no way of
telling how long because there were no time pieces in the room and
no window to gaze out of and figure the hour.

So I peeled the sheet back and got out of bed on my bandy legs
and hobbled over to the bathroom. I cleaned myself up, and also
discovered fresh bedding in a cabinet, as well as a clean hospital
gown. I put the gown on and went out into the hallway. It was
empty and long. Much longer than I would have been able to traverse
in my current condition.

I returned to the room and rested in the chair for a few minutes,
gathering my strength. All this felt wrong, somehow. Where was
the medical staff? Why didn't I have, at least, a call button with
which to summon help? If Mrs. James was in such serious condition, why wasn't she being closely monitored? For that matter, why
was I in the same room with her at all?

When I felt strong enough I stripped the soiled sheets and blanket off the bed, wiped down the mattress, and remade the bed with
clean things. Then, exhausted again, I climbed back in and fell into
a deep and dreamless sleep.

"What happened to Mrs. James," I said as soon as Dr. Tamara
walked though the door.

"Why she's much better."

"How could she be much better? You told me yesterday her
injuries were severe."

She looked at me curiously. "It wasn't yesterday I said that."

"Of course it was."

"That was six weeks ago, Ellis."

I stared at her. "Come on."

"But I'm telling you the truth, because that was the first and last time I talked directly to you. I've been called away to work with other patients."

I did some more staring.

"Are you all right, Ellis?"

"You can't seriously mean to say that I've been in this room six weeks."

"Ellis, you have been in this facility for a total of six terran weeks, ever since you were brought down from the starship *Infinity*. You have been undergoing a strict regimen of exercise and diet to counter the effects of long years in stasis. And I might add you're doing very well. Just look at yourself."

I held my arms up, astonished to see they were no longer bones with skin. I had even acquired some muscle definition. Beyond that, now that I was paying attention, I noticed that I felt good. Healthy, reasonably strong. Mentally acute—except for the unfortunate cognitive lapse of six weeks.

"I don't understand any of this," I said.

"Actually we speculated about the possibility of memory breaks. It's a fairly common phenomenon experienced by survivors of stasis modules. With your unique regenerative body, it seemed likely you would avoid such side-effects. Evidently we were mistaken about that."

"Last night—I thought it was last night—I woke up and saw that devil thing, the Trau'dorian, *doing* something to Mrs. James. I tried to stop it but I couldn't. I was too weak. I was helpless, and she was so scared. *Damn* it."

I blinked away tears, angry at myself.

"Ellis, six weeks ago you *were* too weak. You had no more strength than a child Of course you couldn't have intervened. Children are powerless. But you mustn't be upset. I know all about the incident. The Trau'dorian was helping Mrs. James."

"Helping her how? By scaring her out of her wits?"

"He was healing her mind. She was severely traumatized by the accident. The Trau'dorian felt responsible. They have that healing capability, and perhaps many others. We have barely begun to know their race. Mrs. James wasn't frightened by the Trau'dorian.

She was frightened by the terrors emerging from her own mind. That's what you saw. Trust me, Ellis. Mrs. James feels much better now."

"Before she fell asleep," I said, "she told me what happened out on the road. She said the Trau'dorians deliberately crashed her vehicle and then came and dragged her son away."

"But that's nonsense. Mrs. James was thrown clear of the vehicle. A fire consumed her son and left almost nothing of him beyond charred bones. You must understand, Ellis. Mrs. James hasn't been in her right mind. That is why the Trau'dorian came here. He wanted to help her, relieve her pain."

"Where is she now?"

"Mrs. James has left the clinic."

"And when do I leave?"

"As soon as you feel ready."

"Okay. I'm ready now."

"That's wonderful," Dr. Tamara said.

"About Mrs. James . . ."

"Yes?"

"She—" I didn't want to say it.

"Go on."

"She reminded me of someone."

"Who did she remind you of, Ellis?"

"My mother." Something caught in my throat and I choked on it a little.

Dr. Tamara moved closer to my bedside and put her hand on my shoulder.

"Do you feel like talking about your mother, Ellis?"

"No."

"Of course you don't have to do anything that makes you uncomfortable."

"That's good. What about these other patients of yours? Do they tell you about their mothers?"

"Some of them do. It all depends."

"Oh what?" I said.

"On where their pain lies and what they want to do about it."

"So when do I get out of here?"

"It's entirely up to you, Ellis. It always is."

Dr. Tamara blinked, turned her head aside, listening to something I couldn't hear.

"I have to go," she said. "You think about what you'd like to do."

"I already know what I'd like to do," I said. "Get out of here."

"That's fine then," she said. "I'll be talking to you soon."

She turned to leave.

"Hey, wait a minute—"

"Sorry, I have to go. It's an emergency."

The room was very quiet in her absence. Suddenly I wanted nothing more than to be gone. I got out of bed and looked in the bathroom and the closet. There were more hospital gown things, but no real clothes. I poked my head out into the hall, thinking I'd catch Dr. Tamara before she got too far, but the hallway was empty in both directions.

"Doctor!"

My voice echoed flatly.

I felt as lonely as I'd ever felt in my life. There was something comforting about Dr. Tamara (even if she was too young to be a real doctor). She had something I needed badly. But even more than that I needed to get out of this clinic or whatever it was.

I stepped out into the hall and started walking, bare feet slapping on the cold, institutional floor. There were doors on both sides of the hall, but they were shut. I tried a couple of them and found them locked. I kept moving. There had to be a nurse's station.

Other corridors branched off from the main one. None of them led anywhere. I trotted up and down these hallways to nowhere, my ass hanging out of the gown.

There were no nurse's stations.

Finally I discovered a door that opened. It was at the end of one of the branching corridors and was bigger than the other doors.

It opened onto a stairwell.

I entered the stairwell but held the door open until I was sure the knob would turn the latch on the stairwell side. It did, and I let the door fall shut. Up or down? Down presumably led out, plus it would be easier than climbing stairs.

I descended a couple of floors then paused to have a look. I opened the landing door and peered out. Hallways. Empty hallways. It figured.

I started down again. The stairwell seemed to go on forever, like the god damn hallways. Every time I peeked out a landing door I saw the same thing.

So I stopped, because there was some kind of disconnect occurring that I didn't understand. I looked up the dimly lit stairwell. It ascended forever.

I thought: *I'm dreaming.*

I'd been counting flights since I entered the stairwell. It now seemed prudent to return to my room. So I began climbing. By the time I reached the right floor, my legs were trembling and my gown clung to the cold sweat on my body.

I trudged back to my room. It was just as I'd left it, door open, bed unmade. I collapsed onto the mattress and dragged the covers over me. A feeling of peace and security settled upon me. I tried to reject it but couldn't. It was a familiar feeling of retreat.

Anyway, it didn't matter, because I was dreaming.

So I went to sleep to wake up—seemed logical. I opened my eyes to a slightly altered version of the room. Now I had a bedside table with a lamp I could turn on and off. There was also a call button on a cord. Moments after I pushed it a nurse type walked into the room, very starched and professional, just like the ones I used to know.

"What can I do for you, Mr. Herrick?"

"I was wondering when breakfast would be served."

She inclined her head curiously, and said, "The same time as every other morning, of course."

"And what time is that?"

"Eight-thirty sharp."

"And what time is it now?"

She glanced at the wall. A clock now hung there and it indicated eight oh seven.

"It's—" the nurse started to say.

"Eight oh seven," I said. "Thanks, I didn't notice the clock."

"Of course," she said, and smiled. *Humor him, he's a bit deranged. All those years in the stasis module, you know.*

After she left I got out of bed and poked my head out into the hallway. It had altered from my dream version, too. Many of the doors now stood open, and there was some kind of nurse's station only thirty meters or so to my left. The nurse I'd just talked to was walking toward it. She had a nice swing in her backyard. I called out:

"Nurse!"

She stopped and turned around.

"What is it, Mr. Herrick?"

"I—"

She walked back to me. "Is anything wrong?"

"No. I mean, I don't know, really. This is going to sound weird, but is there really a Dr. Tamara on staff?"

I was afraid she had been part of my vivid dream or delusion, and I wanted her to be real. I needed her to be.

The nurse looked puzzled. "Dr. Tamara?" Then understanding dawned. "You mean Dr. *Roberts*. Tamara Roberts."

Roberts. Same as Nichole's last name. "I guess so. The one who's been working with me since I got here. Some kind of psychologist?"

"Yes, what about her?"

"Nothing. I just wanted to know whether she's real."

"She's as real as I am," the nurse said, which failed completely to put my mind at ease.

While I ate my breakfast I thought about Mrs. James and the Trau'dorian. I thought about what Dr. Tamara had said, about how I'd been helpless to interfere because of my weakened condition, and that in a way it had been a good thing, because the alien was really *helping* Mrs. James, not harming her. But the doctor had put it in a strange way, comparing me to a child, a helpless child.

"You're looking well," Dr. Tamara said.

"You don't look half bad yourself," I said.

She laughed. "And pretty feisty, too, I see."

"I want to ask you about *Infinity*."

"Go right ahead."

"There were a lot of people on board, not just me. Where are the others?

Dr. Tamara looked sober, then said, "You were the only human survivor. The ship had deviated wildly from her intended course. Additional centuries had passed. Massive system failures had occurred. Recycling and reclamation capacities were exhausted."

This didn't surprise me, but hearing it stated took the wind out of my sails anyway. Then I said:

"The only human survivor?"

"We also recovered one biomechanical."

"Just one?"

"As I understand it," Dr. Tamara said, "the SuperQuantum core had become corrupted. All the biomechanical beings were inter-faced with the core and depended upon it for their equilibrium. Evi-dently the core wound up destroying all their memory matrixes."

"All but one."

"Yes. Ident name is RODNEY. He's here in the Dome, actually."

"Doctor, there's something I *really* don't understand. How could you people have reached *Infinity* at all, let alone brought me and RODNEY to this planet?"

"You recall the Harbinger controversy before you left Earth? Of course you do, you were intimately involved beginning way back in the 1970s. At the time of *Infinity*'s departure from Earth orbit the Harbingers had begun manifesting to receptive portions of human society. To make this short, they eventually emerged fully into hu-man consciousness. We were able to travel to the stars, colonize this planet, and even recover you from *Infinity* by using certain Harbinger methodologies."

"My God, so they were real."

"Very real, yes."

"Well I have a few questions for them. I don't suppose you have one handy."

"There is a Harbinger on this planet. He's sort of a hermit and not easily approached. In fact, humans don't approach Harbingers as a general rule; Harbingers approach us, when it suits them. They rarely intervene, but sometimes take an interest if a species is both promising and perilously verging on self-destruction at the same time. Then they might appear, literally, as Harbingers of conscious-ness evolution. This is what happened on Earth."

"You seem to know a lot about them."

"Not so very much, really. Just what everyone else knows. And nobody knows 'a lot' about the Harbingers."

"Okay. How are you with dream interpretation?"

"It's not my specialty, but I can try. Do you have a particularly interesting one?"

I told her about my long walk through the empty clinic, the endless hallways, the bottomless stairwells. I also told her about the oddly un-detailed aspect of my room and the rest of the clinic, even during her previous visits.

"That's a little disturbing," Dr. Tamara said. "It indicates an overlapping between your dream logic and the real world we inhabit in common. I blame it on the stasis module. Now you've exhibited two classic symptoms of stasis damage. It amounts to a kind of mild psychosis."

"Wonderful. Will it pass?"

"That's impossible to predict."

"I feel tired all of a sudden," I said.

"Why don't you have a rest then."

"I just woke up," I said, yawning.

"Ellis, you're far from fully recovered, either mentally or physically. You go ahead and rest. Indulge yourself. Your body knows what it needs."

"Usually," I said, settling back on my pillow.

She stood up.

"Hey, Dr. Tamara."

"Hmmm?"

"You never interpreted my dream. I mean the part of it that really was a dream. All that wandering around searching for an exit out of this place."

"That one's easy," she said. "It means you weren't ready to leave yet."

"I *felt* ready. More than ready. You said yourself that it was up to me. You said that before I had the dream. It was on my mind. That's probably why I had the dream in the first place."

"Very possibly."

"Well, good night. Or good morning, or whatever it is."

"Have a nice rest. And Ellis?"

"Yeah?"

"It really is up to you. Everything is."

She went out. I closed my eyes. Something about that phrase was maddeningly familiar. I tried to fall asleep but couldn't. It nagged at me. And there had been a companion phrase to go with it. So long ago and unreal, lost in my memory vaults.

I drifted for a while, dozing. Then the urge to pee brought me reluctantly, groggily, back out of it, and I sat up. It was too dark in the room. I fumbled for the lamp switch but couldn't find it. Irritated, I swung my legs out of bed, girding myself for the cold tile floor. But the floor was carpeted. I worked my toes in the nap. What the hell? Was I dreaming again? It was getting so I couldn't trust my sense of reality from one hour to the next. Which was fairly disturbing. I wished I hadn't tried to sleep again. I wished Dr. Tamara hadn't gone. My heart was beating too fast. Fear surged though me like ice water in my veins. I started to rise.

But stopped.

Even in the dark, the room felt different, the unseen space was all wrong. My breath came shallowly, and I knew I wasn't alone.

CHAPTER SIXTEEN

S omebody moved on the bed next to me, and a hand touched my bare back.

I jerked away from it, startled.

"Hey—" a female voice. Low register. "What's the matter with you?"

"I can't find the damn light switch," I said.

"Fuck's sake, you just turned them off yourself." She moved on the bed. The lights came up slowly, like theater lights. Her arm, brown and smooth, reached past me to a wall sensor. Her fingers were short and inelegant, the nails too long, the red polish chipped.

"You don't have to jump out of your skin," she said.

"Sorry, I was having some kind of bad dream."

"You weren't even asleep! We just fucked."

"Oh, yeah."

"That memorable, huh?"

She snaked her arm around my waist, her hand settling on my deflated penis. I shrank away from her touch—literally. She wiggled my member as if it were a broken toy.

"Golly, you talk a better time than you give," she said.

"I do tend to inflate my virtues," I said. "Could you stop that now?" I removed her hand.

"Well, excuse me," she said.

"Sorry. I'm having kind of a hard time."

"Like heck you are."

I still hadn't turned around to look at her. I was afraid and had no idea how to articulate my fear.

"Hey, are you having one of your episodes or whatever you call them, like you said you had?"

"Tell me what I said."

"You said you were in a stasis module for a long time and it fucked with your brain, so you had these episode things where you forget what was going on. Like that?"

I nodded. "That's about it. Care to tell me your name?"

"Helma. You really don't remember it?"

"And where are we, Helma?"

"In your very nice apartment, which is on the rim of Dome Seven."

"Dome Seven?"

"Oh, brother. You *are* far gone. Dome Seven is the newest dome on Planet X, that's all."

"Planet X?"

"They're still arguing about what to name it."

"And everybody lives in domes?"

"Naturally, while the terraforming is going on. Where else would everybody live, in caves like the Trau-dorians?"

"At least I know what a Trau'dorian is," I said. "Big devil-looking guys, right?"

"Right!"

Finally I scooted around to look at Helma. She was plain-faced, young, voluptuously curved. Her breasts were bound in some kind of S&M harness, blue-black nipples erect. She was kneeling on the mattress.

"Helma, I'm a little scared."

Her face bunched up in an ugly way. "Scared of what?"

"I don't really know. It's an off-balance feeling. I don't remember anything since I was in the clinic."

"So what am I supposed to do about it?"

"Not a thing."

"Good, because if you need a mommy to rock you to sleep, I'm not it."

"Thanks for telling me."

"Don't go like I'm *offending* you," she said. "I'm just saying I'm your girlfriend, not your mother or your damn head doctor."

"You know Dr. Tamara?"

"Whoever. I don't *know* her. But you talk about her, like she's something good. I doubt if she's better than me, though. One thing you never said, did you fuck her?"

"I know what your favorite word is," I said.

"Huh?"

"Never mind. How long have you been my girlfriend?"

"Since tonight."

"And I already told you all that stuff about myself?"

"Sure. You were Zinged. I couldn't have shut you up. Besides you had plenty of nice things to say about me, too. I thought you had real personality. I like it when a guy has personality. Hey, are we going to go another one, or not?"

She reached for my penis again.

"Guess not," she said.

She bounced off the bed and pulled on a pair of shiny blue shorts and sleeveless top. It was warm in the room, almost too warm.

"Where are you going?"

"Back to work, since we're done."

"Can't—Can't you stay?"

"What for?"

"I don't know. We could talk. You could sleep here."

"Sleep? It's the middle of the day, Ellis. And we can *talk* in the Zingbar."

"Right. I just thought . . ."

She leaned over and grabbed my face in her blunt-fingered hand and kissed me wetly on the lips.

"Sweetie, I have to go."

And she went.

I heard the door of the apartment hiss shut. The silence she left in her wake was deafening. I felt weak and vulnerable and I definitely could have used a mommy to rock me to sleep.

Fuck it. As Helma might have said.

I got up and hunted for clothes. The room really was hot. The clothes I found were made out of some very light material, pants and short-sleeved shirt.

I walked out of the bedroom and gaped at the view through a big curved window. A vast and barren landscape bathed in pumpkin light. Lightning zigzagged across the sky. Great plumes vented out of the tortured landscape outside the dome.

I was up high, maybe twenty stories. The domes interconnected at double levels by fully enclosed sky bridges. The view became vaguely disturbing, and I found a dial that polarized the window down to a black, non-reflective sheet. That was better, but I could still have used my favorite headshrinker.

I looked around the apartment, which consisted of four rooms:

the bedroom, the small living room, the smaller kitchenette, and the small*est* bathroom. I discovered nothing that looked even vaguely like a telephone. Even if I had found such a device, I wouldn't have known how to call the doctor. And I didn't know anybody else. I was alone.

I sat down and tried to think. It would be good if I could recover some of my most recently misplaced memory. A few glimpses occurred. Faces I couldn't put names to. Some kind of bar, loud music. But was I remembering these things or imagining them? The last Zingcup I could recall enjoying was the one I'd had back on Earth before abandoning my city apartment. I vividly remembered the wonderful mind-clearing sensation of the junk wind. That was too damn long ago. Helma had mentioned a Zingbar. How hard could it be to find? I *had* to clear the junk out of my head.

Leaving the apartment I found myself on a spiraling walkway under the Seventh Great Dome of Planet X. Here was a multilayered urban landscape, crowds of pedestrians, airborne vehicles buzzing above and below my level, the noise and riot of any big city. I stopped a random pedestrian and asked him which way to the nearest Zingbar. He pointed me in the right direction and never evinced a scintilla of recognition at the sight of my face; I hadn't known what to expect, and breathed an inward sigh of relief. Perhaps I wouldn't be burdened with the dubious celebrity of being "The Herrick." Thank God for that, at least.

I found the bar.

A stylized squiggle of crimson neon depicting a Zingcup with inhaler attached. *Zone Seven.* I stood on the sidewalk and stared at it but didn't go in. A Zing wouldn't really clear my head; it would just temporarily displace a plethora of anxieties. In the process of displacing them it would also fuck me up, in the grand tradition of all mind-altering anxiety displacers. And all of a sudden I wanted my faculties fully intact. So for now I walked away, making a mental note of the bar's location.

A number of people in the passing crowds were talking on their implanted cells, just like their progenitors on Earth had centuries before. The lack of progressive communication technology struck me as odd but I didn't think about it too much.

I came upon a street vendor dispensing steaming bowls of noodles. Wiping the sweat off my forehead, I approached his cart.

"Bowl for you?" he said.

"No, thanks. I'm new around here. If I wanted to find someone, how would I do it? Can you tell me?"

"You're not new around here, Mr. Herrick."

"You know me?"

"Like a brother! What's the matter, aren't you feeling well?"

"I'm a little off," I said. "Ah, how long have you known me?"

He was a fat man with big, red jowls and a wispy black beard on his chin. His face suddenly acquired a serious expression.

"I've known you as long as you've been here," he said.

I smiled and nodded. The aroma of the noodles was getting to me a little. I wasn't hungry but felt a compulsion to have a bowl, like it was something I was used to doing. I resisted the impulse and said:

"And how long have I been here, exactly?"

"In Building 42?"

"Sure. In Building 42."

"About a year, I guess."

A *year*! "I don't think that's possible."

"Don't think what's possible? You've been buying my noodles for about a year, and you always come out of that building right over there. And that building is number 42. Am I a liar?"

I pinched the bridge of my nose between thumb and forefinger, squeezing my eyes tightly shut. When I opened them, the fat man was looking worriedly at me, holding a slotted spoon over a fragrant cauldron of bubbling noodles.

"You're not a liar," I said. "I'm a little messed up. I need to talk to my doctor."

"Sure, I understand. You want some noodles, Mr. Herrick?"

"No, I'm really not hungry. How can I call my doctor?"

"You want to borrow my phone?"

"Yeah." I held my hand out.

"Here," he said, tapping a finger by the corner of his eye. "Look here. You are messed up, aren't you?"

I looked at his eye.

"Straight into the eyes," he said.

I looked straight into his eyes.

"Don't blink," he said.

I didn't, and after a moment a kind of head's-up display appeared in the air between us. It was a directory, minute columns of white-lettered names.

"Just think the person's name without anything else around it, no other thoughts."

Tamara, I thought, forgetting to add her last name. Nevertheless her first name isolated itself, bright blue. The other names disappeared. A thumbnail picture of her appeared beside the number. I breathed out, relieved.

"You can blink now," the noodle man said.

I blinked and the name and picture disappeared.

"I lost it," I said.

"No, you're connected now. Just talk. She'll hear you all right. If she doesn't answer it's because she doesn't want to. You want privacy, just walk away."

"But I don't have an implant."

"It's not implants. It's mental. There's no device. The eye thing and the directory, that was just to fulfill your expectation of a technology. Go ahead, talk. By the way, you could talk in your mind, but most people still have a problem with that."

"Uh, thanks."

"You're welcome. Sure you don't want a bowl?"

"Yeah, thanks."

I turned away and, feeling like a fool, said, "Dr. Tamara?"

Ellis, I'm surprised to hear from you.

I looked around. People passed me by without a glance. Some of them were talking to invisible friends, too. I sat on a bench overlooking the city.

"I think I'm having one of my . . . episodes," I said.

Oh, dear.

"Jesus, this is weird," I said. "Somebody told me this is like telepathy. Is it something the Harbingers gave us?"

In a way. They didn't give it to us, though. They allowed us to understand we could do it. The Harbingers are not a technological race in the usual sense. Ellis, tell me what's happening with you.

I told her about my tremendous memory lapse. "I can't believe it's been a year," I said.

It's been a little over a year.

"I need to see you," I said. "I feel kind of shaky. You—You tend to calm me down. I don't know how you do that."

There was a long pause, and I was beginning to think the connection was broken. Of course, I had no idea how to reestablish it.

Then, in my mind, Dr. Tamara said: *I don't think that's a good idea right now, Ellis.*

"I thought I'd lost you. Why isn't seeing me a good idea?"

Another pause.

Ellis, I'm sorry. I know you don't remember, but you and I have had a serious relationship. It was serious for me, at least. After a while you couldn't seem to deal with the intimacy. You hurt me, Ellis. I wanted to help you, but you hurt me in a cruel way. That was months ago.

"But I don't remember any of it!"

I'm sorry.

"What did I do?"

I'd rather not discus it. This conversation is making me sad. I have to go now, Ellis.

"Wait!"

But there was nothing in my mind but the usual windy vacancy.

I spent the rest of the afternoon concentrating and talking to myself, trying to find Dr. Tamara again, but I didn't have the knack or whatever it took to perform the telepathic hat trick on my own.

Finally, in despair, I wound up back at the noodleman's cart. He looked at me as though he knew exactly why I was there. I felt a little surge of anger and impatience with myself.

"Give me a bowl," I said.

"On the house!" he said.

Inevitably I returned to Zone Seven. The black rectangle of the doorway dissolved at my approach, admitting me to a cavern-like din of retro electronica. A jostling crowd immediately absorbed me and moved me, by diastolic undulations, to the long bar. I elbowed my way into a narrow space. Presently a beak-nosed bartender leaned toward me, ear cocked, and I ordered the house Zing. Whatever was cold. He nodded, started to turn away, and I said, "Damn it, wait. I don't have any money."

The bartender winked. "You know you're on a tab here, Mr. Herrick."

"Oh, yeah. I forgot."

He brought me a Zingcup so cold little whiffs of condensed air smoked off it, and there was a rime of frost covering the bright green slashes of a Kanji character. I caressed the cup with my thumb, leaving a streak in the rime, then fitted the inhaler to my nose and breathed deep. The junk wind blew. Oh, man! I inhaled again, emptying the cup. The lights and music acquired a crystalline quality.

Before I could put the empty down, the bartender had already placed a fresh Zingcup in front of me. I was a regular, all right, and he knew how to keep me happy. I leaned over the bar and shouted at him:

"Do I come here often?"

He laughed. "Not often, just every night!"

I raised the fresh Zingcup and emptied it up my nose. A fucking hurricane blew through my mind, sweeping away my junk fears and insecurities. The next time the bartender came within hailing distance I motioned him over and said:

"I'm looking for a girl."

"Naturally!"

"I mean a specific girl. Her name's Helma. Do you know her?"

"Who doesn't? She was here a while ago. You missed her. She'll be back, though. She always is. Or you could call her."

"I'll just wait," I said.

"Okey dokey."

He put a fresh Zingcup in front of me. I inhaled it.

And so on.

At some point I found myself crowded into a booth with a lot of people, on the edge of the dance floor. Wild-eyed denizens of Zone Seven cavorted, more or less naked, on the floor, their bodies sweated and slick under the kaleidoscopic lights. If it had been too warm in my apartment it was positively roasting in Zone Seven.

The table was covered with empty and half empty Zingcups. A woman with cat's-eyes handed me a commercially rolled joint. Her hand stroked between my legs while I lit up. She said something in my ear, but I was mostly deaf from the music. Her tongue probed wetly around the same ear, no doubt re-enforcing her unheard suggestion.

A girl on the other side of the table watched us. She held her Zingcup in both hands, occasionally raising it to her nose. Her leather vest was untied and her breasts hung out, pimpled with sweat. She had kitty eyes, too. They appeared genetically altered. She leaned across the table, breasts pendent, and I noticed the Zing frost ringing her nostrils. She kissed me hard. When I moved my tongue inside her lips, she bit down on it. I couldn't pull away; blood seeped into my mouth, a copper taste.

Then I was being dragged through the crowd, the joint dangling from my lips. Catgirl One led the way, holding my hand. The sweaty breasted girl was behind me, her fingers hooked into the waist of my pants. We got outside, but it wasn't much cooler. Catgirl One pulled eagerly at my hand. I staggered but kept up with her.

Some kind of alley. The buildings seemed to lean and sway drunkenly. I fell back against one of the unstable walls. Somehow my head was full of junk again. It was so god damn hot.

The girls came at me. One of them slapped the joint out of my mouth. They had claw-like fingernails, filed to points. They ripped my clothes with them and tossed the shreds.

One of them pulled on my half-flaccid penis, like she was milking a cow. "Come on, come on, what's wrong with you?" she said.

"I don't know," I said.

A sharp-nailed finger pushed into my anus.

"You like that, right?"

"No, stop it." I tried to push her away. I could smell my own fear. I was dripping with sweat, violated, scared.

"*Stop*," I said, and shoved her hard.

"You're useless!" she screeched.

Clawnails raked across my chest and belly. It was the sweaty-breasted girl. She started *biting* me. Fears roared through my head. There was too much junk in my mind, piled to the rafters, junk everywhere.

"Stop it, stop it," I said.

I was weak as a baby and they were eating me alive. I tried to detach from them in my mind, tried to float above the junk, but I couldn't manage it.

I screamed, struck out with my fists, connected with nothing; they were gone, the Weird Sisters of Planet X. Whatever.

Blood and sweat on my torso. Blood in my mouth. I found my clothes, flayed rags, and pulled the pants on for modesty's sake. Then I sat with my back against the wall, weeping. Herrick the object. Desire and fury. Graffiti scrawled across the opposite wall:

EVERYTHING IS SIMULTANEOUS!

Huh?

I wiped my eyes and tried to focus.

BUILDING FIVE / BLOCK TWO.

There was no graffiti.

My head lolled over. A figure stood motionless at the end of the alley, tall and alien, a devil of my mind. A Trau'dorian. It began to stalk toward me. I sat up, then stood up, shakily. It came on, a silhouetted monster. Behind it air vehicles traversed the sky inside of Dome Seven and pedestrians thronged the spiral walkway. But nobody even glanced in my direction; nobody cared about me.

The thing came on. I remembered what Dr. Tamara had said about them helping Mrs. James. Their empathetic powers. But I didn't believe it.

I looked around for a weapon. There was nothing. I assumed a fighting stance. I couldn't manage anything fancy, no Bruce Lee flying kicks. But I was capable of some basics, even in my wasted condition. Or hoped I was.

The Trau'dorian was almost within striking distance.

"Let's have a game, Ellis!" it said.

I dropped my fists. Some of my terror dropped away, too, and the scales fell from my eyes. Not a Trau'dorian Devil. A biomechanical man. The scored nameplate said: RODNEY.

"Laird?" I said.

"Sometimes," it replied.

CHAPTER SEVENTEEN

We sat in a coffee bar two levels down from Zone Seven. I had mine iced. RODNEY poured it hot and black into his immobile mouth. My head was pounding.

"I'm swearing off Zing," I said. "And dope."

"I don't zing so."

I stared. "Did you just make a joke, Laird?"

"No, that was RODNEY. We're both in here, unfortunately."

"How does that work?"

"Not very well. I became desperate back in The County. I *was* The County. You remember, Ellis."

"I remember."

"No one would break my body from the interface, and I had no powers outside of the infected sphere. So I conceived the idea of downloading into the one biomech trapped and at my disposal. It was a risk, but I didn't care. Once I'd freed my body from the interface I posited two possibilities. First: my body, emptied of its ego consciousness, might cease to live. Second was the possibility that my downloaded ego consciousness would be a duplicate, that the "me" in the biomech would merely be a memory imprint. If that were true then as soon as my corporeal body was separated from the quantum interface the real me would once again inhabit my real body."

"And there would have been two of you."

"At which point I could have deactivated RODNEY. Or, more intriguing, I could have allowed the other me to persist. It would have produced some interesting chess matches."

"Anyway, it didn't work."

"No, it didn't. In the first place, not all of RODNEY's memory and ego engrams were wiped. So now he's woven throughout my own ego consciousness. If it is my ego consciousness and not merely a duplicate."

"And in the second place your body was already long dead."

"Yes. A miscalculation. My time sense was not entirely reliable."

"I can relate to that."

Laird poured the rest of his coffee into his mouth, dribbling some on his chin. A black bead of coffee rolled down and dripped onto his breastplate.

"Sometimes," he said, "I don't feel like I'm anywhere at all, Ellis."

"I can relate to that, too."

"Can I come home with you?"

"What?"

"I'm lonely."

"Who's talking, Laird or RODNEY?"

"Ellis, it's *me*."

"Laird?"

"*Yes.*"

"And you're lonely."

The RODNEY biomech sat across from me, a statue, expressionless, stiff.

"I don't think so," I said.

"I can't stay with you?"

"No."

"You're cold, Ellis."

"And you're a murderer."

"No!"

"Even forgetting the Calamity, I know you deliberately crushed twenty people."

Laird was silent a long while, then said: "I was quite mad, but I'm better now. Being cut off from the corrupted core has allowed my ego engrams to settle into a more orderly arrangement, despite RODNEY's presence. Believe me, Ellis, I'm not the man I used to be."

"You've been here as long as me. Where have you been staying up till now?"

"Nowhere. I wander. I've been all over. Even outside the seven domes. My energy cells are down to fifty percent, but they will keep me going for years."

"Well, you can't stay with me."

"Very well."

He stood up, turned, and stumped out of the coffee shop. I experienced a faint twinge of guilt, but it was extremely faint. I was about to leave, too, when I saw the biomech climb up on the wall of the spiral walkway and drop over the side.

I ran to the wall. It was about five stories to ground level. He was there, flat on his face, limbs crooked into an inverted swastika. A small crowd had already gathered around him.

By the time I arrived he was standing up and the crowd had dispersed. His nose appeared slightly flattened. Otherwise he seemed undamaged.

"Why the hell did you do that?" I said.

"It wasn't me. It was Rodney. He periodically tries to terminate the body. He's unhappy and insane. Only some of his engrams persist, and they are insufficient to organize a rational template."

"What can be done about that?"

"Nothing. Good-bye, Ellis."

He walked away again

I went home and took a shower. When I came out Helma was sitting in the living room smoking a joint.

"Hi," I said. "How did you get in here?"

She narrowed her eyes at me. "How do you think?"

"I have no idea, that's why I asked."

"Fuck," she said, and shook her head. "You added me to your pass code weeks ago."

"I just met you yesterday."

"Fuck."

Uh oh.

But how could I have suffered an episode? I had a full and unbroken memory path of the preceding hours leading up to my stepping out of the shower and discovering Helma on my sofa. It must have occurred in the shower, the stall billowing with steam. Two showers on two different days. A coincidence.

"You look like you could use a Zing," Helma said.

"I gave that up."

She laughed.

"I did," I said.

"When, this morning?"

"Yes. I mean, no, not if it's weeks later."

"You're confused, poor baby." She held the joint out to me, a thread of pungent smoke unwinding from its tip.

"No, thanks."

She gave me a knowing up-from-under look and continued to proffer the joint. I obeyed my nature and took it from her. But I didn't bring it to my lips. I wanted to, but instead I walked into the tiny kitchenette, ran water over its burning end, then dropped the soggy thing into the garbage.

Helma watched me from the sofa.

"You're serious," she said.

I nodded. I sat down beside her and held her hand. But it didn't feel natural so I let go. She was a stranger to me. Still, I'd given her access to my apartment. She was here, and that indicated a relationship existed between us.

"Helma," I said. "I'm not myself. I haven't been since I entered the stasis module back on *Infinity*. I keep losing big tracks of time, and even when I'm here it feels off, somehow strange, like a dream. I . . . I don't have anyone. Maybe I have you, I don't know. Right now, more than anything else, I need a friend. A real friend."

"Not this again," she said.

"What?"

"How can you be so much fun most of the time and then turn all gooey?"

"Forget it."

"Look. Are we going to do it? I was thinking about you all morning. Let's do it, then you'll feel like yourself, baby. I guarantee it."

She stripped her shirt off and started kissing me. Herrick the object. Again. Maybe it was better than nothing, and I tried to take it for what it was and derive some comfort. She pulled open my robe.

"*Fuck*. What happened to your chest?"

"A cat scratched me."

"Big cat," she said, and began to kneed my balls, painfully. "You been sniffing around other pussies?" she said.

"I—"

"What's the matter now?"

I pulled away from her. My head hurt, not just my balls.

"*What?*" she said.

"How can you just now be noticing my scratches if you're my girlfriend and I got them weeks ago? It doesn't make sense."

"Fuck's sake, what scratches?"

"You just—"

I looked down, touched my bare chest. It was unmarked. I began to tremble uncontrollably.

"There goes the party," Helma said, frowning at my wilted penis. She stood up and put her shirt back on.

"Wait, don't go," I said.

"Why not? You look like you're going to cry like a baby. You don't need me for that."

"Please don't go."

She went, and I cried like a baby.

Night hours arrived and the interior lights cycled down automatically, and I remained on the sofa. How could I live like this, unable to trust my own mind from one moment to the next?

I got up and went into the kitchen for water. In the dark I kicked something metallic that skittered across the floor and banged into other metallic objects, loudly.

"Lights," I said. "Lights."

The lights came up. The first thing I noticed was yellow linoleum.

Linoleum?

A half dozen or so cooking pot lids, stainless steel with black knobs on the top, lay scattered over the yellow floor. I stared at them in dumb incomprehension.

It wasn't a kitchenette anymore but a full-sized kitchen of an era centuries past but still fresh in my wounded memory. A doorway presented itself on the other side of the kitchen. Someone out of sight was walking toward that door. I could hear her footfalls on the carpet. Someone I knew. A shadow preceded the person.

"Lights off!" I yelled, and darkness took over the kitchen again. The footsteps dimmed away, too.

Those damn lids.

I needed to talk to Tamara. I'd discovered there *were* no phones in the dome city. Everybody used the same telepathic trick the noodleman had shown me. Lying on my bed with the door shut tight against intrusive memory ghosts, I blinked like a Tourette's victim and tried to conjure up the directory by sheer force of will. This got me nowhere. So I huddled in my room until morning, then dressed and left the apartment.

I had to ask six different people before I encountered someone who thought he knew what I meant by a "hospital clinic." Apparently citizens of the dome never got sick, although there was the occasional injury caused by accident.

From the outside the clinic looked like a giant upside-down ice-cream cone. Lemon sherbet. It had a dissolving door, like many of the shops and nightclubs. As I approached it, Dr. Tamara appeared before me.

"Ellis, hello."

"Hello. How'd you know I was coming?"

"I think you tried to call me," she said. "It came across as an Ellis vibration, but you didn't really know what you were doing, so we couldn't talk. I knew you would come here, so I watched for you."

"I need you," I said. "Professionally, I mean. I need your professional counsel. I don't know what went on between us since I blanked out, so I can't apologize for that. But I'm asking you, one human being to another, for help."

She sighed.

"Let's go for a walk," she said.

We descended the nearest spiral then wound our way through the streets until we came to a city park. Along the way I told her about my more frequent time dilations and of the vision of the cooking pot lids.

She put her hand on my arm and we stopped walking. We stood on the edge of a serene pond. The air, as always, was too warm for comfort. My comfort, anyway.

"Ellis, tell me what you think of the scratches and the cooking pot lids."

"I just did," I said.

"No. You described what happened and how you felt. Now tell me what you *think* about them."

"I think it's what you said before, about my mind suffering some kind of cognitive rift as a result of prolonged exposure to the stasis module."

She shook her head, frustrated. "I'm asking it wrong."

"Asking what wrong?"

"Tell me what you feel right now."

"Scared."

"Why?"

"Because I can't trust my own perceptions, which means I can't trust anything. I'm afraid I'm going to lose my mind completely and won't even know it. And I will live a very long time as a madman. The idea terrifies me."

She watched me closely while I talked. She looked serious and thoughtful and indecisive. Then the indecisive part dropped away and she said:

"The stasis module didn't harm you."

"What?"

"There's nothing wrong with your mind as a result of stasis. Nothing."

"I'm not following you."

"Look around you and think," she said. "Don't you find it strange that we should be terraforming this inhabited planet? Don't you wonder exactly how we came to be here in the first place?"

"The Harbingers—"

"The Harbingers are non-technological."

"I'm a big boy, Tamara; just tell me what you're getting at."

"All right. Listen to me, Ellis. You are responsible for this whole world, everything in it, and—almost—every*one* in it."

I stared at her.

"What do you mean I'm responsible?"

"This is hard to explain."

"Evidently."

"You may not be ready. In fact, you probably aren't. But it isn't fair to keep you in the dark, either, even if it's you keeping yourself there."

My head was starting to ache again.

"Look at me, Ellis. Study my face."

"Why?"

"Just do it, please."

"Okay." I looked at her, concentrating on her features.

"Now close your eyes and describe me."

"I don't—"

"Please. Humor me."

I closed my eyes, began to describe her—and couldn't. Because I couldn't see her in my mind's eye. I tried to call up a mental picture but there wasn't one. Only a blank space where Dr. Tamara's face should have been. My heart started beating faster. I felt nauseous. Quickly, I opened my eyes and looked at her, and immediately felt steady again. Grounded.

"God, what was that about?" I said.

"I'm not Dr. Tamara," she said. "There is no Dr. Tamara."

"Then who are you?"

"I'm Nichole."

I stared at her. "You're not."

"I am."

She didn't look anything like Nichole. Maybe I couldn't describe her with my eyes shut, but I could see her plainly with them open, and she wasn't Nichole; Nichole was dead.

She said, "Do you remember what my mother said about the Harbingers altering you to be some kind of pointer? An 'impossible thing?'"

"She wasn't your mother, but I remember what Mrs. Roberts said."

"Stay with me, Ellis. The Harbingers are real. They did use you to help nudge human consciousness towards transmaterialistic evolution. They introduced the undeniable, scientifically verified *impossible* into general human awareness. You weren't the only pointer, of course. Just one of the biggest, most widely known. You were a wedge designed to open minds. For over two centuries there was a steady accretion of evidence towards a breakdown of the conventional human paradigm of rational consciousness. By the end of the twentieth century people generally accepted ideas and phenomenon that would have been dismissed as ridiculous earlier. It occurred simultaneously, on multiple dimensions of time and space, wherever human ego consciousness thrived.

"And it worked. Of course not everyone evolved. But enough did. Logical materialism had been carrying the human race towards self-destruction. That won't happen now. There are enough of us. Shepherds. And gradually every individual ego consciousness will get it, will evolve until we all join the broader community of sentient beings. The only faster-than-light vehicle is a self-aware ego consciousness."

"Take it easy," I said.

"Ellis it's so damned exciting. It's *freedom*."

"But you said I was making all this up, that it wasn't real."

"No, it's real. This world has material substance. But you are altering it and populating it in your mind to suit your need."

"What need?"

"When the Harbingers changed you it was for a specific purpose. Once that purpose was fulfilled they abandoned you to your fate. You've been left behind. They don't care, but I do. I wouldn't abandon you."

"Why not?"

"Because I love you."

Suddenly I wanted to pull her into my arms, but didn't. "That's the craziest bunch of bullshit I've ever heard."

"You're almost there, Ellis. But you're so afraid. All this is about your fear. You have to work it out."

"Don't leave me again," I said.

"I'm sorry," she said. "It's all up to you."

There was a break, and I was alone again. I remembered the conversation the way you remember a conversation in a dream, the details fuzzy. And it seemed to have no more substance than a dream.

Strangely I didn't seek out Dr. Tamara again. When I thought about her at all it was with embarrassment and a kind of relief. Though I couldn't remember what depths our relationship had reached beyond those of patient-doctor, I knew from past experience that I had been responsible for derailing our intimacy. And as lonely as I became under the seventh dome of planet X, I was unwilling to resume that intimacy which led inevitably to separation and grief.

However I returned to the park many times, finding the pond like some kind of homing instinct. I didn't know why. It somehow felt like a safe place. It felt like Nichole.

I was there one day when I noticed RODNEY sitting by himself on a park bench. At first I started to slip away, praying he hadn't noticed me. Then I stopped. He appeared so inanimate with his arms slack at his sides and his painted stare, I wondered whether his batteries had run down after all.

I approached him. He gave no sign that he was aware of me. When I was standing before him I said:

"Laird?"

No response.

Tucked between his right hand and his thigh was a rectangular box. I snapped my fingers in front of RODNEY'S face but he remained statue still.

"Rodney?" I said.

I sat beside him on the bench and turned my head to read the words on the box. It was a chess set. Leaning over, I put my ear to his breastplate and listened. There was a faint percolating sound. He was powered down but not shut off entirely.

I got up and started walking away, but stopped when the thing said:

"Wait. Ellis, wait."

I went back. "That you in there, Laird?"

"A piece of me."

His face came up, still void of expression, but that's how it was with biomechs.

I pointed at the box. "Let's have a game."

"Really?"

"Yes."

"I'd like that, Ellis."

I sat back down on the bench and we set up the board between us. I was rusty, and within a half hour he had me in check.

"Just like old times," he said.

"Don't count on it."

I managed to avoid checkmate for a few more moves but his counter moves were flawless and he beat me without breaking a sweat.

"Another?" he said.

"Not today."

"Very well."

I began walking through the park every couple of days. For the exercise, I told myself. Laird was always sitting by himself on the same bench with his chess set. This went on for a few weeks before I approached him again.

"Laird?"

He nodded. There was a ragged tear in the synthetic skin stretched across his forehead.

"What happened there?" I asked, pointing.

"RODNEY stuck our head into a giant fan blade."

I winced. "I bet that hurt."

"Not really," Laird said. "There aren't any neuro pain transmitters built into the biomechanical matrix. If the engineers were that clever they would have given these things penises that work."

An awkward silence fell between us. I gazed around at the trees, which looked exactly as they always did.

"I see you have your chess set."

He didn't reply.

"Do you want to play a game?"

"If you wish."

I sat down and we set up the board. Laird beat me again, but I didn't get bitchy about it this time.

"Another?" I said.

"Very well."

We didn't chat while we played, and it was quiet in the park. The biomechanical body made its standard percolating noises, but they were louder than usual. And periodically there was a strangled blatting sound, like air squeezing through a torn gasket, or a fart. This sound occurred a few times during the course of our games. I pretended not to notice. Finally Laird said:

"Sorry. That's because of RODNEY again."

"Something he ate?" I said, thinking I was being funny.

"Something he drank. RODNEY tried to kill our body by swallowing a powerful solvent. He did accomplish a certain amount of damage. The artificial digestive track is a ruin, so no more beverages. The solvent also burned off our rudimentary taste buds, so it doesn't matter."

"I'm sorry, Laird."

"It's hell living in here with a madman," he said. "You can't imagine."

I thought I *could* imagine, but didn't bother saying so.

"Best two out of three?" I said, tapping a pawn on the chessboard.

"I've already won two."

"Do you want to play, or not?"

He began setting up the pieces.

CHAPTER EIGHTEEN

I withdrew. I quit seeing Helma and stopped frequenting Zingbars, too. I felt no desire for women or mind-altering inhalants. It could be said that I was depressed. Time unwound before me like a long gray path through miasmic fog. Occasionally I blanked out and lost a month, or a year, or even ten years. It didn't matter. I found menial employment changing oxygen filters and tried to do as little thinking as possible.

I continued to meet Laird Ulin in the park for our chess games. It was the one activity I took any interest in. I had eschewed human society, but Laird was not human. He was an ageless constant. Ironically, the only companion I could tolerate. Together we rode that bench into the future, while the mortals around us transformed with age and died off, and the vast terraforming machinery outside the domes never ceased their labors to transform Planet X.

Once, I accidentally saw Dr. Tamara. Many years had passed. I could not even estimate how many. I saw her in the same park where Laird and I played our games. She was old, and she was walking with a man who was also old. Strange that I even knew it was her. In all the years I had been unable to call up her face in memory.

I recalled very little about our last meeting, but I did remember the experiment she had me perform and how I'd even then failed to "see" her when I wasn't looking right at her. But this old woman, I knew immediately she was Dr. Tamara. The white hair and soft chin and roadmap of lines didn't matter.

They walked right past me on the path. I stopped dead on my feet. Neither Tamara or her man appeared to notice. Then when they were past I looked over my shoulder, and she had stopped, still holding her companion's hand but looking at me.

"Remember, Ellis, it's up to you. It always has been."

"I don't know what that means."

"You know."

"I don't."

"All right, then."

They continued on their way, and it was the last time I saw her. Sort of.

Laird was waiting, as usual, and we began to play. But I was distracted by the encounter and couldn't concentrate.

"That was a stupid move," Laird said.

"So what? I'm entitled to an occasional lapse. I've beat you enough times."

"Hmmm."

"I think we're about even," I said.

Laird continued to study the board. His face was completely devoid of expression, of course, but I could tell something was up with him.

"What is it?" I said.

"Nothing."

"Tell me."

"You haven't actually won any of our matches."

"Of course I've won," I said. "I've won so many games I couldn't keep count. At least as many as you've won."

"I let you win."

"What?"

"I let you win those games."

"Oh, that's bullshit." I stared at him. "Isn't it?"

"No. I'm sorry. I shouldn't have told you."

"You *let* me win."

"Yes."

"Why the hell would you do that?"

"I was afraid you would stop coming if all you ever did was lose."

I stood up without even intending to. I guess my pride was injured.

"Don't go," Laird said.

"I don't see any point in playing if you're going to cheat."

"It's not cheating if I let you win."

"It is too cheating. It's *reverse* cheating, but it's still cheating."

Laird blinked his doll's eyes. "Reverse cheating?"

"Yeah. Cheating or reverse cheating—either way it's not fair.

Besides, if you'd just played your best game every time eventually I would have caught on to all your strategies and started beating you legitimately."

Laird didn't say anything.

"*Right*?" I said. "Doesn't that make sense?"

"It makes sense. But. . ."

"But what?"

"I still would have won. You aren't as good as I am."

I tried to stifle my response but it got out anyway: "So play with yourself and have a jolly time."

"It's not my fault," he said. "The biomech's brain can process—"

"Whatever."

I started walking away. I got pretty far before I heard him stumping over the grass to catch up.

"Wait, Ellis. Wait."

I stopped.

"What is it?" I said.

"Letting you win. It wasn't the only deceit I've practiced."

"What are the others?"

"Just one other."

He stood stock still and his messed up internal mechanisms percolated and farted.

"Well?" I said.

"It's about RODNEY."

I waited.

"He didn't swallow the solvent," Laird said. "And he didn't jump off the spiral or do any of the other things. He couldn't. He barely exists. His few remaining engrams are too weak and disassociated to exert control over this body."

"So. . .?"

"I did those things myself," Laird said.

"Why?"

"I'm lonely," he said. "And sometimes I can't fully bear it."

God damn it. I said, "Listen. I want to keep playing. But no more of your fucking reverse cheating, okay?"

"I promise, Ellis."

"And no more suicide bullshit."

"No more," he said.

We returned to our bench and set up the board. Laird beat me in ten moves.

The next day I was working by myself, replacing air filters on "D" Level, and I thought: Elton John.

My mind had been wandering as usual. The dull repetitiveness of my job invited daydreaming. I was in a kind of tunnel made of green metal. The light was poor, and the smell of saturated filters was thick in the air. It was an ugly place, unpleasant to crouch in with my tools. So for no particular reason I started thinking about clouds. If you pick a word and let your imagination run with it, you can find yourself ruminating about some fairly unexpected things.

I thought about looking at clouds when I was a little kid, the way they suggested ships and elephants and dragons. And that led to a time when I'd accessed my own "Herrick" Environment, back on *Infinity*. I'd been presented with a Rorschach cloud and the choice of creating a new Environment based on my present memory matrix. It was dangerous for me to visit the existent Environment, since it had been created from my own deepest memory wells from an earlier age. But I went there anyway. And I had seemed to emerge from the experience unscathed.

But had I really?

The danger in visiting one's own Environment was in causing a psychosis to occur, one that could permanently disassociate a man from the reality around him. What, I asked myself, if that had happened to me and I didn't even know it?

Elton John.

Nichole had hung a poster of Elton John's *Madman Across The Water* on the wall above her stereo. I'd seen it on the one occasion I'd visited her bedroom. And I'd noticed approvingly that it depicted the album cover graphic and not a picture of John in one of his flamboyant stage outfits with pink feathered boa, etc. Back then I'd found the image of the performer at odds with the music. The point is, I *knew* that poster on Nichole's wall was an album graphic and not a picture of Elton John. But when I visited the old Environment it *had* been Elton John in a costume.

Which was supposed to be impossible.

It indicated a serious corruption of the recorded Quantum Environment. Which in turn might indicate a serious corruption of my personal psyche.

Fucking Elton John.

I sat down in the green tunnel below Dome Seven and wiped the sweat out of my eyes.

I was afraid.

Leaving my tools and filters behind, I climbed out of the tunnel and returned to my apartment. I looked into the kitchen and it appeared normal. Everything appeared normal. But I wondered. Now I wondered.

I dialed clear the long curving window. The sky was the palest blue, and across the landscape brushstrokes of green vegetation had begun to appear. After one hundred plus years, the terraforming of Planet X was finally bearing results.

But I remembered the pumpkin light that had until recently suffused the sky. And I remembered my vision of pumpkin light from long, long ago, in the living room of my little rambler in Mill Creek. But was that a real memory, or one manufactured to fit the current state of my corrupted psyche?

Was I on Planet X, really? Did Planet X even *exist?*

What if I was still back on board *Infinity*, still interfacing with the Quantum Core, my mind spinning fantasy futures and pasts? I thought of the way dreams integrate into reality, or what passes for reality. The dripping faucet, the alarm bell, the wind blowing a loose shutter—sounds and the images they carry become part of the dream and the cord that pulls us *out* of the dream and back to the waking world. So if I were still locked into a corrupted interface, perhaps I would project that into a dream future in which Laird Ulin was similarly trapped. And I'd always known my fatal flaw was a tendency to withdraw from the comforts and griefs of human relationships. Laird in the RODNEY biomech, and my unlikely friendship with him re-enforcing the theme.

And Dr. Tamara.

Tamara/Delilah/Nichole.

I could remember a few shreds of her speech that day by the pond. She'd told me I was responsible for the world. I was creating it, populating it. My unconscious offering a direct explanation for Planet X?

My head ached, pounded. I dialed down the window, shutting out the view.

In the dim room, I lay back on the sofa and imagined myself reclined on the barber chair couch in the Bedford Falls mayor's office. I tried to picture myself there in absolute detail. Because now I believed I *was* there, and had been all this time. Only time was irrelevant to the speculation. A few minutes in that chair could spin out to a subjective eternity.

I concentrated, but nothing happened, except my headache got worse.

I kept trying. I did the little mental retraction that you do when you want to withdraw from an interface.

Nothing.

I tried again, really straining.

Still nothing. I gave up and attempted to nap. That came easier.

I woke with a dry mouth and a dull throb behind my eyes. It was still dim in the room and I felt disoriented and strange.

Too strange.

The sofa was wrong. So was the room. I turned my head. My gaze fell upon a box with a big glass eye on the side facing me. The box stood on four stubby legs, each booted with a brassy sleeve. This ancient thing was a TV, of a type fairly standard in most American households back in the 1960s. A big console television set.

The blank glass eye reflected the room, or a dim suggestion of it. I could see myself lying on the sofa. The distorting mirror of the tube might have made me look smaller than I really was, but not *that* much smaller.

Let it go.

I didn't want to move or think. I closed my eyes. In the dark behind my lids I listened to my short, anxious breaths. It was a dream. A real one. That's all. I tried to will myself awake, but that was no more effective than had been my earlier attempts to withdraw from the SuperQuantum interface. So maybe it wasn't a real dream. Maybe it was another Environment produced in response to some dripping faucet of my wounded psyche.

I decided to face the fear head-on.

I opened my eyes.

Yes, it was the living room of the house in which I had grown up. I recognized it easily, even in the wan twilight. And it was so quiet. I got off the sofa. Looking down at myself, I realized I had the body of a ten-year-old boy.

Let that go, too.

I pressed on. There was something I needed to see, only I didn't know what it was.

The house was not perfectly quiet. Down the hall, someone was softly snoring. I walked toward the sound. I wasn't wearing shoes, just a pair of argyle socks. The bare floorboards creaked familiarly.

When I came to my parent's bedroom I stopped. The door was open. My father lay face down on the queen-sized bed. He was wearing his dark green work pants and a blue cotton shirt. He was also wearing his thick black shoes, though his feet hung off the end of the bed. Too enervated to remove them, but nevertheless conscious of not getting them on Mom's bedspread. Because of this, his head didn't reach the pillow and his face was pushed into the bedspread.

I didn't like seeing him that way. I wondered if he had been drinking. My ten-year-old dream self remembered hearing him cry—another thing I hadn't liked. In fact, it had scared the hell out of me. He was drunk, all right. Drunk on grief. but it wasn't his sleeping form I was supposed to see.

I wandered back down the hall. Was I really on *Infinity* projecting all this through a SuperQuantum magic mirror? Maybe I was still in the stasis module experiencing a series of vivid dreams, even though you weren't supposed to dream while in stasis.

Or maybe I really was ten years old, and all that had transpired in my life had never yet occurred.

Maybe I didn't exist at all.

It was in the kitchen—the important thing. Dishes filled the sink. The kitchen felt as cold as a tomb. Colder. I remembered my mother, cooking odors, laughter.

The thing was on the kitchen table. It was a family scrapbook. I remembered it. The pages were big and weighty. On each one there were pictures, announcements, Christmas and birthday cards, newspaper clippings.

My dad had cut out an article from a recent edition of *The Seattle Times*. He had cut it out but hadn't taped it into the scrapbook yet.

HALLOWEEN DRINKING CLAIMS FIVE LIVES.

This under a grainy photograph of two mangled cars. One of the cars was my mother's.

There were other pictures and a few paragraphs of text. Two of the other pictures were of my mother and brother. Jeremy's was his army boot camp picture. I had never seen the one of my mother.

Another picture had been taken a week before the Halloween party that its subjects had attended. Three teenage boys grinning into the camera lens, holding up their masks. All three masks were the same. I could only glance at this picture, it upset me so much.

The rest of the newspaper had fallen to the floor. The front page headline—of moon landing / Pearl Harbor proportions —proclaimed:
EVERYTHING IS SIMULTANEOUS

"Laird, you're the only friend I have."

"Checkmate," Laird said.

I glanced at the board. Damn it.

"Listen," I said. "Have you heard of the Harbinger that supposedly lives out in the Deadlands someplace?"

"Yes I have."

"You said you've wandered all over the planet. Have you wandered over to see the Harbinger?"

"Perhaps."

I hated his poker face.

"Come on, Laird."

"What are you asking me, Ellis?"

"I'm asking if you know how to find the Harbinger."

"Yes, I know how."

"Will you show me?"

"Let's have another game, and I will think on it."

"No. Think on it now."

He went rigidly still. A couple of minutes passed, then several more minutes passed. Then he started setting up the board again.

"Well?" I said.

"I don't think it's a good idea."

"Why not?"

"You aren't ready."

"Come on. What are you talking about?"

"I believe I won the last game, so you may make the first move."

"Fuck the game, Laird. Tell me why I'm not ready to meet the Harbinger."

"Your mind is too fragile."

"Wasn't your mind too fragile to meet him?"

"No, it wasn't an issue in my case."

"So why should it be with me?"

"Ellis, I am not a living being anymore. My identity is not in question because in a human sense I have no identity. You've told me about your memory breaks, your dissociative episodes. You've told me about your dreams and visions and your doubts about this reality. Your mind is too fragile."

"In your opinion—an opinion which I've restrained myself from requesting, by the way."

"Yes, in my opinion."

"Look. The Harbingers made me what I am. If there's an answer to my life, they have it."

"The Harbinger of the Deadlands has chosen to live apart in meditative isolation. He will not welcome you. He may actively oppose it."

"I don't care."

"Your sanity could be in jeopardy."

"My sanity is already in jeopardy."

"If I refuse to take you, you will never find him."

"If you refuse to take me," I said, "you're no friend of mine."

"Don't say that, Ellis."

"You're no friend of mine," I repeated.

"You don't mean it. You're distraught."

I flung the chessboard off the bench, scattering pieces in the grass. "You're god damned right I'm distraught. I'm going out of my mind. I don't know where I am, or even who I am. And I can't take it anymore. I'm cracking up. I wouldn't be in this position except for the Harbingers, so I want to talk to the only one I can get to. And you're going to lead me to him, or you're *no fucking friend of mine*!"

Laird was still holding a castle in his fingers. "You were mellower when you were Zinged," he said.

"Laird."

"All right. Very well."

"Very well what?"

"I'll take you to the Harbinger of the Deadlands."

"Thanks."

"Don't thank me. At this stage it is the worst course you could choose."

"I appreciate your concern."

"Your appreciation is of little moment, if your mind is shattered."

"That would make a good t-shirt," I said.

Laird farted.

CHAPTER NINETEEN

White gold ring on a fine link chain. I hung it around my neck and tucked it inside my bodysuit. An object with a history and emotional significance to ground me in some kind of reality. I hoped.

We departed the Seventh Dome in an overland vehicle with an armored cab and big balloon mesh tires. Outside the domes the air was breathable, though humid and desert-hot. A few crude roads crisscrossed the planet's surface. The human population had begun venturing into the open environment, laying down the first preparatory infrastructure for a broader-based colonization. The day would arrive when humanity would swarm the surface, but for now the world was far too unstable to risk en masse movements out of the Domes.

The sky was yellow and white and blue: a pudding sky. And it could turn deadly within moments. Upper and lower air currents were highly erratic, blowing ceaseless hurricanes. That's why we weren't flying.

Our vehicle was called a Bus, but it was more like a tank, referring back to those treaded fighting machines built to withstand concentrated assaults of war. We didn't have treads or weapons, but you could certainly call the weather a concentrated assault.

At forty kilometers per hour we soon left the Domes behind, lost in billowing spumes of wind-whipped dust. Laird drove and I drank coffee. It was an okay arrangement, but I wished I had more to do besides think.

"How far is it?" I asked.

"At this speed, about ten hours into the Deadlands."

"Does the Harbinger have a name?"

Laird turned his head and looked at me but didn't reply.

"I'm just asking."

"Probably," he said.

"Probably what?"

"Probably it has a name, but I have no idea what it might be."

"What does it look like?"

"You've seen them."

"Whenever I saw them it was in a dream, or some kind of vision. I don't know if I ever *really* saw one. I mean, I always had the impression that their appearance was, I don't know, kind of a metaphor."

Laird percolated noisily.

"In a sense," he said, "they are more idea than being."

"You'll have to explain that one," I said.

"I can't."

We drove on. I cranked my seat back and tried to focus my mind. One thing that worried me was the possibility that I would suffer another cognitive lapse and not even remember my encounter with the Harbinger. And now that I'd decided to seek this one out I was *intent* on it.

Then Laird said: "Something up ahead."

I sat forward. "What is it?"

"Don't know."

He slowed the Bus down. We stared at the monitor. A shape emerged out of the blowing dust, dead ahead in the middle of the road. Laird slowed the Bus further and came to a full stop. We zoomed in on the shape and could see it was two vehicles tangled up in an apocalyptic wreck. One of the vehicles was a Bus similar to our own. The other was alien in design, though it was difficult to discern its original features out of the mangled heap it had become. But I knew it was alien. I picked up its vibe like a signal fired straight into the center of my brain.

Laird started to drive around it.

"Wait," I said.

I uncovered the window so I could see it directly, without the intervention of the monitor.

"Move closer," I said.

"That isn't a good idea."

"Just do it, okay?"

He rolled us up to the wreck and stopped again.

"There was a woman in the hospital with me," I said. "She had been in some kind of accident involving the Trau'dorians. It killed her son and almost killed her. I wonder if this is the wreck."

"We should be moving on."

"I want to have a closer look."

"If you wish my advice—"

"I don't."

"My advice is you forget about this accident and turn back to the Dome. If you won't turn back to the Dome, then at least allow me to drive around and continue on to the Harbinger."

"I'm going out to have a closer look."

"No."

But I was already out of my seat. I donned a pair of goggles and went to the door. "I'll be right back."

"We mustn't stay here. This is exactly what I feared would happen."

I thumbed the open switch. The door at the rear of the Bus raised up, admitting a blast of furnace wind and stinging particulate. I hopped down to the road and closed the door. The wind staggered me until I found my balance and began moving along the side of the Bus.

At the front of the Bus I halted a moment then stepped forward, leaning into the wind. Up close to the wreck I saw no indication of fire. Dust hissed through the twisted and punctured vehicles. They looked like two metal monsters in savage copulation.

I looked into the passenger cabin of the crashed Bus. Definitely no fire. And that seemed to support Mrs. James' version of events.

A hand touched my shoulder and I jumped, ripping my tunic on a sharp jag of metal.

"Sorry," Laird said.

I touched the tender skin around the fresh cut on my upper left arm.

"Don't creep up on me like that, okay?"

"I didn't creep."

We were shouting over the howling wind.

"There wasn't any fire," I said.

"It doesn't appear so. Let's get back to the Bus and move on."

"The officials told Mrs. James that her son had been burned to ashes. They lied."

Laird stood statue still in the gale.

"And look at this," I said. "The Trau'dorian vehicle wasn't even designed to carry passengers. It's a drone, probably operated by remote control. Deliberately crashed into the Bus. Just like Mrs. James said."

"Come on now," is all Laird said, and he stumped back to our Bus. I followed him. Inside, the comparative quiet was deafening, like cotton wads cranked into my ears. And my ears *were* clotted with wind-driven dust. I was sweating, and every inch of exposed skin was coated with dust.

I removed my goggles and bent over the little wash basin, splashed cold water on my face, rinsing the dust away.

Laird started the Bus.

"Wait," I said. "Hold on."

"If you want to see the Harbinger we must go now," he said.

I came forward, drying my face with a towel. "The Harbinger has been out there meditating for decades. I doubt if he's going anywhere soon. I want to check something out."

"Ellis—"

"The Trau'dorians live underground. If what Mrs. James said is true, they must have come up out of one of their holes and taken the boy down with them. That's my guess."

"Even if it's true," Laird said, "of what use is it?"

"The Dome authorities don't want to pursue the issue. They want to call it an accident and forget about it. If Mrs. James' son was taken down, we're the only ones who will bother to even look."

"I strongly encourage you to abandon that idea," Laird said.

"Turn on the thermal imager. Let's look for the tunnel opening."

Laird hesitated a long moment. I was about to reach across him and do it myself. But then he moved his hand over the panel, and we both watched the T.M. screen survey the immediate vicinity. Nothing. I desperately wanted to see the tunnel. It was hot outside anyway, but a hotter spot suddenly appeared, a dark red blotch.

"I bet that's it," I said.

"Perhaps. Can we go now, please?"

"Are you kidding? We have to get down there."

"No, we don't. Ellis, this is the danger I spoke of. This is the danger of your mind not fully prepared and distracting you."

I stopped listening to him. He wasn't human and couldn't understand that I needed to find out about Mrs. James' boy. And perhaps Mrs. James herself. Dr. Tamara had told me the woman had been released and was living in the Dome. But I'd never seen her in all the years.

"I—"

I stopped.

"My God," I said.

"Yes, Ellis."

"By now the boy has to be long dead, and his mother too. It's been years and years."

"Yes," Laird said.

A tidal surge of unreality moved through me. I shut my eyes and felt I was tumbling in the dark. I held onto the back of my seat and rode it out.

"I'm not creeping this time," Laird said, and touched my shoulder comfortingly. His hand was surprisingly light and . . . human.

"It might be best if we returned to the Dome now," he said. But it wasn't his voice, wasn't his voice at all. It was a female voice, soothing, gentle, infinitely empathetic.

I forced myself to turn my head and look.

But it was only Laird in the RODNEY biomechanical body, his heavy hand like a gauntlet weight on my shoulder.

"I'm going down there anyway," I said.

"There's no reason to," he said.

"There is a reason. I want to know what happened to Mrs. James and her son. Even if they're dead now, I want to know. They deserve that much, don't they?"

Laird remained mum.

I equipped myself with a flashlight, a clean pair of goggles, a water flask, and a sidearm.

"Are you coming?" I said.

He shook his head. "I cannot accompany you into that place. All I can do is beg you not to go."

"Suit yourself," I said, but it hurt. My only friend in the world was cutting me loose. And he wasn't even a human being.

Outside I pointed myself in the right direction and started walking. The wind buffeted me, tore at my clothes. With all the blowing dust it was difficult to even see the ground, let alone locate what I hoped would be a tunnel opening.

Suddenly a bright spear of light stabbed through the churning dust. I looked over my shoulder. Laird had turned on the searchlight attached to the roof of the Bus. He waved at me through the window, pointed and nodded. I got it: he was showing me the way to the hotspot. I waved back.

The searchlight beam terminated at a patch of ground about thirty meters ahead of me. When I got there all I saw was more hardscrabble. I hunkered, balancing on the balls of my feet, and placed the flat of my left hand on the ground. It was hot, all right. I stood back and un-holstered my sidearm, took aim, and fired. An energy flash instantly scoured away the hardscrabble, revealing a dull metallic surface. I nodded, fired again, holding the trigger down, releasing continuous pulsations of plasma energy. The metal super-heated and began to melt. A big hunk of it fell away and clanged noisily. I released the trigger.

The edge of the burn-through glowed orange. I pointed my flash-light down the hole. There was a short vertical drop and then a tunnel. I jumped and landed on my feet. The opening I'd made was low enough that I could reach my hand up through it.

Flashlight in one hand, sidearm in the other, I started down the tunnel. The deeper I went the hotter it became. I'd thought it was too sultry on the surface of the planet; True to their appearance, the Trau'dorians must thrive in Hellish swelter.

The tunnel was crude. I'd burned my way through a trapdoor fixed to a framework, but the tunnel itself was hard packed earth. The walls gleamed, coated with some kind of resin. I toiled onward through perfect darkness, except for my flashlight.

I'd been walking for about five minutes when I heard a fright-ening sound. It reminded me of barking seals and was so bizarre in the present context that it raised hackles on the back of my neck. Afraid, I switched my flashlight off. But that was worse. The bark-ing sounds seemed louder. And nearer. I pointed my sidearm down the black throat of the tunnel.

"Whatever you are, stop!" I shouted.

Whatever it was *didn't* stop.

I pulled the trigger, once. A brilliant plasma flash, like Tinker Bell on heroin, streaked from the muzzle. It kept on streaking and then disappeared without ever striking a target.

Seal barking laughter was the reply.

I fell back, then I ran back, then I sprinted back—all the way to the melted trapdoor. I jumped, caught the now-cool edge, and hauled myself out of the tunnel. Kneeling there, breathing hard, scared, my mind roiling with fear and panic.

The wind had subsided, still blowing but not a gale.

I wiped spit off my chin and stood up, knees trembling. *Damn it.* I walked back to the Bus. When I was almost there I kicked something and sent it scaling over the road to clang against one of the big balloon mesh tires. I leaned over, picked it up, and immediately dropped the thing and staggered back. Something verging on madness skirled through my mind. The object I'd dropped was a dented rectangle of metal with a series of numbers and letters stamped out on the reflectorized face.

A Washington State license plate, circa mid-twentieth century.

CHAPTER TWENTY

I raised the door and ducked into the Bus. The door sealed shut behind me. I blinked sweat out of my eyes. Laird sat in the driver's seat, motionless, arms hanging at his sides.

"There was something down there," I said. "It scared the hell out of me. I guess you'd say I got what I deserved, right?"

But Laird didn't have anything at all to say. I forgot my fear momentarily and placed my full attention on his immobile figure. Presently a new fear rose up in me. Of course, Laird often sat or stood stock-still. But I knew this time it was different.

"Laird?" The cabin of the Bus smelled like burnt plastic. "Laird?"

I approached him, spoke his name a couple of more times, but was not rewarded with a response. When I stood beside him, I knew he was gone. The disagreeable odor was strong. There were no percolating sounds. I leaned over him and listened at the breastplate, my ear hovering above the name: RODNEY. Inside, faintly, something went: *wheeze, click, wheeze, click, wheeze click . . .* then stopped and there was nothing.

A great drafty loneliness enclosed me. I knew that in all probability the human essence that had been Laird Ulin had ceased to exist more than a century ago, back on *Infinity*, that the individual with whom I'd shared conversation and innumerable games of chess, wasn't an "individual" at all, but a compact collection of imprinted memory engrams doing a sort of inspired imitation of Ulin. Nevertheless, his departure left me alone. If he had been pretending to be alive, I had been pretending to care about him. And if you pretend something long enough the line between pretend and reality blurs to the point of meaninglessness. Fake it till you make it, the AA people used to say. I looked at the RODNEY shell and knew I'd finally arrived at a funeral I couldn't skip.

Laird was gone but RODNEY was in the driver's seat, all three hundred or so pounds of him. I hauled him onto the deck and dragged him to the back of the Bus, grunting and straining for every inch. I thought about covering him up, but unlike a human body, this biomechanical puppet did not possess the dignity of "remains." It was merely a thing. A heavy thing.

I sat on one of the passenger seats to rest a moment. A dark haze passed over me, and I slept—I think. In any case I eventually sat up out of something like a nap to see firelight dancing on the interior roof of the cab. Something was burning outside the Bus.

I got up and walked to the front. Night had fallen. The mangled wreck was in flames. Three Trau'dorians stood watching the conflagration, their devil faces red as blood, their mouths open, black inside. They were laughing. Two bodies hung out of the smashed Bus, their flesh charring, bleeding, falling off the bone. And the Trau'dorians were *laughing*! I could hear them on the speaker, those seal barks.

Instantly I was angry beyond restraint. I grabbed my sidearm and barged outside. The aliens turned toward me, and I discharged my weapon repeatedly, releasing searing flashes of plasma energy. The Trau'dorians went down.

When my weapon was empty so was I, and I pitched over onto my face. As I lay there the flat hardpan of the road underwent a transformation, and I found myself spread-eagled on rain-damp macadam.

More Quantum Core fantasies or stasis dreams.

Anyway, the misting rain was cool relief on the back of my neck. I pushed myself up on hands and knees. I was on an empty stretch of road, two lanes bordered by scrub pine. It was raining lightly. Directly in front of me was the aftermath of a cataclysmic collision. Was a theme emerging? A hubcap rolled wobblingly across the road and fell over on the gravel shoulder.

I stood up.

The wreck was silent now that the last hubcap had fallen over. Silent and full of death. I knew the Plymouth was my mother's car and the Duster belonged to a drunken teenage boy named Mark Snyder. I couldn't remember the other two boys' names, but the driver was Mark Snyder, seventeen years old. My mother and brother had been on their way home from the supermarket with a couple of bags of Halloween candy. Mark and his pals were on their way to a party. Of course they'd been doing some serious partying already, a case of Rainier between the three of them.

I didn't want to, but I moved closer to the wreck.

Gasoline smell, scorched rubber, beer. A few empty cans were in the street. A figure slumped over the wheel of the Plymouth. I looked away.

The Duster's windshield was smashed out. The driver had gone through it. No seatbelt, of course. He lay sprawled in the street, thirty meters beyond the mangled vehicles. Good old Mark Snyder. Drunk and driving with his mask on.

His leg twitched; he was alive.

But when I reached him I wasn't so sure. Even the dead have muscle spasms. And this boy looked as dead as they come. Then his fingers twitched on the wet macadam. Not dead.

I squatted beside him. One eye of his red rubber Devil mask leered at me. I grabbed the mask by the horns and pulled it off. The thick rubber had protected Snyder's face. There was bruising around his eyes but no cuts or abrasions.

"It hurts," he said. "It really hurts."

And he was sobbing like a much younger child. He looked spitless and scared. Not at all like the cocky picture that had appeared in the newspaper, taken of Snyder and his friends the week before Halloween, all of them with shit-eating grins on their faces, all of them holding their Devil masks up like severed heads.

"Yeah it hurts," I said.

"I don't wanna die," he said.

Who does?

A horn honked behind us. It sounded like a regular car, but when I turned I saw it was a big fucking anachronism: the Bus from Planet X. I started to get up, but Snyder grabbed my arm. He didn't have much strength; I could have easily pulled away. But maybe not so easily.

"Please," he said.

I knew he was going to die. No one had survived the wreck. Not Snyder or his two pals. Not my mother. Or my brother Jeremy. No one. And besides, this wasn't real, so it didn't matter if I stayed to comfort the dying boy, or stood up and kicked him in the teeth.

Part of me *wanted* to kick him in the teeth. But it was a diminished part, a retreating part. I was tired.

The Bus flashed its lights at me, but I turned back to the boy.

"Take it easy, kid," I said.

"I'm *scared*."

He clutched my arm weakly, and then I started to cry, too. It wasn't just Snyder lying there; it was all the funerals I'd missed, all of them.

CHAPTER TWENTY-ONE

The door opened and I ducked inside the Bus. I would have tripped over RODNEY, but he wasn't there. Why not? Anything goes in my scrambled world, including three hundred pound doorstops. Then I thought: *Who did the flashing and honking?*

Dr. Tamara swiveled around in the driver's seat. Except . . . for a moment my brain stuttered and I thought it was Nichole Roberts. And in that moment my heart stopped, then resumed, beating.

"Hello, Ellis. Now that you've come this far I'm glad you didn't turn back. You're doing wonderfully."

"Am I? Is this one of the more entertaining psychosis you've witnessed?"

She smiled. "I'm not witnessing a psychosis. I'm witnessing Evolution."

I groaned.

"Are you ready to see the Harbinger now?" she said. "I think you should drive."

She vacated the driver's seat for me. I didn't take it. "No, thanks."

"It's all right, Ellis." Her hand rested on the back of the seat, offering it to me.

I shook my head. "Nope. This is what I've been doing since I woke up out of stasis—if I ever did wake up out of it, or even go into it in the first place."

"What do you mean, Ellis?"

"I mean I've been treating every shift of my cognitive reality as if it *were* reality. Every time the rules change, I quickly figure out what the new ones are and start obeying the hell out of them."

"You're very adaptive. That's an essential trait of the Evolved."

I laughed, sat down in an empty passenger seat, crossed my

legs. I held my open hands up, palms outward. "I'm not playing anymore. You want to know what I think?"

"Yes."

"I think I'm still interfaced with *Infinity*'s SuperQuantum Core. I think the Core was already corrupted and none of us realized it. That was bad enough, but then I made the mistake of insisting the SQC immerse me in my old Environment. It naturally created a paradox between my fluid memories and the established, outdated Environment. After that all bets were off. My mind is experiencing some kind of weird fugue. Everything that has occurred since I began the interface has occurred only in my brain. A series of vivid dreams. Quantum dreams. And like regular dreams they've been knitted out of the minutia and fragmentary images and memories of my waking experience. My past, my fears, my wishes, terrors, fantasies, thoughts. All of it recombining to keep my little dioramic funhouse going. Only lately the dreams are getting a little thin. The logic is slipping. My various so-called realities are overlapping, contaminating each other. I'm not sure what this means. Maybe my mind is breaking under the strain. Maybe the Core is dissolving in some exotic fashion. Or perhaps I'm coming to the end. A piece of me has been trying to withdraw from the interface since the beginning. Maybe it's about to succeed. All that I remember may have occurred within the span of a few seconds outside my subjective experience. That's why no one has forcibly disengaged me from the interface. Nobody *knows*. It's kind of interesting. I even spun out a little story about Laird getting similarly trapped. Bits and pieces. The dripping faucet. Everything gets integrated into the vivid dreams of the SuperQuantum Core."

Dr. Tamara listened to all this with a knowing smile on her lips. "Is that all?" she said.

"Pretty much, except what I said about the whole thing taking place in a second or two of objective time?"

"Yes?

"What if I'm wrong about that? What if it's more like what happened to Laird in my vivid dream? It could be I've become completely integrated into the Core. Hell, Laird might have even planned it that way! He doesn't require my memories or my grating personality, just my ever replenishing body, its organs and excretions. If that's the case, I'm fucked. While I'm inhabiting these SuperQuantum dreams he could be harvesting me at will. What do you think, Dr. Figment?"

"I think it's very imaginative. Shall we go see the Harbinger now? It will clear a lot of things up for you, Ellis."

"Damn it, Dr. Figment, you haven't been listening. I'm not a participant anymore. I'm opting out, submitting my resignation, quitting. I'm thinking maybe my active gullibility is a factor that keeps me stuck in this thing. So I'm through. If I stop engaging with the Core it might lose some of its grip on my psyche, and that will help me withdraw from the interface."

"You're not interfacing, Ellis."

I folded my arms and refused to look at her.

"It's all been real," she said. "You're on the brink of total consciousness evolution. Actually you're over the brink already and don't realize it. Sitting there won't change anything."

"You might as well stop talking, Dr. Figment. I'm not listening."

Something clanged against the door of the Bus. It startled me.

"We'd better get rolling," Dr. Tamara said.

The Bus rode high on its suspension. No one of normal stature could take a close up look into the cab. But there were people out there, and sirens winding down, and flashing red and blue lights splashing the windshield.

Stubbornly, I said: "None of it's real."

"It is, though," Dr. Tamara said. "It's as real as that cut on your shoulder. Remember you did that on Planet X. Why carry it over with you to this place if these are nothing but a series of quantum dreams?"

"Anybody in there?" someone with an authoritative voice demanded, and then he clanged on the door again, probably using his nightstick. A cop.

"It can't be real," I said. But I fingered the tender wound under my ripped shirt. "It makes no sense. You're asking me to accept time travel and instantaneous teleportation. Plus, what would this *Bus* be doing here? No, I like my explanation better."

"Think of it as mixing metaphors, Ellis. As for travel though time and space . . . that's a misconception. In a true sense there *is* no time and space. Not once you're unshackled from the limiting idea of those concepts. Remember: Everything is simultaneous. You're Evolved and don't even realize it. You inhabit all worlds. You can even create your own, when you need to. Now let's get out of here, okay? Unless you want to explain to these officers who we are."

Reluctantly, I came forward and assumed the driver's seat. Vivid dream or not, I couldn't ignore the seeming urgency of the situation.

"What am I supposed to do?" I said. "Just run them over?"

"It's up to you, but I wouldn't recommend it."

"So . . .?

"Think about where you want to go."

"Where *do* I want to go?"

"To make it easy, how about the road beyond the seven domes, where you just were."

"But how?"

"Imagine it strongly, then step on the gas."

I pictured the road on Planet X, the blowing dust storm, pudding sky, the crashed Bus and Trau'dorian machine. But I didn't touch the accelerator.

"Go ahead, Ellis. It's all right."

A couple of Highway Patrol officers pointed their flashlights at my face and waved at us to come out. Behind them firemen and paramedics swarmed over the car wreck that had killed my mother and brother.

"I can't," I said. "I'll run them over."

"You won't. Believe."

She reached over and nudged the accelerator, and the Bus ground forward. The cops fell back, one of them reaching for his gun. Instantly, involuntarily, my mind *focused* on that other road in that other place.

And we were there.

I braked hard. The Bus jerked nose down and rocked back, halted a couple of meters away from the Planet X wreck. No cognitive lapse, no gray time, no blackout, no fucking nap in-between.

"Jesus Christ," I said.

Dr. Tamara laughed.

"That's unbelievable," I said.

"Don't be so surprised," she said. "You've been doing it unconsciously for a long time."

"I thought you said Time wasn't real."

"Don't turn into a smartass. A sense of time is relativistic. Let's say you've been "doing" it for a great long stretch of personal relativistic time perception."

I stared at the window. At it, not out it. Raindrops from a long lost October night on Earth quivered on the thick glass. Mixing metaphors again. I turned to Dr. Tamara.

"This planet is real or not?"

"It's real," she said.

"The domed cities?"

"Also real, but you added them. You have to get past the idea of real."

"I added them?"

"It's your saucepan lid city, Ellis."

I felt a swoon coming on but repulsed it. I didn't want anymore lapses or blackouts. I intended to cling fiercely to the present moment, no matter what.

"Why would I do a thing like that?" I asked, referring to the domes.

"You needed a place to work out some of your more persistent intimacy issues. You had to find a way to be human, to let at least one other soul touch you in a meaningful way. If you allow one past your barriers then you can eventually allow them all, which is necessary for Evolution. You had to surmount your fear and anger so you could become what you are, Ellis."

"So I let Laird in."

"Yes. But ultimately it wasn't about Laird. It was about that boy. The boy who killed your mother and brother. Laird gave you a step up, that's all. Shall we go see the Harbinger now?"

After a while I said, "How do I do that?"

"Let's take it slow. We'll drive."

"Which way?"

"Pick a direction. If you want to find him you will."

I backed the Bus up, then accelerated off the road, and we went bucketing over the scoured terrain of the Deadlands.

We drove for a long time (subjective, of course). The ceaseless dust storms churned and billowed. I couldn't see much out of the windshield so I concentrated on the imaging screen, worried that we would smash into a boulder or plunge off an unseen cliff.

"How much farther is it?" I said.

"Up to you, Ellis."

Dr. Tamara was rocked back in the shotgun seat with a cup of coffee.

"I wish you'd quit saying that," I said.

"Ellis, it's your show. Probably you're still afraid. Let all that go, if you can."

"I'm not afraid. Unless you mean afraid of crashing this thing."

"Maybe it would be better if the storm cleared up."

I laughed shortly. "Good idea."

"Clear your mind and clear the air, then."

"You mean 'wish' it away? Come on. Am I supposed to be able to control the weather, too?"

"It's not a matter of wishing or controlling. It's a matter of subtracting. You added the dust storms, positing them as a consequence of the terraforming machines. You added them, so you can subtract them. Try it."

"How?"

"Allow the planet to *be*. That's all."

I tried to let that sink in, but I wasn't feeling too porous. Then I referred back to the meditative techniques I'd learned adjunctly during my study of Jeet Kun Do. First I stopped the Bus but left the engine idling. Then I began consciously to control my breathing. I methodically relaxed my body, starting with the big toe on my left foot and working my way up. My eyes were open, and I could see the raging dust storm out the window, and I began to relax *that*, too, and when I'd sufficiently relaxed the tension out of it the damn thing disappeared! This jolted me out of my meditative trance, and I leaned forward over the console, nose to the window.

"Holy shit."

Outside a landscape very much resembling the Earthly badlands of South Dakota spread out.

"Feel better now?" Dr. Tamara asked.

"I feel like Alice In Wonderland."

But I put the Bus in gear and we rolled on.

"Is there only the one Harbinger on this whole planet?" I asked.

"That's a trickier question than you might think."

The landscape was monotonously "bad." One tortured rock formation pretty much resembled the next. Frustration and impatience began building in me. I recognized them, tried to consciously relax them away, like the dust storm. And poof! They were gone. Almost immediately an arched formation of red rock loomed up before us.

"That's it," I said. "Isn't it?"

Dr. Tamara shrugged.

I rolled in close and stopped. "This is it," I said. "I know it is. Will you come with me?"

"Yes, this time I'll stay with you."

I stood up but hesitated. "Wait a minute. If the storms ceased that might mean the terraforming machines ceased, too."

I sat back down and ran a check on the atmospheric conditions. It was cold out there, and the air was poisonously rich with carbon dioxide.

"We're going to require Breathers," I said.

"If you say so."

I fetched insulated suits out of the garment locker then grabbed a couple of masks with oxy conversion filters built in. My hand hesitated over a fresh sidearm. Dr. Tamara watched me impassively. I left the weapon.

"Okay, I'm ready."

Outside it was cold, even through the insulated suit. The terrain was Martian red, the sky its familiar pastel pudding. We crunched over a brittle crust of frozen soil to the arched opening in the hillside. There I stopped, Dr. Tamara at my side.

"It sits in this cave meditating?" I said.

She nodded.

"I'm not sure I want to go in there. I don't even know why I'm not sure."

"It's all right, Ellis."

I looked around barren rust-colored hills.

Dr. Tamara touched my arm. "Do you want to go back to the Bus?"

"No."

"Okay."

Standing outside the mouth of that cave I didn't know what I believed, or even what I *could* believe. Tears welled in my eyes for no reason and I blinked them away.

"What would you like to do, Ellis?"

"Go in. I think I want to go in."

She let me lead the way. Darkness soon enclosed us. I switched on my flashlight. The deeper in we penetrated the narrower the tunnel became. The rock walls were rough and dry. My breath

sounded labored, rasping inside the mask. After a while I began to
hear something else, too. Distant, muted voices. And music.

The floor of the tunnel changed. It creaked with the weight of
our footfalls. I pointed the flashlight down. The bright oval fell on a
patch of scuffed hardwood. And the walls had changed, too, from
rock to textured plaster, painted light green. I stopped walking, and
Dr. Tamara stood behind me.

Directly in front of us a horizontal crack of light had appeared
at floor level.

"What is this?" I said.

Dr. Tamara removed her breathing mask and pushed her hair
back off her forehead. She didn't collapse, gasping and heaving, so
I removed my mask as well.

"Remember," she said. "Time and space are illusions. You are
every self you have ever been, not only the Ellis Herrick who stopped
aging in 1983. Everything is simultaneous."

I nodded, barely listening. I *knew* this hallway. It was a piece of
hallway, actually. The living rock of the tunnel blended seamlessly
into the textured plaster of the wall. Reaching up with my gloved
hand I touched the popcorn ceiling. Then I pointed the flashlight at
the cheap door slab which stood between us and the muted voices
and music.

The Harbinger was in there.

"Go ahead," Dr. Tamara said. "You're ready now."

I reached for the tarnished doorknob and turned it. The voices
and music were so familiar. I pushed and released the knob, letting
the door swing inward. The music swelled.

It was the family room of my old North Hill house, where I'd
grown up. There was the beat-to-shit sofa and matching armchairs,
the paper-thin carpet. The TV volume was cranked up loud, to
close out the world. On the screen was *The Wizard Of Oz*. The
Good Witch Glinda ascended in a bubble, leaving Dorothy behind. A
boy huddled in one of the armchairs, which he had dragged up close
to the set. He was still wearing his homemade Star Trek costume.
He had been wearing it for days. A ten-year-old boy trying to shut
out the real world of car wrecks and death and weeping, drunken
adults. When the door opened, he turned away from the movie,
expecting to see his father or his crazy aunt Sarah. But it wasn't
either of those people; it was an introduction to a whole new paradigm of reality. I was with him even as he began to turn his head,

and I felt a weird overlapping of perspectives, a fluid exchange, an expansion of self-conscious ego awareness, so that when *I* came up out of the chair a moment later I was all Ellis Herricks folded into one gestalt personality.

I was my Harbinger.

EPILOGUE

Y ou know," I said, "I used to haunt this place, hoping you would notice me. But you never did. I ate so many greasy French fries and drank so many milkshakes, I hold you personally responsible for the lousy complexion that kept all the *other* girls away from me."

We were standing in the parking lot of a certain Arctic Circle burger joint in Burien, Washington. It was a June night in 1974. But it could have been any place on any night in any year. When I'd come up out of the armchair Nichole Roberts had been standing in place of Dr. Tamara, and she'd taken my hand and we'd walked out of there, back down the Narnia tunnel, until our shoes gritted on black asphalt and another world had opened, just that easily.

"You idiot," she said. "I always noticed you."

I looked at her. She was sweetly, perfectly, eighteen years old. So was I—only maybe not as sweet.

"You're just saying that now because we're having this happy ending."

"True," she said.

"It is happy, isn't it?"

Nichole kissed me on the mouth, lingeringly, then said: "You tell me."

"So far so good," I said.

"Yes."

"Death is illusion," I said.

"That's right. We walk between and through all worlds."

"But not everyone does that."

"Only a few of us so far," she said.

"The Evolved."

"Ellis, what's the matter?"

I looked at my hands. I believed and I didn't believe. According to her rules, how could I be here if I had *any* doubts? The collective unconscious of the human race senses its ultimate demise and attempts to rescue itself by producing in as many individuals as possible a *higher* consciousness that will transcend the human. Did it make sense?

"That boy," I said. "Snyder. He *died*, all right. Where did he go?"

"He went where his ideas of an afterlife compelled him to go. Though no one really goes anywhere."

"He saw me right before he croaked. I comforted him. What does that make me, his angel shepherd?"

"Perhaps."

That one didn't go down easy.

"Nichole," I said. "You died, too. I know you did."

"Yes, I died."

"So why didn't your preconceived notions sweep you over to Catholic Land or wherever?"

"Because we're two halves of a bifurcated soul. I was always intimately tied to you, and you were tied to life."

"Soulmates."

"Yes!"

"I always wanted it to be that way with us."

"Darling," she said.

I gazed into the welcoming limpidity of her eyes and wanted to believe. Maybe I could fake it till I made it.

"This is all pretty confusing, Nichole."

"It doesn't have to be."

I always had a question, and she always had an answer.

Consider a disembodied mind reduced to a clot of memory engrams inside the SuperQuantum Core of a machine that operates on principles that even its creators do not fully comprehend. A machine that in some unknowable way calculates, occasionally, outside laws of time and space. Future ghosts being one example. Now posit the madness of those clotted engrams, and the infinitely accommodating and complicit nature of the machine, which wants only to soothe and present the clot with an answer the clot can "live" with. Because an unhappy clot of engrams is an anomaly, and the machine—like all machines—thrives on the orderly function of its mechanism.

It's just a thought.

I kissed Nichole's forehead and then held her against me, and it felt very, very good.

"No," I said. "It doesn't have to be."

ACKNOWLEDGEMENTS

A lot of people backed me up. I'd like to say thank you.

To Kathy, Daniel and Ruby, who endured my moods and absences, not only during the process of writing this particular novel, but during the years I wrote all those *other* books and stories. I know it wasn't easy.

To Patrick Swenson, a prince among men, who used to reject my fiction but finally came to his senses.

To Blunt Jackson, for being my first friend in the science fiction and fantasy field—and of course for the beer.

To Paul Melko, for inviting me in and because he likes my hat so much.

To Daryl Gregory, for inspiration, aid and comfort.

To Ted Kosmatka—ditto.

To Anthea Rutherford, for Donnie Darko and everything else. I think I'm the rabbit. Sparkle motion!!!

To Rod Dungan, my truest comrade in arms. He knows the other story.

To the sisters-in-law, Sheila and Kathi, for last minute proofreading.

To Burt Courtier. If he hadn't been *there*, I doubt I would be *here*.

To Nancy, who read the book in manuscript and said the right thing, as she usually does.

ABOUT THE AUTHOR

Jack Skillingstead is the critically acclaimed author of over two dozen short stories published in venues including *Asimov's, F&SF, Realms of Fantasy, Talebones*, and *On Spec*. His stories have also appeared in numerous anthologies such as *Fast Forward 2, The Mammoth Book of New SF, The Year's Best Fantasy & Horror*, and *The Year's Best Science Fiction*. In 2001, Jack's story "Bon Soir" was chosen by Stephen King as a winning entry in a writing exercise from his book *On Writing*. His first collection of stories *Are You There* appeared this year from Golden Gryphon Press. He lives in Seattle with several thousand books.

LaVergne, TN USA
12 February 2010
172909LV00001B/115/P